"James just keeps getting ... ligent read, so well-written that I couldn't ... Every single time I turned out my light for the night, I found myself thinking about the story, flipping the light switch again and reading just 'one more chapter.'" —MyShelf.com

"Libraries, books, and a big, lovable cat is just purrfect perfection. Author Miranda James weaves out an excellent plot that leaves you hooked until the end. I can't wait to read and review the next in the series." —A Cozy Girl Reads

PRAISE FOR THE *NEW YORK TIMES* BESTSELLING CAT IN THE STACKS MYSTERIES

"Ideal for Christie fans who enjoy a good puzzle."
—*Library Journal*

"Filled with Southern charm . . . Will keep readers guessing until the end. Miranda James should soon be on everyone's list of favorite authors."
—Leann Sweeney, *New York Times* bestselling author of the Cats in Trouble Mysteries

"Combines a kindhearted librarian hero, family secrets in a sleepy Southern town, and a gentle giant of a cat that will steal your heart."
—Lorna Barrett, *New York Times* bestselling author of the Booktown Mysteries

"[A] pleasing blend of crime and charm."
—*Richmond Times-Dispatch*

"Humor and plenty of Southern charm . . . Cozy fans will hope James will keep Charlie and Diesel in action for years to come."
—*Publishers Weekly*

Berkley Prime Crime titles by Miranda James

Cat in the Stacks Mysteries

MURDER PAST DUE
CLASSIFIED AS MURDER
FILE M FOR MURDER
OUT OF CIRCULATION
THE SILENCE OF THE LIBRARY
ARSENIC AND OLD BOOKS
NO CATS ALLOWED
TWELVE ANGRY LIBRARIANS

Southern Ladies Mysteries

BLESS HER DEAD LITTLE HEART
DEAD WITH THE WIND

A Cat in the Stacks Mystery

NO CATS ALLOWED

Miranda James

BERKLEY PRIME CRIME
New York

BERKLEY PRIME CRIME
Published by Berkley
An imprint of Penguin Random House LLC
375 Hudson Street, New York, New York 10014

Copyright © 2016 by Dean James
Penguin Random House supports copyright. Copyright fuels creativity, encourages
diverse voices, promotes free speech, and creates a vibrant culture. Thank you for buying
an authorized edition of this book and for complying with copyright laws by not
reproducing, scanning, or distributing any part of it in any form without permission.
You are supporting writers and allowing Penguin Random House to continue to
publish books for every reader.

BERKLEY is a registered trademark and BERKLEY PRIME CRIME and the B colophon
are trademarks of Penguin Random House LLC.

ISBN: 9780425277751

Berkley Prime Crime hardcover edition / February 2016
Berkley Prime Crime mass-market edition / February 2017

Printed in the United States of America
3 5 7 9 10 8 6 4 2

Cover art by Dan Craig
Cover design by Lesley Worrell
Book design by Tiffany Estreicher

*This book is dedicated
with great affection, admiration, and respect
to Natalee Rosenstein, who opened the door—
and kept it open.
I can never thank her enough.*

ACKNOWLEDGMENTS

As always, many thanks to my long-suffering, ever-supportive editor, Michelle Vega. Blessed was the day you became my editor; another reason to thank Natalee. My agent, Nancy Yost, and her staff, Sarah, Adrienne, and Natanya, work hard on my behalf, and they are much appreciated. Thanks also to Bethany Blair, Michelle's hardworking assistant, and my publicist, Danielle Dill, for all that they do.

My fellow critique group members only got to look at a small portion of this one, but they deserve thanks for their encouragement and support. Thanks to Amy, Bob, Kay F., Kay K., Julie, and Laura, as ever. And to Susie and Charlie for all they do to provide a happy place to meet (even when I'm viewing it through a computer screen). My cohorts in the Femmes Fatales keep me entertained with their lively wit and humor on a daily basis. Thanks to Donna Andrews, Dana Cameron, Charlaine Harris, Toni L.P. Kelner, Catriona McPherson, Kris Neri, Hank Philippi Ryan, Mary Saums, Marcia Talley, and Elaine Viets, for inviting me to join in the fun.

I needed answers to a few questions, and I'd like to thank several people for their help. They can't be held accountable for any mistakes I've made. Thanks to Linda Burciaga,

Christina Torbert, Julianna Davis, and Scott D. Deleve, for answering my questions, odd though they might have been.

My new coworkers at the Rowland Medical Library, University of Mississippi Medical Center, welcomed the stranger into their midst and made me feel like one of the family right away. I cannot thank them enough for providing a rewarding, interesting, and collaborative work environment.

Finally, I come to my two first readers, Patricia Orr and Terry Farmer. Mere thanks are not enough for their continued support, love, and encouragement. They are always there for me.

ONE

||||||||||||||||||||||||||

"He's out there again today, Charlie." Melba Gilley made the announcement as she strode hurriedly into my office at the Athena College Library. "Do you think we should call the campus police?"

"No, I don't think *we* need to do anything." I turned from staring at my computer screen to face my longtime friend. "This is, what, the second day you've seen a strange man sitting in a car across the street from this building?"

Diesel, my Maine Coon cat, jumped down from his perch on the window ledge behind my desk and ambled around to greet Melba. The two adored each other, and if anyone could calm Melba down, Diesel could. I couldn't figure out why she was so agitated by this. I figured there was an innocent explanation for the so-called lurker's presence.

Melba plopped down in a chair near my desk and commenced rubbing the cat's head. Diesel's rumbling purr brought a smile to her face.

"I know you think I'm imagining things." Melba's tone was defensive. "And for your information, Mr. Smarty-Pants, this is the *third* day I've seen that man out there." She sniffed. "He's hard to miss, sitting in that little bitty car. He's way too tall for it, and I don't know how he manages to scrunch himself into it."

"Maybe he's simply waiting for someone to get off work so he can give them a ride home," I said. "Have you thought about maybe approaching him and asking him if he needs help? On the other hand, if he's lurking for some purpose, and you let him know you've spotted him, he might go away."

Melba shot me a look tinged with utter disgust. When she spoke, she addressed the cat. "After all these years somebody ought to know me better'n to think I don't know most of the people who've got legitimate business around here." She darted another barbed glance at me when she paused for breath. "Or think I'd do something so dumb as to go up to a complete stranger and ask him why he's trying to hide in a teeny-tiny car way too small for him."

Diesel warbled as if he agreed with Melba, and this time the glance I got was triumphant. My cat was smart and a good judge of character, but he loved Melba so much he'd probably warble at anything she told him.

I resigned myself to the fact that I wouldn't be able to work again until I allowed Melba to get whatever this was out of her system.

"So if he's not here to pick someone up from work, and

you don't feel like simply asking him," I said, "why do *you* think he's sitting out there every day?"

"I don't know, but I'd be willing to bet you it has some-thing to do with *him*." She pointed down at the floor, and I knew whom she meant—her new boss, Oscar Reilly.

My new boss as well, actually. The previous library director, Peter Vanderkeller, departed abruptly a couple of months ago, right before classes resumed after the holi-days, with no explanation that I ever heard. While the college searched for a new library director, the president, Forrest Wyatt, appointed an assistant vice president of finance as the interim director. I thought the interim should be a senior member of the library staff, but the president didn't concur—not that he ever asked my advice in the first place.

"Reilly hasn't so far impressed me as being anything other than slimy and obnoxious, and I know you don't care for him, either." I had observed him leering at two of the youngest and prettiest female library staff several times when he evidently thought no one was watching him. "He sure doesn't know anything at all about what a library does or how it should function. But why would you associate a stranger on the street with Reilly?"

Diesel warbled loudly when he heard the name *Reilly*. My cat and the interim director had met twice since Reilly stepped into the interim position, and both times Diesel took one sniff and backed away.

The first time it happened, I should have taken it as a sign that things were about to get unpleasant. Upon ini-tially meeting the man, I found Reilly charming, sympa-thetic, and eager to do his best for the library while it was in his charge. What became quickly apparent afterward, however, was that he was mercurial in temperament, harsh in his criticisms, and contemptuous of his staff.

The president couldn't find a new director soon enough to suit me or the rest of the staff. In the meantime, if Reilly aggravated me too much, I could simply hand in my notice. I had sufficient income that I wouldn't really miss the part-time salary, but I would definitely miss the work I did cataloging the rare books and maintaining the archives. Others, like Melba, didn't have that option. They needed their jobs, and they were all terrified Reilly would fire them at any moment.

"You never know what might crawl out from under all sorts of rocks when that man's around," Melba said darkly. She continued to scratch Diesel's head. "I wouldn't put anything past him. Maybe the guy watching him is out for revenge."

"Revenge for what?" I asked. "Reilly hasn't been in Athena all that long." He had come from a small school in New England only four months ago, in fact, to take the job here. "Surely you've had time to dig up most of what there is to know about him." Melba always managed to find out details about the lives of anyone who interested her—or who annoyed her, in this case.

Melba shook her head. "All I've heard is that he's a widower with two grown children who live up North some-where. I don't know the girl who was his assistant over in the finance office, but I'm going to make her acquaintance right soon. I'm sure she has a few tales to tell."

"You'd better be careful." I tried not to sound like a stern father admonishing his daughter to behave, but as much as I loved her, Melba sometimes tried my patience. She could worry at a subject until it was in rags. "Reilly impresses me as the vindictive type, and you don't want to lose your job. He'll be replaced eventually, and we can hopefully get back to business as usual."

My reward for what I thought was a well-tempered speech was a look full of irritation.

"He'd better not try to fire me," Melba said in a fierce tone. Diesel trilled loudly, alarmed by the shift in his friend's demeanor. "I've been here a long time, and I know a lot of people. People with influence, and if I have to call in favors, I'll do that." She further stated that if Reilly crossed her too much, she would hand him a certain part of his anatomy on a platter and make him kiss it.

Melba was a lot more riled up than I had realized. Normally she was an easygoing sort, but once her temper started rising, she could turn into a gale-force wind.

Before I could speak in an attempt to calm her down, she went on. "He had the nerve this morning to accuse me of lying to him. Can you believe that? Why would I run the risk of lying to my new boss?"

"That is utterly ridiculous." I could feel my own temper start edging toward the red. Melba was one of the most forthright people I knew, and she wouldn't lie. "What could he possibly accuse you of lying about?"

"My lunch hour yesterday. He left for a meeting around ten, and he wasn't back at noon when I left to go to lunch with a friend. He claims he was back by ten to twelve, and I didn't come in from lunch until a few minutes after one." Melba's face reddened as she talked, and I feared for her blood pressure. "When I told him I was late by only about five minutes, he said it was obvious to him I was goofing off the whole time he was gone and had left for lunch a lot earlier." She paused for a deep breath. "Then he said he would see about putting in a time clock to keep me from cheating the college out of work time."

"That's outrageous." I could understand now why Melba was so angry with the jerk. She didn't tolerate any aspersions against her character, particularly against her truthfulness. She did like to gossip more than she probably should, but she never passed along dirt just for the sake of it. She was invariably right, at least in my experience.

"He asked me if I could prove my story, and the way he said it made me want to scratch his eyes out right then." She shook her head. "I tell you, Charlie, that man is crazy."

"Why did he wait until this morning to talk to you about it?"

Melba shrugged. "I don't know. I was so surprised by the whole thing I never asked him." She glanced at her watch. "Break time is over in two minutes. I'd better get back downstairs." She gave Diesel a couple more scratches on his head before she rose.

"Don't do anything rash," I said, even though I knew I risked annoying her further. "I think you ought to talk to human resources and file a complaint for harassment. He's creating a hostile work environment, and he shouldn't be allowed to get away with it. You need to document his behavior toward you and let them handle it."

"Good idea," Melba said. "I'll go call right now and make an appointment." She strode briskly from the room, and moments later I heard her clattering rapidly down the stairs.

Diesel came back around the desk and jumped into his window again. I gave him attention briefly before I turned back to the computer.

I found it difficult to concentrate on work, though, because I was concerned for Melba. What was the matter with Reilly? Why was he so combative?

My thoughts then turned to the strange man in the car. What *was* he doing, sitting out there every day? Keeping someone under surveillance?

I stared at the computer screen blankly for some time while Diesel napped. The ringing of my office phone finally roused me. I picked up the receiver and identified myself.

"Hi, Charlie. Penny Sisson from HR. Sorry to bother you, but I'm afraid I have an issue I need to discuss with you."

"Hi, Penny, what's up?" I didn't know her well, but the college's chief HR officer was known to be intelligent, thoughtful, and highly competent. I wondered if her call had anything to do with Melba's problem with Reilly.

"There's been a complaint."

I couldn't interpret the tone in Penny's voice. There was a bit of hesitancy to it, and that made me uneasy.

"A complaint about me?" I couldn't imagine what I could have done to upset anyone.

"In a way," Penny responded. "Can you come over to my office this afternoon sometime?"

"Sure." I glanced at my watch. Ten minutes after three. "I'm about ready to wind things down here, and I can be over there in about ten minutes." I paused a moment. "Can't you at least tell me what this is about?" Curiosity was one of my besetting sins. I had to know now; otherwise I'd work myself into a tizzy.

Penny exhaled into the phone, and for a moment I thought she would refuse to answer until I was in her office. Then she said, "It's about your cat. We've had a complaint about you bringing him to work with you."

TWO

▪▪▪▪▪▪▪▪▪▪▪▪▪▪▪▪▪▪▪

That—as Aunt Dottie used to say—flew all over me.

I was ready to storm downstairs and have it out with that jerk Reilly, because I had no doubt whatsoever who'd made the complaint. It was exactly the kind of under-handed, childishly vindictive action he would take. All because Diesel wouldn't have anything to do with him. And, I realized, because he knew I'd seen him leering at women.

I forced myself to take a couple of deep breaths so that I could respond in a civilized manner to Penny.

"I'll be over in a few minutes," I said. "Diesel will be with me, and I hope there won't be a problem with that."

"No, not at all," Penny said.

I said good-bye and put down the receiver, still in a fog of rage. Diesel sat up on the window ledge and meowed at me. He had picked up on my distress. I forced myself to calm down and give him some attention to keep him from getting upset as well.

"We're leaving work now, but we're not going straight home," I told him as I stroked his head and down his back. "We're going to talk to a nice lady for a little while, and *then* we're going home." I continued stroking for a few moments, and he relaxed.

Diesel stood patiently while I put on his harness and attached the leash. I powered down the computer, gathered up my backpack and a bottle of water, and we left the office. I made sure the door locked securely behind us. After an unpleasant incident in the fall, I had been overly conscious of the safety of materials in the archive.

As the cat and I made our way downstairs, I prayed that we wouldn't encounter our nemesis. The last person I needed to see right now was Oscar Reilly, because I was still way too angry with him.

My prayer went unanswered, however. Diesel and I made it halfway to the front door from the foot of the stairs, and then I heard Reilly call out to me.

"Leaving early today, Charlie?"

I turned to see Reilly consulting his watch rather ostentatiously. He leaned against the door frame that led into the outer office where Melba worked. I wondered briefly where she was, because I was afraid she would go after him herself for that remark.

I stared at Reilly for a moment, careful to keep my expression neutral, while I longed to walk over and punch that smirk off his face. I seldom had such strong adverse reactions to people, but there was something about Reilly that brought out the worst in me.

Instead, I consulted my own watch, making a grand gesture of it. "Why, no, Oscar, I'm not," I said in a tone that I
might have used to respond to a toddler. "My normal hours
are eight to three, and it's now nearly twenty past. So actually I'm leaving late. I won't claim overtime, though, so you
don't need to worry about that."

Diesel meowed loudly, and Reilly's face darkened,
whether at my tone or at the cat's timely contribution, I
had no idea. I had to suppress the sudden urge to laugh.

Before Reilly could respond, I said brightly, "Diesel
and I have an appointment with the head of HR, Penny
Sisson. So if you'll excuse us, we'll be on our way."

I didn't wait to gauge the effect of my statement on
Reilly. Instead I turned and headed for the door, and Diesel
trotted beside me.

The mid-March afternoon had turned cool, but not
unpleasantly so. I could have used a light jacket, but the
walk to the building that housed HR would warm me.
Diesel had his own coat to keep him warm. The thick ruff
around his neck had started to thin out as the spring and
summer loomed.

The Athena College campus had never looked lovelier—
leaves on the trees beginning to show new canopies of
green, the buildings basking in the glow of the afternoon
sun, the whole scene one of solidity and respectability. The
college had been founded before the Civil War, and a few
of the original buildings remained. I sometimes fancied
that, if I closed my eyes and listened intently enough, I
would hear echoes of students and faculty of generations
past as they went about their business on this historic
campus.

I smiled at my own whimsy and realized that my mood had lightened. *Good for my blood pressure.*

The few students and faculty we encountered during our brief walk to the HR office all smiled and nodded pleasantly at Diesel and me. I knew I had a reputation around campus as an eccentric because I was often seen walking a large cat on a leash, but Diesel and I had not encountered anyone unfriendly in the several years since I'd adopted him and started bringing him to work with me.

The building that housed the human resources department occupied the corner of a street a couple of blocks past the main part of the campus. Though designed with a nod to harmonizing with the older architecture, the structure looked too square and boxy to be anything other than what I called municipal modern. Diesel and I headed up the walk to the front door and stepped inside, where a blast of frigid air greeted us.

I shivered from the onslaught, having warmed up from our walk over. I consulted a directory on the wall to find the number of Penny Sisson's office, and I hoped that her space would be warmer.

"Down the hall this way," I told Diesel, who stood sniffing the air and staring in the opposite direction. He trotted obediently beside me as I strode toward the correct office.

I identified myself to Penny's administrative assistant. She smiled at me and the cat and told us to go right in. I thanked her, and we moved around her desk. Penny awaited us in the doorway with a welcoming smile.

After an exchange of greetings, Penny invited me to have a seat. Diesel settled on the floor beside me, and I glanced around the office. Sun streamed in the windows, helping temper the cold air from the vents. Colorful photos and posters of various scenes in Mexico decorated the walls, and I recalled that Penny's husband was a distinguished anthropologist who worked extensively in Mexico.

"I appreciate your responding so quickly, Charlie." Penny smiled again, a bit nervously this time. She ran a hand through her thick, black curls, and then pushed her horn-rimmed glasses up her nose. "As I mentioned during our phone conversation, there has been a complaint about your bringing Diesel to work with you."

I nodded. "The previous library director gave me permission to have Diesel with me, and it was approved by the president."

"Yes, I'm aware of that." Penny laid her hand on a folder on her desk. "I have copies of both letters in your file. The issue at hand is that the complainant claims to be highly allergic to cats and that having Diesel in the building is making him sick."

My blood pressure rose drastically, but I held on to my temper as I spoke. "I am assuming that the person who lodged the complaint is Oscar Reilly. Is that correct?"

"Yes," Penny said.

"Then he's a liar." I saw no reason to hold back. "I saw him when I left to walk over here, and he displayed no signs of an allergic reaction of any kind. No sneezing, no tearing eyes, no blotchy skin. No sign at all. Surely if he were truly allergic, I would have seen signs of it before now, and I never have in the entire time that he has been working in the building with Diesel and me."

"Oh, dear." Penny's eyes widened. "That's a serious accusation, Charlie."

"I will stand by it," I said. "I am truly sorry that you have been put in the middle of this. I have no idea what game he's playing, other than trying to harass me enough to make me quit. It's not going to work, however. If he wants to keep Diesel out of the building, then he's going to have to prove that he is severely allergic."

"I will note your response." Penny opened the folder, picked up a pen, and started writing. After a few moments, she looked up. "Do you want to lodge a countercomplaint?"

"Not at the moment," I said. "Any further communication on this complaint can go to my lawyer, Sean Harris. Pendergrast and Harris is the firm."

I rose, and Diesel sat up and looked up at me. I smiled down at him. "I don't think there's anything more to say at the moment. Thank you, Penny."

She stood and came around the desk to extend her hand. I shook it, and we exchanged smiles. "I will be *delighted* to share your response to the complaint with Mr. Reilly," she said. "Have a good day."

I bade her good-bye, and Diesel warbled for her. We left her office and wended our way through the building and back outside. As we headed in the direction of home, back the way we had come, I reflected on Penny's choice of words. Why would she be *delighted* to tell Oscar Reilly how I had responded to his complaint? I wondered whether he had made other such malicious, and frivolous, complaints. If so, Penny was no doubt tired of having to deal with them. And him.

Diesel meowed loudly, and I realized I was walking too quickly. I spotted a bench underneath a tree nearby and decided we should sit for a few minutes until I'd had time to cool down a bit. "Come on, boy," I said. "Let's rest here for a while. Sorry for going so fast."

Once I'd made myself comfortable on the wrought iron, Diesel hopped up on the bench and leaned against me. I put my arm around him and rubbed his chest. He purred happily, and as I petted the cat, I could feel my temper cooling down.

My thoughts couldn't stay away from Oscar Reilly for long, however. What did he have against me? I wondered. I couldn't think of a single thing I had done to make him annoyed or angry with me. He might have seen my disgusted expression, I supposed, when I observed him ogling women. Maybe he thought I would report him for that, and this was his way of launching a preemptive strike.

I simply didn't get it. The more I thought about it, the odder it seemed. Was he simply paranoid? Or overly sensitive? Perhaps he had picked up on the fact that I didn't think he was fit for the position he held. Had I somehow given myself away?

Then the memory surfaced, and I knew exactly why he was targeting me through Diesel.

THREE

||||||||||||||||||||||||||||||||||

I hadn't given much thought to the incident at the time, but now that I reconsidered it, I figured it had to be the source of Oscar Reilly's petty-minded attempt to get rid of me.

The occasion was the first senior staff meeting held after Reilly stepped into the suddenly vacant position. He opened the meeting by giving us a short sketch of his background, chiefly as a financial administrator in various university positions. Having grown up poor in New England, he had worked hard to save money and to earn scholarships to put himself through school, although he had taken a couple of years longer than usual because he had to drop out at one point to work several jobs to help pay for his mother's hospital bills. I thought the level of personal detail unnecessary in the situation, and it made me a bit uncomfortable.

After he finished the story of his life before Athena, he

stated twice how important the library was to the college's reputation and accreditation and mentioned that he personally made great use of the online resources. He looked forward, he told us with an ingratiating smile, to working with the university's board of trustees to raise money for a much-needed library addition. In particular, he said, he enjoyed working closely with the Ducote sisters, Miss An'gel and Miss Dickce, and gushed about how gracious and generous they were.

The Ducote sisters had been trustees for many years and were always involved in fund-raising efforts, so I had no doubt Reilly had encountered them. But he mispronounced their surname, giving it two syllables rather than three. He did it several times, and after the meeting ended, I decided I had better tip him off to the fact that the sisters got annoyed when people didn't get their name right.

"Oscar"—he insisted that we address him by his given name—"if you have a moment," I said as we rose from the table, "I need a quick word with you."

"Certainly, Charlie," he said, offering me an expansive smile.

I waited until the room was clear before I explained why I wanted to talk to him. He frowned when I told him the sisters' preferred pronunciation of Ducote (du-COH-tee). I smiled when I finished and added, "I know you wouldn't want to offend them."

Reilly shook his head. "Certainly not. Now, if you'll excuse me, I have another meeting." He turned and strode from the room.

At the time I thought his manner and abrupt departure merely rude, but now I wondered whether he had also been angry because I caught him in a mistake and dared to correct him. At least, I reflected, I hadn't done it in front of the group. He wasn't particularly friendly after that incident, but I never suspected he would act maliciously or vindictively against me because of it.

I could, of course, be letting my imagination run a bit too wild with this, but I couldn't come up with any other reason or explanation for Reilly's making a frivolous complaint.

"I don't know, Diesel." I rubbed the cat a few more times before I stood. "Come on, boy, let's go home." We resumed our walk across campus but took a different route this time, one that would take us by the main library building. I remembered I had a book to return, and I could put it in the book drop by the sidewalk in front.

As we approached the book drop, I glanced past it and noticed Oscar Reilly in the small parking area between the antebellum home that housed our mutual offices and the main library. He was talking on his cell phone, holding it to his left ear, while his right arm gesticulated wildly. He didn't look happy, I decided as I put my book in the drop. He stood in front of his car, a late-model Mercedes, and he kept looking at the windshield while he talked and gestured.

"Come on, Diesel, let's cross the street here." I looked down at the cat, who blinked at me a couple of times and meowed. I wanted to avoid Reilly, and thus far I didn't think he had seen me and my cat. I was curious about what had him so worked up, but I didn't care enough to go find out.

When Diesel and I reached the sidewalk across the street, we walked a bit faster than usual. I wanted to be out of Reilly's sight quickly. I didn't trust my temper if I had to talk to him right now.

"Harris."

My name boomed out at me from across the street, and with great reluctance I halted and turned. Reilly beckoned with his free hand.

"Get over here. Now."

My blood pressure rose rapidly. For a moment I stayed where I was, furious at the peremptory summons. Diesel scuttled behind me and huddled against my legs. I tightened my grip on his leash. The last thing I needed was for him to bolt in fear.

"It's okay, boy," I told him, though it took great effort to speak in a calm tone. "We'll go see what he wants, and then we'll go home." I stepped forward. "Come on, now. It will be okay."

Diesel responded with a plaintive meow but came docilely enough behind me. I checked the street for traffic before we crossed. Reilly waited beside his car, his phone now put away.

"What is it you want?" I asked, my tone barely civil.

Reilly glared at me, his face flushed with anger. He pointed to the windshield of his car. "What do you know about this?"

I almost laughed when I saw what had infuriated him. The windshield bore the slogan *Oscar the Grouch* in large, lurid pink lettering. The words took up the center portion of the glass. The rest of it was covered with what looked like petroleum jelly.

I turned back to Reilly. "I believe that refers to a character from *Sesame Street*."

Reilly cut loose with a string of obscenities, but I simply stared at him. I really shouldn't have tried to goad him, but I was still furious with the man. When the flow trickled to a halt, I said coolly, "If you are asking whether I know who did this, the answer is no, I don't."

Reilly took a step forward, right hand curled into a fist, and I thought he was about to strike me. Before the scene degenerated further, however, a voice interrupted.

"Step back, Reilly. Now."

My erstwhile attacker faltered, no doubt startled by the commanding tone. He turned to see who had spoken.

I had already recognized the voice. The chief of campus police and a retired marine, Martin Ford brooked no nonsense, student, staff, or faculty. Relieved to see him, I stepped away from the still-glowering Reilly, making sure Diesel stayed by my side.

"Look at my car." Reilly gestured imperiously. "What are you going to do about that?"

Chief Ford approached the car and examined the windshield. "I don't think there's any permanent damage. Looks like lipstick and petroleum jelly." He turned to Reilly. "When was the last time you used your car?"

"When I came back from lunch," Reilly said. "Around one."

Ford checked his watch. "Ten to four. That's well over two hours, say two and a half, for someone to do this." He gestured toward the windshield. "Any idea why you're being targeted like this? Third incident, right?"

"Yes, it's the third practical joke." Reilly rubbed his forehead. "Why haven't you caught the jackass who's doing this?"

"It would help," Ford responded in a mild tone, "if I had an idea about *why* these things are happening to you. I repeat, any idea why you're being targeted?"

I figured I could have thrown in a few cents' worth of reasons, but I kept my mouth shut. I was curious to hear what Reilly had to say.

"None of this happened before I took over administration of the library." Reilly's fists clenched. "I'm simply trying to do the job I was asked to do by the president, but obviously some jerk doesn't like what I'm doing. I haven't done anything to provoke this kind of juvenile behavior, I can assure you."

"I see." Ford pulled out his phone and took several pictures of Reilly's windshield. "Probably the work of a student you've somehow annoyed." He put the phone back in its holster on his belt. "We'll keep looking into these incidents, and eventually we'll track down whoever is responsible."

"That's what you told me two days ago," Reilly said, obviously angry. "And yet it's happened again. The president isn't going to be happy when I report this to him."

Ford appeared unruffled by the threat. "I'm not happy, either, Reilly. Don't blow this out of proportion. I told you, we're working on it."

Reilly stared at the chief for a moment, then turned and strode to the back of the library administration building. Moments later, the back door slammed behind him.

Ford turned to me. "Afternoon, Mr. Harris. And you, too, Diesel."

I returned the chief's greeting, and Diesel emerged from behind my legs to let Ford rub his head.

"Any idea what's going on here?" Ford asked.

I shrugged. "He's not popular with the library staff. He has no idea how to run a library, and the staff resent him. I didn't know about the practical jokes, but I guess someone is trying to get back at him for being such a jerk."

Ford arched an eyebrow. "Pretty strong words coming from you. Don't think I've ever heard you speak that way about anyone."

"I haven't had much cause to, I guess." I grinned. "But Reilly brings out the worst in everybody." I was tempted to share the story of Reilly's complaint about Diesel, but I realized that wasn't a good idea.

Ford grimaced. "I want to catch whoever's behind this and put a stop to it before it escalates any further. Right now it's pretty harmless, but it could get ugly if it's unchecked."

"I'll keep my eyes and ears open." Despite the fact that I found the current prank amusing, I knew Ford was right. This behavior had to be stopped before someone got hurt.

Ford nodded as he left. Diesel and I continued on our way home. I thought about the words in pink lipstick on Reilly's windshield. They were innocuous enough, but the prankster had to be pretty annoyed to go to such lengths.

Could Melba have done it? I wondered. She was certainly angry, but surely she wouldn't do something so childish. I could picture her as she was earlier, ranting about Reilly to me.

I stopped suddenly, and Diesel chirped in surprise.

Pink lipstick.

Melba was wearing pink lipstick today.

FOUR

||||||||||||||||||||||||||||||||||

Diesel meowed loudly several times and pulled against his leash, and I realized I still stood in the center of the sidewalk, oblivious to what was happening around me. I heard a loud "Excuse me," and I hastily stepped to one side. Diesel, clever boy, moved nimbly with me so that the woman and her two stuffed canvas bags passed us without further fuss.

Led by my cat, I headed homeward again, a distance now of only about three blocks. My thoughts reverted to Melba and the problem of the pink lipstick. I grimaced at the words; they sounded like the title of a Golden Age detective story by John Dickson Carr. But this situation was happening in the present. I knew there were other women besides Melba who wore pink lipstick, but the coincidence struck me as worrisome.

How to approach the subject with Melba—that was the

question plaguing me as I fished out my keys to unlock the front door. Diesel darted inside the moment the door opened wide enough. I knew the quick entry meant he was eager to visit the litter box.

While my hands coped with the fastenings of the cat's leash and harness, I thought about Melba. I couldn't blame her if she had played that prank on Oscar Reilly. His behavior toward her was inexcusable, and I knew when she had her dander up, she could be a bit unpredictable.

The trouble was, the tenor of this particular prank seemed more like something an undergrad would do, not a woman of Melba's age and experience. If Melba wanted to get her own revenge against Oscar, I figured she would come up with a far subtler, and in the end more devastating, plan.

In the kitchen I headed right for the fridge and helped myself to a glass of ice-cold water. I thought more about Melba and the lipstick. I could just call her and tell her about the scene I had unwillingly witnessed and gauge her reaction. No, upon reflection, I decided it would be better to wait until we were face-to-face again. The direct approach was best.

Loud crunching noises emanated from the nearby utility room. Diesel did enjoy his dry food, though I knew it wouldn't be long before he started campaigning for his nightly serving of wet food. He often had tidbits from the dinner table as well, but I tried to ration them carefully. I also tried to make sure that none of the ingredients of the people food he ate were harmful to cats.

Moments later my gentle giant of a feline ambled purring into the kitchen. That loud noise, the source of his name, always made me feel better. He rubbed his head against my knee for a moment before he stretched out under the table near my feet.

My thoughts shifted to a different topic, though one still connected to the odious Oscar Reilly. What *would* I do if he persisted in his attempts to keep me from bringing Diesel to work at the archive? I could quit, as I'd reasoned earlier, because I didn't absolutely need the money from the job, helpful though it was. I would certainly miss the work I did there, though, because I loved it.

Or, I thought, I could take a leave of absence until the college found a new full-time director of the library. Oscar Reilly was only temporary, after all. *And the more temporary the better.*

That sounded like the superior option, I decided. First, though, I had to find out whether part-time employees could actually take a leave of absence. I pulled out my cell phone and checked the time. Thirteen minutes to five, so perhaps Penny Sisson was still in her office. I had a good memory for phone numbers, and I punched in her number after only a few moments' thought.

As the phone rang several times, I figured I had missed her after all, but then she answered.

When I identified myself, she said, "I'm glad you called, Charlie. I was going to call you first thing tomorrow morning anyway."

"Do you have some news for me?" I asked, a bit surprised.

"Yes, and I don't think you'll be happy with it." I could hear the tension in her voice. "I spoke with Mr. Reilly and passed along your message about proof of allergies and

25

your lawyer's name. Mr. Reilly said he'd be happy to provide proof. He needs time to get in touch with his physician back East, though."

"How much time?" I asked, dismayed by the news. I really expected Reilly to back down after I called his bluff.

"It might take as much as a week, according to him," Penny said.

"In the meantime, do I have to leave Diesel at home when I go in to work?"

Penny sighed. "That would be best. I know it's annoying, but I don't think you should antagonize Mr. Reilly."

"I've been thinking about taking a leave of absence from the archive," I said. "Are part-time employees allowed to do that?"

"Yes, provided that you have the approval of your supervisor," Penny said. "Do you think Mr. Reilly would approve your request?"

"I don't know," I said. Frankly, I doubted he would, simply to be difficult.

"It can't hurt to ask," Penny said. "There's a form in the faculty and staff handbook. Fill it out and give it to him. Let me know the outcome."

"I'll do that," I said and told her good-bye.

I put the phone on the table and looked down at my cat. Diesel stared up at me with his trusting, loving eyes, and I knew whatever decision I made about the job, I would consider his best interests first and foremost. After all the years of taking him along with me everywhere I went— except to church, the grocery store, and the occasional visit to my doctor—I couldn't suddenly start leaving him at home. Azalea wouldn't mind looking after him, though she pretended half the time that he was a pest and got in her way. The rest of the time she sneaked him bites of bacon and sang gospel music to him. Despite his newfound friendship with my housekeeper, I knew Diesel would be unhappy without me. I would certainly be unhappy at work, worrying about him.

Thoughts of Azalea reminded me to check to see what she'd left for my dinner. I checked the fridge and found the casserole dish I had overlooked earlier. Resting atop the plastic wrap that covered the food was a note from Azalea with instructions on reheating the food. She went on to say that there was a bowl of salad as well, along with a freshly made jar of her homemade Thousand Island dressing.

Diesel and I would dine alone tonight. My son, Sean, would be with his fiancée and law partner, Alexandra Pendergrast. He still claimed my house as his home in Athena, but he spent most of his nights with Alexandra at her place. Though engaged, they had not yet set a firm wedding date. I fretted about that, wishing they would finalize things, but my son was every bit as hardheaded as I was, and I knew it was useless to discuss the matter with him.

One of my boarders, Justin Wardlaw, now in his junior year at Athena College, was in England for the semester. I knew from his occasional e-mails that he was having a wonderful time there, but I did miss his cheerful, albeit at times rambunctious, presence in the house.

My other boarder, Stewart Delacorte, did not often dine with me. He spent any spare moment he had with his boyfriend, Haskell Bates, the taciturn sheriff's deputy, whenever Bates was off duty. I had thought Stewart might move in with him, but for now he seemed content to remain in his suite on the third floor.

After deciding that it was too early for dinner, I headed for the den and my laptop computer. I might as well find the necessary form and submit my request for a leave of absence. If Oscar refused, then I would simply hand in my resignation. I didn't want to have to deal with him any more than I had to.

Diesel hopped on the couch beside me while I waited for the computer to boot up. He nestled his head against my thigh, and I rubbed along his spine. He rewarded me with loud purring and the occasional warble.

I hadn't had much call before now to consult the Athena College employee handbook, but it took me only a moment to find it on the website. I downloaded the form I needed, then exited the browser. The form didn't require much work, but I did have to think carefully about what I entered under the reason for the request. I couldn't say what I really wanted to, that I didn't want to deal with a jerk of a boss. Instead, I finally settled on the vague statement that I had urgent personal matters that needed my complete attention. In the blank for amount of time requested, I put six months. Surely by then, I hoped, there would be a new library director. The search had started right after Peter Vanderkeller left, and that was a couple of months ago.

Once the form was done, I attached it to an e-mail message to Oscar Reilly, and I copied Penny Sisson. I clicked on the Send button and stared at the screen for a moment. I had an odd feeling, as if having crossed a personal Rubicon, but I was glad I had done it.

I set the laptop aside and regarded the dozing cat lying

next to me. There were no doubt many who would question my decision, separating myself from a job I loved because of a household pet. Those who would question, however, were not people I particularly cared to know. Diesel was as much a member of my family as my children, their partners, and my own dear friend, Helen Louise Brady.

The front doorbell chimed, and Diesel perked up at once. He hopped down from the couch and trotted out of the room. I followed more slowly, thanks to legs and a back that stiffened up while I sat on the couch.

The bell chimed a second time before I could get to the door. "Coming," I called out loudly. Diesel already waited beside the door. He chirped to let me know he wanted the door open.

"I know, boy, I know," I muttered. I unlocked and opened the door.

Lisa Krause, the head of circulation and reference at the Athena College Library, stood on the doorstep, her expression one of mixed anger and anxiety.

"Thank goodness you're home, Charlie," she said. "I hope you don't mind my coming by without calling first, but I'm just so upset I had to talk to someone I could trust."

"Of course not," I said. "Come on in."

Lisa stepped in far enough for me to close the door, and Diesel warbled for her. Her face cleared a little as she regarded the friendly cat. She rubbed his head for a moment and then began to smile.

"He really is good at making me feel better." Lisa took a steadying breath. "I don't suppose you'd let me borrow him for a couple of days?" She smiled.

"I'm afraid he's a noncirculating item most of the time,"

I said, and she rolled her eyes at the intentionally bad pun. "Come on in the kitchen, and let me get you something to drink. Tea, coffee, a soft drink? What would you like?"

"A bottle of bourbon," Lisa said as she followed me. "But a soft drink will do."

"That bad, eh?" I asked as I motioned for her to take a seat at the table.

"It's so ridiculous I still can't believe it happened." Lisa dropped her purse on the table and plopped into the chair. "I swear, Charlie, if you hear that someone ran down Oscar Reilly in the street, you can bet it was me."

FIVE

||||||||||||||||||||||||

I couldn't say that I was surprised by the source of Lisa's distress. Oscar Reilly appeared to excel at annoying everyone around him—or at least everyone in the Athena College Library. Perhaps he was a joy to work with in his normal role—but I wouldn't want to bet on that.

I handed Lisa a cold can and a glass. "I think there might be a few people ahead of you on that." I sat in my usual spot to her left.

Lisa offered a wry grin as she popped the top on her can and poured some of the liquid into her glass. "Wouldn't surprise me if the line stretched halfway around the football stadium." She set down the can and had a sip of her drink.

"What did he do to you?"

Her expression turned grim. "He basically called me a liar. He didn't come right out and say I was, but he might as well have." She paused for another sip of her drink. "At first I was so stunned by it I was absolutely speechless. I've been stewing about it most of the day."

I didn't know Lisa anywhere near as well as I knew Melba, but based on my knowledge of her character, I would have said she was not a prevaricator. I had always found her straightforward and open.

"Exactly what did he say?" I asked.

Diesel had been sitting next to me but the obvious distress in Lisa's voice caused him to move to her side and bump his head against her leg. She smiled down at him and rubbed his head. "Thank you, sweet boy. You are just the kind of tonic I need right now." She raised her head to look at me while she continued to stroke the cat.

"He called me to his office this morning to discuss the preliminary budget I'd turned in for the coming fiscal year," she said. "At first everything seemed fine, then suddenly he started questioning me on some of the line items from the current year's budget. He seemed particularly interested in the travel budget." She frowned. "It's been cut repeatedly the last few years, but we still have some money for a couple of us to attend meetings. I went to a meeting back in the fall in San Francisco for a committee I'm on, and he peppered me with questions about it." She paused for another sip of her drink. "I answered him as best I could, though he didn't seem really interested in my answers. Then all of a sudden, he said, 'So if I got in touch with other members of the committee, they'll say you actually attended the sessions?'"

I felt her distress level rise with every word, and so did Diesel. He began an anxious warbling, but Lisa appeared not to hear. When she broke off, he butted his head against her leg, and she focused on him with an apologetic glance. "I didn't mean to upset him, Charlie. I'm so sorry."

"It's okay," I said. "He's simply worried because he knows you're upset. It's all right, Diesel. Lisa is going to be fine."

Lisa continued to stroke him while I considered what to say in response to her encounter with Oscar.

"I can't reveal the details, but I heard a similar story earlier today involving Oscar." I smiled at her. "In that instance, too, he chose as his target someone who is honest to a fault. I have no idea what he thinks to gain by behavior like this, but my advice to you is to go to HR and file a complaint. He is creating a hostile work environment, and that constitutes harassment."

"I considered that." Lisa sighed. "But frankly the thought of it makes me feel like throwing up. Now that I know he's pulled the same thing on someone else, though, I know I really need to do it. Is this other person going to file a complaint?"

"Yes, and this person has been with the college for a little over thirty years. She has a lot of credibility, as do you. You have an excellent record, as far as I'm aware. Don't let him continue to get away with this kind of nastiness." I considered telling her about my own issue with Oscar but decided that it would sound slightly frivolous when compared to her situation.

Lisa nodded. "Thank you, Charlie. I can't tell you how much I appreciate you letting me vent and giving me good advice." She grinned suddenly. "I wish you would apply for the director's job. You'd be terrific to work for."

As always, my first reaction to such praise was embarrassment. I struggled to speak for a moment. "Thank you, Lisa. I'm touched by your kind regard and your faith in my abilities. But my days of being in charge of a library are done."

"I can't blame you for not wanting to take it on," Lisa said. "It's bound to be full of headaches and politics."

"True," I said. "I had enough of both during my years as a branch manager at the public library in Houston."

Diesel seemed to be satisfied that Lisa was okay. He moved away from her and back beside my chair. He stretched and ended up with his head against one of the chair legs.

"Our loss." Lisa stood. "Thanks again for the tea and sympathy, so to speak. I'd better get home and let my dogs out for a run in the backyard."

Diesel and I escorted her to the door and let her out. She turned to wave as she headed down the walk to where her car was parked on the street. Diesel and I watched until she was safely in her car, and then I closed the door.

What the heck was Oscar Reilly up to? I considered that as Diesel and I wandered back into the kitchen.

I couldn't fathom the method to his madness—for surely it was madness to antagonize one person after another in the library. I wondered if he had bullied other library personnel in this manner. Or had he made Melba, Lisa, and me targets for a particular reason?

Could he be trying to make us all quit of our own accord? I couldn't imagine why he would, but in my case at least he was doing a darn good job.

I decided I might as well start getting my dinner ready.

I took the casserole dish out of the fridge and put it in the oven, following Azalea's instructions about the proper temperature and timing. Then I went to the utility room to open a can of wet food for Diesel. I left him scarfing it down while I went back into the kitchen.

I would've loved to talk all this over with Helen Louise, but I knew she would be too busy right now to chat. I would have to wait until later tonight. For a moment I was tempted to take the casserole out of the oven, pack Diesel into the car, and drive over to the bistro and have dinner there.

But then I realized that I was being selfish. Helen Louise needed to be able to focus on work, not sit and hold my hand and listen to my troubles when she had customers lined up, waiting to be served.

The noise of a key turning in the lock of the kitchen door brought me out of my reverie. I looked in that direction to see Sean stepping into the room.

"Hi, Dad, how are you?" Sean came over to the table and set his briefcase down. He went to the fridge and rummaged around for a beer.

"Doing okay, Son, how are you?"

"Better now," he said, brandishing the bottle of beer. He popped the cap off and came back to the table to join me.

"Rough day?" I asked.

Sean shook his head. "No, not that bad really, just intense. Crazy family members challenging a will. Like something out of a really bad movie. Hard to believe lunatics like these guys are free and on the street." He grinned suddenly. "They're going to make a heck of a chapter in my memoirs one of these days."

"With the names changed to protect the not-so-innocent," I said, and he grinned even more broadly.

"Something like that." Sean sipped at his beer. "What about you? You were looking pretty serious when I came in."

Diesel chose that moment to amble back into the room. He chirped several times and approached Sean for attention. Sean complied, rubbing the cat's head until Diesel purred.

"Actually I do have a matter to discuss with you. I might need your professional services."

Sean regarded me with concern. "What happened?"

He had already heard me talk about Oscar Reilly, so now I simply related what had happened today. As an afterthought, I included the incident in the parking lot. I wouldn't put it past Oscar to try to blame me for it.

Sean listened without comment until I finished. Then he shook his head. "Wonder what his game is?" He thought for a moment. "Until he produces his proof of allergy to cats, I think it's probably best that you don't take Diesel with you. Or simply don't go to work at all."

"That's my plan," I said. "I don't want to deal with him. In fact, I put in for a leave of absence. I figured I could take time off until the college finds a new library director." I sighed. "The only problem is, Oscar has to approve the leave."

Sean drained his bottle and set it on the table. "You think he will?"

"I don't know. He might, but I think it's more likely he'll refuse."

"If he does turn out to be allergic to cats, and he won't approve your leave request, what will you do?"

"I'll quit," I said. "I don't want to, because I love what I do there. But I'm not going to leave Diesel at home. It's not fair to him after all this time."

Sean suddenly looked a bit uncomfortable. "We've never talked about this, Dad, and it's not really my business, but will you be okay financially if you quit?"

I had never told either of my children the full extent of my aunt's legacy, beyond the fact that she left me her house and some money to keep it up. In truth, she left me quite a considerable inheritance that, combined with my pension from the city of Houston, made it unnecessary for me to work.

"I'll be fine," I said. "Aunt Dottie left me pretty comfortably well-off, and I don't really have to work. I do it because I like to keep busy and I like to think I'm providing a useful service to my alma mater."

"What do you know?" Sean grinned. "Had no idea my old, doddering father was a rich man. You'd better watch your coffee from now on."

"Ha ha." I had never fully discussed my financial status with either of my children. They knew I was comfortably off, but this was the first time I had admitted to one of them that I didn't have to work to make ends meet.

"Seriously, though, I'm glad for your sake. I don't like to see you treated this way, and if necessary, I'll act on your behalf, of course. But for now, I think we have to wait to get the doctor's report."

"If it ever shows up," I said. Diesel warbled loudly, and both Sean and I laughed. "Diesel agrees with me. Neither of us thinks that Oscar is really allergic to him. The man seems to be a born troublemaker."

The front doorbell chimed and startled me. I rose from the table.

"While you see who that is," Sean said, "because it's bound to be for you, I'm going to run upstairs and pick up a couple of things from my room."

Diesel accompanied me to the door while Sean climbed the stairs two at a time.

I opened the door to find a distraught Melba standing there.

"You're not going to believe this," she said as she entered the house. She paused for a moment to scratch Diesel's head while I shut the door.

Melba looked at me, her expression stormy. "That man is now saying I vandalized his car with lipstick. Can you believe it? I would never do anything so stupid."

I glanced at her lips. Their pink hue looked uncomfortably like the color of the lipstick on Oscar's windshield. I said that to her as tactfully as I could.

"I know that, Charlie," she said. "The thing is, it probably is my lipstick. But I didn't do it."

SIX

 ⅏⅏⅏⅏⅏⅏⅏⅏⅏

"Wait a minute," Melba said with a puzzled expression. "How did you know about Oscar's car?"

"Come on in the kitchen, and I'll tell you." I motioned for her to precede me, and Diesel escorted her, meowing every few steps. That was how he expressed concern for his friend.

Before I got involved in a long conversation with Melba, I figured I'd better turn the heat down on the oven, or my dinner would get completely dried out.

That done, I continued with my story once she was seated. Diesel leaned against one of her legs. "Diesel and I happened to walk by the parking lot not long after Oscar discovered the vandalism. He summoned me over and demanded to know what I knew about it."

"So he was trying to blame you first," Melba said in a tone laden with disgust. "Figures."

"How about something to drink?"

"Got a bottle of bourbon?" She gave me a wry grin. "Water will do, thanks."

I started to remark on the coincidence of her asking for bourbon the way Lisa had, but I caught myself in time. I couldn't betray Lisa's confidence, just as I hadn't told Lisa about Melba's issue with Oscar. I had to watch what I said to Melba carefully.

Once Melba had a couple of sips of water, I posed a question. "You said that it probably was your lipstick that was used to do this. Did somebody steal it out of your purse?"

"Out of my top desk drawer," Melba said. "I put the day's lipstick there so I don't have to dig in my purse." She brandished the large, bulging handbag, then set it down again. "Some creep went into my desk and took it."

"Did the creep put it back after he or she was done with it?"

"No, they didn't." Melba scowled. "Not that I'd want it back anyway after the way it was used, but it wasn't cheap, let me tell you. Oscar made a stupid joke about all my pink earlier in the day." She indicated the pink pants and jacket she wore with a white top. "So I knew he'd noticed my lip color."

Diesel rubbed against Melba's leg. He knew she was still upset. For his sake and hers, I hoped Melba would calm down a bit, and soon.

"Did you tell him someone stole the lipstick out of your desk?"

"At first, when he accused me, I didn't know it *was* stolen," Melba said. "Then when I was going to whip mine

40

out and show him it was practically a new tube, it wasn't there."

"I'll bet he took that as proof." I shook my head at the man's hardheaded obtuseness and lack of judgment.

"He sure did." Melba downed the remaining water. She set the empty glass on the table and leaned back in her chair. One hand stroked Diesel's head while the fingers of the other beat a tattoo on the table.

"I don't know what I'm going to do, Charlie," she finally said. "I can't work for that man one more day. He might fly off the handle any minute and accuse me of the good Lord knows what. But I don't have much vacation time at the moment, after I took that month off at Christmas to go visit my cousin in Orlando."

"I suppose you could try what I'm trying," I said, though I realized now it wouldn't work for either of us.

Melba perked up. "What's that?"

"Ask for a leave of absence. I submitted my request form a little while ago."

She slumped back in her chair again. "Fat chance of him agreeing to that." She shot me a curious glance. "Why are you wanting a leave of absence all of a sudden? What has he done to you?"

"Complained to HR about me bringing Diesel to work with me. He's claiming he's allergic to cats." I snorted in derision. "Have you seen any signs of him having allergies? I haven't."

"Not a one," Melba said. "I swear, if someone doesn't get rid of that jerk, I may do it myself. Imagine picking on this sweet, darling boy." She looked down at Diesel. "We don't like that nasty man, do we, boy? You knew right away he was a stinker."

Diesel warbled in response, as if he had understood every word. Frankly, I often thought he did. Or if not all the words, the sense of them and the emotion with which they were spoken.

"Let's talk about the stolen lipstick," I said, "and see if we can figure out who had the opportunity to take it. When was the last time you remember seeing it or using it today?"

Melba thought for a moment. "I did a little touch-up about nine thirty, after I finished my coffee. Usually I check it before I leave for lunch, and then when I get back. But I was in a hurry to get out the door for lunch and didn't check. Oscar had so much urgent work waiting for me the minute I got back from lunch, and I never even thought about checking my lipstick."

"I saw Oscar in the parking lot with his car not long after three thirty," I said. "That's a big window of opportunity for someone to steal the lipstick. Depending, of course, on when the lipstick was used on Oscar's windshield. Who came into your office today?"

"Lisa Krause, for one," Melba said right away. "Oscar wanted to talk to her about something, and it was after nine thirty when she showed up." She frowned. "I'm pretty sure I went to the ladies' room while she was with him, so I guess she had the opportunity."

"Was she still with him when you came back from the ladies' room?" I asked. "You weren't gone that long, were you?"

"No, I wasn't," Melba said. "But I didn't leave my desk for probably a good ten minutes, though, after she went in to Oscar's office. I was gone probably five minutes, max, and she'd left by then."

Lisa was so distraught over Oscar's accusation that I supposed she could have decided to get back at him with a prank. I didn't think, however, that she would do such a juvenile thing.

"Anyone else come into the office?" I hoped there were more viable suspects besides Lisa.

"Delbert Winston came along right after Oscar and I finished our little meeting." She grimaced. "I went to the ladies' room again and stayed there for at least ten minutes. Delbert was gone by the time I came back."

Delbert Winston, the head of the cataloging department, who also did minor repairs on damaged books, had a small run-in with Oscar the first week Oscar took over, I recalled. Something to do with supplies Delbert ordered and that Oscar canceled. Delbert, only a couple of years away from retirement, didn't strike me as a strong candidate for the role of practical joker. I didn't think he would risk being fired if caught doing something like this. I figured Oscar would make sure the culprit lost his or her job, if the truth ever came out.

"That's two people," I said. "Nobody else?"

Melba shook her head. "Not while I was in the office. Oscar was gone part of the time, and then I was up in your office for a good ten minutes. Anyone could have come in and stolen the lipstick then."

It was more like twenty minutes, but I hadn't begrudged her the time.

"I hope neither Lisa nor Delbert was involved," I said. "I like them both. This one's up to Chief Ford to handle."

A thought struck me. "There's another question. Where did the petroleum jelly on the windshield come from?"

"Beats me." Melba shrugged. "I didn't have any in my desk or in my purse. I guess the joker must have had it on him. Or her."

I nodded. "I suppose so. Well, enough of that. I have something to share. Penny Sisson called me this afternoon and told me about the complaint. I went to talk to her, and I told her that I thought Oscar wasn't telling the truth." I grinned. "She didn't say anything outright, but I could tell she doesn't care much for Oscar, either."

"Probably she's had to deal with other complaints from him, or about him." Melba laughed. "At least we know we're not the only ones who hate his guts."

"You need to go to HR first thing in the morning. Tell Penny about this, and get your own complaint on record. If they receive enough complaints, they'll have to do something."

Melba nodded. "I already made an appointment for tomorrow morning. Remember, you suggested I do that this afternoon."

"You're right," I said. "It slipped my mind, thanks to all the goings-on." I laughed. "I have a feeling Penny's going to be busy tomorrow."

Melba's eyes narrowed. "What is it you're not telling me?"

I shook my head. "Sorry, I can't break a confidence. All you need to know is that Oscar has targeted another person besides the two of us. This person is also going to file a complaint. I realize now that I need to file a countercomplaint myself."

"You darn sure should," Melba said. "I'd talk to that

gorgeous lawyer son of yours." She grinned suddenly. "I think maybe I'll do that myself. He sure is good to look at."

"Sean is here," I said. "I was talking to him about all this right before you arrived. He ought to be down soon, if you want to stay and talk to him."

"I'm surely tempted." Melba rose from her chair. "But I'm going to wait till I've had time to talk to Penny tomorrow morning. Then I may give him a call."

I rose to escort her out with Diesel right behind us. At the door, Melba turned and gave me a quick hug. She let me go before I could gather my wits enough to hug her back. She smiled and slipped out the door after one last scratch of the head for Diesel.

The door shut, I stood there for a moment with Diesel staring anxiously up at me. I rubbed his head while I thought about the situation at work. Peter Vanderkeller, the director who suddenly quit, wasn't the best library director I'd ever worked for, but he was smart enough to let his staff do their jobs. As a consequence, the library ran smoothly, from everything I'd seen the past several years.

Now we were saddled with a man who did not have the right kind of personality to be an effective leader, nor did he have any understanding of the workings of an academic library. He might be a wizard with financial machinations, but as the person in charge of a library, he was a complete dud.

I wondered if it would do any good to approach the president of the college directly and express my concerns. He had seemed like a sensible man, a good leader—until he foisted Oscar Reilly on the library. That was a spectacular error in judgment. I feared that, if no action was taken soon to stop Oscar's bizarre behavior, excellent staff members might quit, even if they really couldn't afford to. Or Oscar might start firing people he didn't like.

Diesel trilled loudly, and I came out of my reverie to see him regarding me with what looked like alarm.

I smiled at him. "I'm okay, buddy, I promise. I was only thinking hard about something. Let's go back to the kitchen so I can check on my dinner."

The cat gave a couple of happy meows, and back to the kitchen we went. I checked the casserole and adjusted the heat upward again. My dinner ought to be ready in less than ten minutes.

"Who was at the door?" Sean asked as he strode into the kitchen carrying a small canvas tote bag in one hand. He set the bag on the table after a wary glance at the cat. He had learned early on not to set anything like that on the floor unless he wanted Diesel to pull everything out and then try to insert himself in it.

"Melba." I recounted her story to Sean, and he rolled his eyes.

"This guy is really rocking for a knocking," he said. "What is he hoping to accomplish, I wonder? Is he deliberately trying to screw things up, or is he just a nutcase?"

"I can't decide," I said. "I've been thinking I might go to the president and talk about the situation with him."

Sean shook his head and fixed me with his stern gaze. "No, Dad, you shouldn't do that. If this Reilly finds out about it, then the situation gets more complicated. You don't want trouble from that." His gaze softened. "I know you want to help Melba, but in this case you have to let things work out without you getting any more involved than you have to."

"You're right." I sighed. "I have to stifle this impulse I have to rush in and try to make things better. The good Lord knows this situation doesn't need any more complications." I went back to the oven and checked the casserole. It looked ready, so I grabbed oven mitts, pulled it out, and set it on a trivet on the table.

"Do you have time for a bite?" I asked. "One of Azalea's specialties, chicken and mushrooms with rice."

Sean gazed hungrily at the casserole, then shook his head. "Much as I'd love to, I'd better get back to the office. Alex and I have a little more work to do, then I'm taking her out to dinner." He picked up his bag. "Take care, Dad, and I'll talk to you tomorrow. Diesel, you try to keep him out of trouble."

The cat chirped, and Sean grinned as he headed to the door. I called my good-bye and good wishes after him, and the door shut behind him.

After I prepared myself a bowl of salad and poured a glass of water, I sat down to eat. Diesel sat beside me and tapped my leg a few times in hopes of snagging a treat. I had to deny him, however, because the casserole contained onions—truly bad for cats. Also, I wasn't too sure about the mushrooms.

While I ate my delicious meal, and occasionally gave attention to the always-famished feline by my leg, I mulled over the prank played on Oscar. Surely there were other possibilities besides my library colleagues.

Besides my library colleagues. Of course, you idiot.
Why did the culprit have to be a library staff member?
Why couldn't it be someone from the finance office, where
Oscar had been working before he was transferred?

SEVEN

||||||||||||||||||||||||||||||||||||

Yes, I decided, I shouldn't limit the suspects to library staff. Surely, unless his current behavior was a bizarre aberration, he had caused similar turmoil among the staff in the financial department.

I did not know anyone personally who worked in that area, however. Even though I knew it was Chief Ford's job to uncover the culprit, I couldn't help my overlarge bump of curiosity. I wouldn't call it overlarge myself, but Sean and Laura often did.

Then I remembered Melba saying she intended to scrape up an acquaintance with a young woman who worked in the finance office. Perhaps she wouldn't go through with that, however, since she planned to file a complaint.

After I finished my meal, I cleaned up the small mess I'd made and put my dishes and utensils in the dishwasher.

I checked my watch and saw that I had another four hours to wait before I could call Helen Louise. I didn't like to call her at work and usually waited until I figured she was home. That meant not until ten. The bistro closed at nine, and Helen Louise and her staff had to balance out the registers and perform a few other tasks before they all went home.

Television didn't appeal, and I had plenty of books, so I headed upstairs with Diesel to read. Soon my cat and I lay in comfort on the bed. Diesel stretched out beside me, head on his own pillow. His eyes regarded me groggily for a few minutes while I read. Then he fell asleep.

I awoke later when the insistent ringing of my cell phone roused me. I put aside the book that had lain across my chest and fumbled for the phone. My eyes registered the time, ten fifteen, and the caller's number a moment before I answered.

"Hello, love." I couldn't hold back a yawn.

"You fell asleep reading again, didn't you?" I could hear the smile in Helen Louise's voice. "I figured you had when you didn't call right on the dot at ten."

"Yes, I did, sorry. Told myself that for once I wasn't going to do it."

Diesel was awake now, too, because he knew that one of his favorite humans was talking to me. He warbled.

"Diesel sends his greetings," I said.

"I heard," Helen Louise replied. "Scratch his head for me. How was your day, love?"

"Eventful," I said. "Nothing earth-shattering, so no need to worry. I'll fill you in on the details tomorrow night." We had plans for dinner, just the two of us. Diesel warbled again, as if to remind me that there would be three, not two.

Helen Louise laughed, a sound I loved. "No need. Melba came by on her way home from your house to pick up dinner. She filled me in on all of it."

"I hope she didn't alarm you over any of this," I said.

"She didn't alarm me, but naturally I'm concerned," she said. "I find it curious that he waited this long to complain about Diesel. Surely, if he were that allergic, he would have mentioned it the first day."

"Of course he would," I said. "Another reason I'm sure he's lying about it. He claims he's getting proof from his doctor, but whatever the so-called doctor says, I won't believe it. The man apparently lives to antagonize people."

"Sounds to me like one or both of his oars aren't hitting the water." Helen Louise laughed again. "I'm curious now to see this guy for myself."

"I don't have any plans to introduce you," I said in a wry tone. "I've applied for a leave of absence from the archive, but since Oscar has to approve it, I doubt I'll get it. I may end up quitting so I don't have to put up with his craziness."

"I'd hate to see you quit a job you love so much. I want you to stay busy so you don't have time to run around town, chasing other women." She laughed.

"Oh, I could fit it in if I really wanted to," I said in an arch tone. "But why do that when I've already found you?"

She laughed again, and after that, the conversation turned a bit soppy, as Sean would have called it during his teenage years. A few minutes later we said good night, I turned out the light, and Diesel and I went back to sleep, me with a huge smile.

The next morning, after a delicious breakfast cooked and served by Azalea, I decided to take Diesel for a morning walk. This wasn't one of my workdays at the archive, and I felt restless. Diesel chirped happily when he saw the harness and leash in my hands. He enjoyed these little rambles as much as I did, for we invariably ran into at least one or two of his admirers in the neighborhood.

The air had a cool, crisp edge to it, and I wore a light jacket as we started out. I would probably shed it before we returned home. Diesel liked to trot along at first, eager to encounter his friends, and I had to walk briskly to keep up.

By habit, Diesel turned onto the sidewalk in the direction of the college. I thought about turning to go the other way, but I decided I wasn't going to let the possibility of an encounter with Oscar spoil our morning. I checked my watch—a few minutes past nine. Oscar should be safely in his office by now.

We met two neighbors along the way, and I stopped to chat while Diesel received the attention he enjoyed. By the time we neared the campus and the library administration building, it was almost nine thirty. Now a bit too warm, I shed my jacket and slung it over my shoulder. Diesel continued toward the library building, because we didn't usually come this way unless we were headed for work.

"Not today, boy." I halted, and Diesel stopped to look up at me with what I called his interrogative expression. "We're not working today." He meowed in disapproval. He was no doubt eager to go inside to see his buddy Melba.

In my peripheral vision I caught a blur of motion. I

turned my head slightly to observe a tall man extricating himself gingerly from a small car.

He had to be the man Melba talked about yesterday. I had forgotten about him until now, but, my curiosity piqued, I started walking toward the library, even though I knew it would confuse the cat.

"Good morning," I called out when Diesel and I were about ten feet away from where the man stood by his car. "Lovely day, isn't it?"

Evidently startled, the man whipped his head in my direction, his expression confused at first. Confusion quickly turned to blandness, however. "Good morning to you, and to your companion. Yes, it is a beautiful day." He leaned back against the car and crossed his arms over his chest. He continued to regard Diesel and me—warily, I thought—as we moved to within five feet of him.

Closer up, I realized the stranger—clearly a Yankee, by his accent—had to be at least six foot seven. I felt a bit puny in contrast, though I was by no means a small man. The stranger had broad, muscular shoulders, with upper arms that strained against the tight fabric of his cotton shirt. He had a vaguely menacing air about him, though I couldn't determine why I felt that way. Perhaps it was simply his size. I had seldom seen so big a man in the flesh.

"I don't think I've seen you around campus before," I said in my best chatty manner. I thought giving him the impression of a dotty Southerner might disarm him enough to let something slip. "I work in the building right there, but today is one of my days off."

I caught the direction of his gaze and went on. "This is my Maine Coon, Diesel. He goes to work with me.

Actually, I take him with me almost everywhere. Do you like cats?"

Startled, the man raised his eyes to mine. "Not so much. I'm more of a dog person, I guess. He's really big. Shouldn't he be on a diet?"

"No, he isn't overweight. Well, maybe only a pound or two," I admitted. "Maine Coons are big cats, although Diesel is much bigger than the average male."

The object of the conversation remained by my leg. His usual practice was to approach a stranger and sniff, then wait to be petted. When he hung back like this, I knew it meant there was something about the person that put him off. My cat was an excellent judge of character, and I decided I should heed his judgment.

"So am I." The stranger guffawed. "Bigger than the average male, I mean." He flexed his shoulders and stared down at me.

Was that meant as a warning? Or was he simply showing off his superior size and musculature?

He had made no attempt to answer my question, I realized, so I created another opportunity.

"If you've never been on campus before," I said in a fatuously pleasant tone, "Diesel and I would be happy to show you around. In addition to working here, I'm also an alumnus." I held out a hand. "I'm Charlie Harris."

The stranger eyed me for a moment, then stuck out his hand. "Porter Stanley. Thanks, but I don't need a tour."

That's something, I thought. *At least I have a name.*

Then Stanley appeared to reconsider. "Tell you what, though, I wouldn't mind seeing inside that building." With a jerk of his head, he indicated the administration building.

"I really like antebellum architecture, and I never pass up the chance to see inside old places like this."

"I'll be happy to show you." I wondered how Melba would react when she saw me bringing her mysterious and menacing stranger into the building. "Come on, Diesel, let's show the nice man where we work." I turned toward the building and didn't wait to see whether Stanley followed me.

I launched into a history of the building as I headed up the steps to the verandah. I felt Stanley's presence beside me. I paused on the verandah to point out a few features before I opened the front door and motioned for him to precede the cat and me. He had to duck his head to enter, and his massive frame filled the doorway.

Inside I chattered away about the staircase, the antique carpets and furniture in the entrance, and the hallway. I saw that the door to Melba's office stood open, as usual, though she wasn't there. Then I remembered she had an appointment this morning with Penny Sisson, to file her complaint. I really would have liked to see her reaction to Porter Stanley, but there might be another opportunity.

Stanley nodded now and then during my peroration on the house, and to my surprise he didn't look bored. He appeared to be taking in the details with considerable interest. Perhaps he really was fascinated by antebellum architecture.

Diesel remained silent. He made a couple of attempts to go up the stairs but I called him back. "Our office is upstairs," I said. "He thinks we're here to work today, but it's actually my day off."

Stanley nodded. He pointed toward Melba's door. "What's in there?"

"The outer part of it is the office of the administrative assistant to the library director," I said. "She must be off from work today. She and Diesel are big buddies, and she would have been out here to see him the moment she spotted us."

Stanley didn't respond to that. "What else? Another office in there?"

I nodded. "Yes, the library director's office is there, too. The room next to it." I wasn't eager to see Oscar myself, but I was too curious to see Stanley's reaction if the two men did meet. "He's probably in his office. Would you like to meet him?"

Stanley shrugged. "Why not?" He appeared not to be particularly interested in Oscar, but I still wondered.

"Let's go knock on his door," I said. "Come on, Diesel." We headed into Melba's office, and the cat sniffed and looked around for his friend. The door into Oscar's office stood slightly ajar. As we moved nearer, I heard voices emanating from it. I heard Oscar's usual rumble, followed by the strident tones of a voice I recognized all too well.

The head of the library's collection development and acquisitions unit, Cassandra—"Don't ever call me Cass"—Brownley rarely spoke in anything other than an irritable tone. I had never known anyone who always appeared to be annoyed at something, but Cassandra invariably seemed to be. I wasn't in the least surprised to hear her arguing with Oscar.

I turned to Stanley with an apologetic expression. "I think we should continue our tour and come back a bit later. The director appears to be in a meeting." Diesel had shrunk back against me. He hated arguments, especially one as loud and apparently rancorous as this one. I couldn't make out the words, but I could tell Cassandra was mighty upset over something.

"Okay," Stanley said with a speculative glance toward Oscar's door.

Before we had moved three feet toward the hallway, I heard Oscar's door bang against the wall. I turned to see Cassandra storming out. She did not acknowledge the fact that two men and a cat were in the room. She pushed past us in an apparent fury, and seconds later I heard the front door open and then slam.

Stanley quirked one eyebrow at me. "Looks like he's free now."

He seemed intent on meeting Oscar. I wasn't keen on seeing my boss right after such a tempestuous meeting, but I was curious to see what happened when the two men met. "Sure, let's go in."

I headed back toward Oscar's office, a reluctant Diesel in tow. Stanley followed right behind us. I walked into the room to see Oscar smiling broadly. That smile vanished the moment he saw me. Then his eyes moved past me and focused on the larger man behind me.

Oscar paled and stood on shaky legs. "What the hell are *you* doing here, Porter?"

EIGHT

|||||||||||||||||||||||||||||||||||||||||

I wasn't sure what I had really expected from bringing Porter Stanley and Oscar together, but I didn't think Oscar would react as though he was terrified.

Stanley moved past me to approach Oscar's desk. Though Stanley paused about three feet away, Oscar backed up against the built-in bookshelves behind him as if he were trying to climb into the wall to get away.

I moved back a couple of paces, making sure Diesel was behind me. Then I pulled out my cell phone in case I needed to call the campus police. I was afraid Stanley might attack Oscar by the way my boss had reacted.

"Aw, now, is that any way to greet an old buddy?" Stanley sounded amused. "You can do better than that, Oscar."

Oscar's voice sounded higher than usual when he spoke. "Why are you here, Porter?"

"I don't think that's anything you want to discuss in

front of your coworker here, is it?" Stanley made himself comfortable in one of the two chairs Oscar kept near his desk for visitors.

Oscar's glance flicked nervously in my direction. "Um, no, I guess not. You can leave, Charlie."

"If you're sure everything is okay," I said. Stanley had his back to me, and I held up my cell phone so Oscar could see it clearly. I mimed punching in three digits. He gave a slight shake of the head. "Okay, then, Diesel and I will resume our morning walk. Nice meeting you, Stanley."

The big man didn't acknowledge me. All his attention appeared focused on Oscar, who showed no signs of relaxing. He still stood with his back pressed against the shelves.

Stanley spoke in a firm tone. "Sit down, Oscar."

Oscar sat, though he continued to eye his erstwhile friend warily.

I turned and walked out. Diesel scampered ahead of me, eager to be out of the tension-filled room. I couldn't blame him. I was glad to be out of it myself, though part of me wanted to eavesdrop on the conversation.

I stopped and turned, trying to decide whether to sneak back, but before I could make up my mind, Oscar's door shut. Given the thickness of the walls and the door, I knew I had little chance to overhear anything now, so I led Diesel out of Melba's office and back out to the street.

We hadn't made it twenty feet down the sidewalk toward home when I heard Melba hail me. I turned, and Diesel almost jerked the leash out of my hand. He was that eager to see Melba. I held firm, though, and we walked back slowly toward her.

"Morning, boys," Melba said with a bright smile. She

scratched Diesel's head as he rubbed against her leg and meowed.

"Good morning to you, too. You sound pretty cheerful. Did your meeting with Penny go well?"

Melba nodded. "Yes, it sure did. I filed that complaint, and now I feel fine. Penny told me from now on I should call her the minute Oscar gets nasty over anything." She nodded in the direction of the building. "Why don't y'all come in with me, and let's have some coffee?"

"I don't think that's a good idea right now," I said.

"Why?" Melba looked startled. "Don't tell me you've had another run-in with him this morning."

"Not exactly." I filled her in on the encounter with her mysterious stranger and his meeting with Oscar.

Her eyes widened at first, then she grinned when I finished. "Maybe this Stanley guy will solve the problem for us. If he beats Oscar up real bad, he won't be able to annoy the rest of us."

"Melba, surely you don't mean that?" I was a bit shocked at her bloodthirstiness, though I had to admit she had provocation.

She rolled her eyes. "No, I don't really want anyone to beat Oscar up that bad, but I wouldn't mind if this guy scared the daylights out of him. Maybe after this he'll be too shaken up to bother me or anybody else." She laughed. "Once he finds out I've filed a complaint, he *really* ought to calm down."

"I don't think he'll be a problem much longer, frankly. He'll have to behave properly because of the complaints, or he could lose his position." I paused for a moment to consider that. "Once all this gets to the vice president for finance and the president himself, I imagine he could get fired right away."

"I hope so," Melba said. "That would be the best outcome for the library, that's for dang sure."

I considered telling her about the argument I'd over-heard between Oscar and Cassandra but decided I had best keep that to myself for now. Melba would probably hear about it from another source eventually anyway.

"If they do get rid of him," Melba continued, "I wish they'd make you the director, or at least the interim. You've got the experience, and everybody likes and respects *you*."

"Thank you," I said and tried not to blush. I have always had a hard time accepting praise, even from an old friend. "It's a kind thought, but frankly I'm not interested. I don't want the responsibility anymore. I like my life the way it is. Diesel does, too, don't you, boy?"

As ever, when I addressed him directly, he responded right away, this time with a loud meow.

"Diesel has spoken." I grinned.

Melba laughed. "Since he's in charge, not you, I guess that's the end of that." She turned to look toward the front of the administration building. "You think we ought to get in there and check on Oscar? How long has that stranger been with him?"

"Not quite fifteen minutes," I said. I had been facing the front of the building, and I hadn't seen anyone come out. Maybe we should go in and make sure nothing had happened to our boss. I still felt uneasy about leaving Oscar alone with Porter Stanley when Oscar was so clearly afraid of the man. "We probably should. Come on."

Diesel for once did not appear happy to enter the

building. I was sure he remembered the unpleasantness from earlier and was still unsettled by it. I stopped for a moment to talk to him and stroke his back.

"Poor baby," Melba said in an undertone as we resumed our progress. "He must have been terrified by it all."

I nodded. "I'm hoping we won't encounter more of the same." I opened the door and held it for Melba. Diesel and I stepped inside and followed her toward her office.

All was quiet as we entered, but the door to Oscar's office remained shut. Melba moved quietly to it and put her ear against it. She listened for about ten seconds before she stepped away.

In a hushed tone she said, "I can't hear anything in there. Usually you can at least pick up a faint sound, but this time, nothing."

We looked at each other, no doubt both thinking similar terrible thoughts. After a moment, I handed Diesel's leash to her. "You two step back. I'm going in."

Melba, eyes round with fear, did as I asked. She and the cat retreated toward the door to the hall while I approached Oscar's door. I knocked loudly and waited.

After a few seconds I knocked again, and when there still no response, I opened the door and braced myself for what I might find.

What I found was an office empty of men. I expelled a pent breath in relief. "No one's here," I announced.

"Maybe they're upstairs," Melba said. "Let's go look."

I passed her and walked to the bottom of the stairs. "Stay here."

Melba didn't argue. Diesel didn't look happy, but I

didn't want him with me, in case I did make an unpleasant discovery on the second floor.

At the top of the stairs I called out Oscar's name. After a moment of silence, I did it again, this time more loudly. There were no other offices on the second floor besides mine. The rest of the rooms up there were dedicated to the archive, archival storage, and storage for a few other things, like old library personnel files and discarded furniture.

I pulled out my keys and went to each in turn, but there was no sign that Oscar and Porter Stanley had entered any of the rooms. I walked slowly back downstairs and shook my head at Melba's interrogative glance. "Not up there," I said.

We checked the other rooms downstairs, a small conference room across the hall from Melba's office, another room full of files and books, the rather dilapidated kitchen, and finally the room that had been turned into a staff lounge eons ago. All vacant.

I peered out a window in the lounge that looked onto the small parking lot behind the building. "Oscar's car is gone," I said.

"Then he must have taken the other man with him," Melba said.

I didn't remember seeing a car come out of the side street that gave access to the parking lot. "They must have gone the other way. I didn't see a car, did you?"

"No, I didn't, and Stanley's car was still parked on the street." Melba handed Diesel's leash back to me, and we stood there a moment, both puzzled.

Melba clutched at my arm suddenly and startled me. "Surely you don't think he's made Oscar go somewhere with him so he can execute him, do you? Maybe he's a gangster."

My old friend's imagination really did run amok sometimes, and this was one of those times, I was sure.

"No, I don't think he took Oscar away to execute him, but I do believe he has some kind of hold over Oscar. Surely if Oscar had been truly afraid for his life, he would have let me call the campus police when I offered to."

"Maybe." Melba looked doubtful. "But what if Oscar didn't realize at first this guy meant to kill him?"

I couldn't keep the exasperation out of my tone when I replied, "Melba, you're getting a bit too carried away with all this. Obviously there's something wrong between the two, but it doesn't necessarily mean murder."

She looked chagrined. "You're probably right. I guess having that man sitting out on the street the past few days spooked me. He seems sinister to me."

Diesel meowed and butted his head against her, his anxiety obvious. Melba reassured him with soothing words and rubs on the head.

"I think Diesel and I had better head home," I said. "I'm sure Oscar will turn up before too long, acting as if nothing happened."

"We'll see." Melba walked out of the lounge and headed for the front of the building. Diesel and I followed.

When we reached the entryway, she turned. "Sure you don't have time to have a cup of coffee?"

I didn't want any coffee, but I realized that Melba didn't

want to be on her own in the building, so I nodded. "Sure, that sounds good."

"I'll put it on and be right back. Only takes about six or seven minutes." Melba smiled and hurried back to the kitchen to make the coffee. Diesel and I went into her office. I chose my favorite chair, and the cat stretched out on the floor by my feet.

I pulled out my cell phone and checked my e-mail. Nothing urgent, I decided after a quick scan. The phone went back in my pocket.

The front door was in my line of sight, and when I heard it open, I glanced that way. I didn't think it would be Oscar, who would surely come in the back way from the parking lot.

Cassandra Brownley stormed into the entryway, accompanied by Lisa Krause and Delbert Winston at a calmer pace. She walked into Melba's office and right by me without acknowledging my presence. She approached Oscar's door—I had shut it before I searched the rest of the building—and jerked it open.

I had no chance to tell her Oscar wasn't inside. She strode in while Delbert and Lisa paused, manifestly nervous, near me. Lisa greeted me softly.

Cassandra came marching out of Oscar's office and addressed her companions. "The jackass isn't there." She finally appeared to notice me. "Where is he?"

"I don't know," I said. "Melba and I have been wondering the same thing. If you don't mind, can I ask why you're so upset?"

Cassandra looked ready to tear the room apart. "Because the bastard fired all three of us this morning."

NINE

||||||||||||||||||||||||||||||||||

"Fired you?" Melba said from the doorway, having returned from putting on the coffee. "What's going on here?"

At the same time, I asked, "Exactly *when* did he fire you?" I wondered when he'd had the time to do it today. "Was it when I saw you earlier coming out of his office, Cassandra?"

"No, the jerk didn't have the courage to tell me to my face." She snapped out the words.

I felt a tug on the leash and glanced down. Diesel was trying to get under Melba's desk. The poor boy didn't like the loud voice of my irate colleague. I got up from the chair and moved to stand behind the desk so the cat could seek refuge there.

"I don't understand." Melba looked as bewildered as I felt. "How could he fire you if he wasn't present when it happened? Who actually fired you? HR?"

"No, we all got letters in the campus mail a little while ago." Delbert Winston spoke in a much calmer tone than Cassandra had done. He pulled a letter-sized manila envelope out of his jacket pocket and waved it for a moment before replacing it. "I didn't think such a thing was legal."

"I doubt it is," I said. "If Oscar intended to fire you, he'd have called you all together at one time, in the same room, with an HR officer present, and then you would have been escorted off campus immediately." I shook my head. "This reeks to high heaven."

"If this is Oscar's idea of a practical joke," Lisa said, "I don't think it's funny. It's downright cruel." She appeared ready to burst into tears.

Melba and I exchanged a glance. I felt sure she was thinking the same thing I was. This looked like another prank against Oscar, but Lisa, Delbert, and Cassandra got caught in the crossfire.

"I think we'd better call Penny Sisson," I said. "HR needs to know about this." After a brief thought, I added, "The campus police, too."

"Why the police?" Cassandra demanded.

I explained my reasoning without going into unnecessary detail. "Oscar has been the victim of several pranks recently, and given the circumstances of this so-called firing, I suspect this is another one. Unfortunately, it involved the three of you in a nasty way."

"I'll call Penny," Melba said. "Y'all have a seat." She waved toward an old sofa near the window and a second chair kept for visitors. "I'll get ahold of the campus police, too."

Lisa and Cassandra chose the sofa, and Delbert pulled

his chair close to them. They all kept their eyes trained on me, Cassandra with her usual glower, and Lisa and Delbert with more hopeful expressions.

I pulled my chair closer to the side of Melba's desk, facing my three colleagues, so I could keep an eye on my cowering feline under the desk. Now that the atmosphere was calmer, he peeped out from his hiding spot, and I reached down to rub his head. "It's all okay, boy," I told him in soft tones. "You don't need to worry." He inched his way out into the open about half a foot, until his head could rub against my shoe.

"Guess we scared your cat with all the commotion." Delbert cast a sideways glance at Cassandra, the true source of the "commotion." "Sorry about that, but we were all really upset."

"Understandably so," I said. "Diesel's okay now, as long as nobody starts ranting again." I stared pointedly at Cassandra, but she appeared not to notice.

"Penny's on her way over," Melba said. "Chief Ford, too. I'll go make some coffee. More coffee, that is."

"None for me," Cassandra said. "I do not imbibe caffeine."

"I'll take some, and thanks," Delbert said.

"Me, too." Lisa rose from the sofa. "I'll come with you."

"Sure thing, honey." Melba smiled at the younger woman.

I itched to question Cassandra and Delbert about their encounters with our mutual boss, but I figured I should keep out of it for now. I wondered where Oscar was, and whether he was okay. Where could the two men have gone?

I would tell Chief Ford about the meeting between the two men. He had the resources to investigate.

Lisa came back with mugs of coffee for herself and Delbert, and Melba, with cups for the two of us, arrived seconds before Penny Sisson hurried into the office. Chief Ford was almost on her heels.

Cassandra jumped up at once and launched into her grievances over her "callous mistreatment at the hands of that incompetent idiot," and it took Chief Ford a few moments to get her to shut up. Finally, she subsided, albeit with a resentful glance at the campus cop, and resumed her seat.

"Thank you, Ms. Brownley," Ford said, and much to his credit, I thought, he sounded polite, rather than irritated. "Now, let's talk about this calmly. You three all received letters saying you were fired, right?"

Lisa and Delbert nodded. Cassandra just glared. The chief turned to Penny Sisson. "Was HR aware of this?"

Penny shook her head. "No, we were not. We haven't had any kind of communication from Mr. Reilly that he intended to lay off any of the library staff. I'd like to look at one of your letters, if I may."

Delbert rose and again pulled his letter from his jacket pocket and handed it to Penny. Before she could grasp it, however, the chief said, "If you would, Mr. Winston, please open the letter and place it flat on the desk here. I'd rather no one else touch it for now."

Delbert complied with the chief's command and then stood back. Penny and Ford moved closer to examine it. After a moment, Penny turned to face the three fired librarians. "This is absolutely *not* the way this college handles the laying off of employees. I don't know what Mr. Reilly was thinking, but this violates our procedures completely."

All three of them looked relieved, even Cassandra, who forgot to glower for at least three seconds.

"Ms. Gilley," Chief Ford said, "you're the administrative assistant. Is it normally your job to type the director's letters and mail them?"

"Normally, yes," Melba said, "but Oscar certainly didn't give me any letters like this to process. I don't know anything about them." She approached the desk in order to inspect the letter. After a moment she said, "That does look like his signature, though." She straightened. "But it's not the letterhead stationery he usually uses." She pointed to the top-left-hand corner of the sheet of paper. "The library's logo should be there, along with the phrase *Office of the Director*. This is just plain Athena College stationery."

"I never noticed that." Lisa Krause turned to Delbert. "Did you?" He shook his head. She glanced at Cassandra, who appeared not to have heard the question.

"This is all really strange," Penny said. "What was Mr. Reilly thinking, to do something like this? It makes no sense whatsoever."

"We don't know that Mr. Reilly is responsible," Chief Ford said. "Even though it looks like his signature, according to Ms. Gilley. I need to talk to Mr. Reilly and find out whether he knows anything about this." He turned to Melba. "Where is he?"

"I don't know," she answered, then looked at me.

"If I could speak to you in private for a moment, Chief," I said. "I need to talk to you about that."

Ford responded with a curt nod and headed for the entryway. I handed Diesel's leash to Melba and then followed the officer.

"What is it, Mr. Harris? Do you know where Mr. Reilly is?" Ford looked and sounded impatient.

"No, I don't, and in fact, Melba and I are worried about him." I quickly explained the situation.

Ford didn't interrupt with questions. When I finished, he got on his radio and instructed his officers to start a search for Oscar's car. Then he called the Athena police department and had a brief conversation with them, ending with a request for their patrol cars to look for the car as well.

Ford restored his cell phone to its holder. "You said Ms. Gilley noticed this stranger sitting in a car on the street outside this building for three days in a row?"

"Yes," I said. "Four days, if you count today."

"Why didn't one of you report this to us?" Ford shook his head.

"Sorry," I said, "but frankly I didn't think it was that serious. I figured the man was simply waiting to pick up a student or a faculty member to drive them home. Something innocuous like that."

Ford stared at me for a moment before he turned and walked back into Melba's office. I felt foolish and resentful at the same time as I followed him.

Ford didn't share with the others what I told him. Instead he said, "Ms. Krause, Ms. Brownley, do you have your letters with you?"

Lisa nodded and delved into the small handbag she had brought with her. Cassandra shook her head. "No, it's on my desk in my office. You'll have to send someone for it."

I could tell the chief didn't care for her patronizing tone any more than I did. His shoulders stiffened, but he regarded her with a bland expression. "Thank you, Ms. Brownley." He asked Lisa to lay her letter, still in its envelope, on top of Delbert's.

"Thank you all," he said. "You can go back to work now." He turned to Penny. "That should be okay, right?"

"Yes, of course," Penny said. "You all are still employed by the college. Those letters are not legitimate. I would like to have copies of them, if you please, Mr. Ford."

"I'll arrange that," he replied.

My three fellow librarians and Penny all began to move toward the door and out into the hallway while Melba, Diesel, the chief, and I remained in the office.

I heard the front door open, and I moved to a vantage point from which I could see who had come in.

Oscar Reilly stood just inside the door frame, glaring at Penny and my coworkers. He looked fine and completely unfazed by whatever had gone on between him and Porter Stanley since I had last seen them together in Oscar's office.

TEN

||||||||||||||||||||||

"Why are you all here?" Oscar demanded in a harsh tone. "Shouldn't you be actually *working*?"

All three of the librarians began speaking at once, and Chief Ford ordered them to be quiet. "Mrs. Sisson, I think it will be helpful if you remain. The rest of you can go."

Cassandra appeared angry at the chief's words, but to my surprise, she didn't argue. She swept out through the still-open door, brushing Oscar aside. Lisa and Delbert followed more calmly in her wake. Delbert pulled the door shut behind him.

"What's going on here?" Oscar said. "I demand to know why all these people were here."

"If you come into the office here, Mr. Reilly, I will explain everything." Chief Ford maintained his calm, commanding manner, and Oscar subsided. He nodded and walked past the campus cop and toward his office.

"No, Mr. Reilly, this office, not yours," Ford said. Oscar stopped and turned back toward the chief with a frown.

"Mrs. Sisson." Ford indicated that Penny should precede him.

Melba and I had remained by her desk, silent witnesses to the scene. I was about to ask the chief whether he needed me any further, but he forestalled me by asking both Melba and me to remain. Diesel stayed out of sight under the desk.

Oscar glared at Chief Ford. "*Now* will you tell me what the devil has been going on here? I come back from a meeting and find half the library here when they should be doing their jobs."

Melba and I looked at each other. What kind of *meeting* had Oscar had with Porter Stanley? It seemed much more like a confrontation to me.

"Have you ever seen this letter before, Mr. Reilly?" Chief Ford indicated the paper Delbert Winston had placed on the corner of Melba's desk earlier. "Please examine it, but don't touch it."

Oscar looked puzzled, but he complied with Ford's request. He stared down at the letter, scanned it quickly, then exclaimed, "I never wrote this letter. This has got to be another practical joke."

He sounded sincere, and I believed him. I didn't think he'd written the letter, or the other two like it.

"Does that look like your signature?" Ford asked.

Oscar glanced down again and studied the paper for a moment. "It does, but I swear to you I didn't sign this letter. What is going on here? Who's doing these crazy things to me?"

"I will investigate this, and I will uncover the perpetrator," Ford said in a confident tone. He turned to Penny. "Mrs. Sisson, do you have any questions for Mr. Reilly?"

"Not at the moment," she said. "I will be in touch with you later." She nodded at Oscar. "We have several matters to discuss, and we need to do so later today, if possible."

"I'll check my schedule and see when I can fit you in," Oscar said.

I admired Penny's restraint in the face of such a condescending tone. The man was insufferable, no matter what.

"As I expect the vice president for financial affairs to be a part of the meeting, I am certain you will find time this afternoon to attend." Penny's icy tone could have chilled a gallon of water, and Oscar blinked, no doubt surprised that she had just trumped his ace, so to speak. She turned without saying anything further and left.

Oscar muttered a few words under his breath, and what little I could catch was not complimentary to Penny. I felt like slugging the man right then and there. He was crass on top of all his other deficiencies.

Ford stared hard at Oscar. I didn't think he appreciated Oscar's behavior any more than I did. When he spoke, his tone had a definite edge to it.

"Can you tell me where you've been the past hour?"

Oscar looked startled. "What has that got to do with anything? I told you I was in a meeting."

"It wasn't on your calendar," Melba said sweetly. "It must have been a last-minute thing."

Oscar glared at Melba, but before he could speak, Ford posed another question.

"This meeting of yours," he said, "was it with a Mr. Porter Stanley?"

That shot hit the mark. Oscar paled but recovered quickly. He pointed at me. "You need to keep your nose out of my business, Harris." Then he jabbed his finger in the air at Melba. "You're every bit as bad as he is. I know you two are cronies. I'd be willing to bet the two of you are behind this campaign to drive me out of this job." He turned to Ford. "She's probably the one who wrote these letters and forged my name. I'm sure if you examine the letters, you'll find out they were printed right here in this office." He waved vaguely in the direction of the combination printer-scanner-copier that occupied a corner of Melba's office.

"You jackass." Melba looked ready to pick up her computer and throw it at Oscar's head. "How dare you accuse me of such a low-down, low-class thing. I'd never do anything like that to save my life. I'm not going to lie and say I don't despise you and wish you were gone, but I know for damn sure I'm not the only one." She snorted. "There'll be a line around the block before long, people just waiting for their chance to tell you what they think of your sorry rear end."

I decided there was no point in my adding any remarks to Melba's forceful tirade. Oscar appeared shell-shocked. I almost laughed. He had no idea what tangling with my old friend could cost him.

"We will be examining every possibility, Reilly." Ford spoke in a calm tone, though I would have sworn I caught his mouth twitch ever so briefly into a smile while Melba ranted at Oscar. "I would like to say, and I want you to consider my words carefully, that both Ms. Gilley and Mr. Harris have outstanding reputations here at the college. You had better think carefully about flinging around accusations like that."

Oscar glowered, and I was surprised he didn't have a comeback to offer. Ford exuded authority, and evidently even Oscar, brash as he was, knew when to shut up.

The chief continued, "Now, back to my earlier question. Was your meeting with Porter Stanley?"

After a stiff nod, Oscar said, "It was. However, the subject of it is a private matter that has nothing to do with my job or the situation here."

"That might be," Ford replied. "Can you give me contact information for Mr. Stanley, in case I need to talk to him as part of my investigation?"

I thought Oscar paled slightly at that question, but he made a quick recovery. "No, I'm sorry, I have no idea where he's staying nor do I have any kind of phone number for him." He paused a moment. "As a matter of fact, I believe he said he was leaving town right after our meeting." His facile smile was not convincing.

"Sure he is," Melba said in a low tone. I heard it, but I couldn't tell whether Ford or Oscar did, since they didn't react.

I agreed with Melba. I thought Oscar had lied—a really stupid thing to do, but then the man wasn't nearly as smart as he thought he was. The more I was around him, the more contempt I felt for him and what a miserable human being he was. I didn't even have much sympathy for him as the target of practical jokes. I had no cheeks left to turn for this man.

"Then I will have to trace him another way," Ford said.

"His car." Melba smiled in grim satisfaction and looked right at Oscar. "I can give you the license plate of his car." She pulled open the top drawer of her desk and retrieved a small notepad. She tore off the top sheet and handed it to the chief.

"Mississippi tag, I see. And you have the make and model." Ford gave a brief smile. "Good work, Ms. Gilley."

"If you've finished interrogating me, I have work to do." Oscar crossed his arms over his chest and regarded Ford steadily. "I don't think there's anything else I have to say to you."

"Idiot," I muttered under my breath. I couldn't help myself. How stupid did you have to be to antagonize the investigating officer with such an obnoxiously patronizing tone? I wondered. *As stupid as Oscar*, I thought. The man must be a financial whiz to have remained employed over the years if he behaved like this on every job.

That gave me an idea. When Diesel and I got home, I would do some digging on the Internet. I might find interesting information about Oscar. You never knew what you could turn up until you tried.

"You might as well go back to work now," Ford said in an even tone. "I will probably have more questions for you, but I have enough to work with at the moment."

Oscar waited barely long enough for Ford to complete that last sentence before he turned and strode to his office. He opened the door and slammed it shut behind him.

"Melba, are you going to be comfortable working here today?" Ford asked. "It might be better if you told your boss you aren't feeling well and go on home."

I agreed with Ford. I didn't trust Oscar not to try to browbeat Melba once we were gone. He was furious with her; anyone could see that.

Melba smiled, and I recognized that smile. She was loaded for bear, as the saying went—a bear named Reilly. She reached back into that same desk drawer and pulled out a can of room deodorizer and plunked it on the desk.

"If he tries any of his mess with me," she said, "he'll get a face full of this before he knows what hit him. He's not going to intimidate me anymore, so don't you worry."

"If it comes to that," Ford said, "he could bring charges against you for assault." He didn't sound overly concerned about that.

"Don't care." Melba laughed. "I've got a good lawyer. By the time Sean Harris gets through with Mr. Jerkhead Reilly, there won't be much of him left over."

"I still think you ought to go home," Ford said.

"I do, too, for what it's worth." I shook my head at her. "You know I love you dearly, but sometimes, as my mother used to say, you let that big mouth of yours overload that tiny rump you sit on."

Melba gave me a sweet smile. "I love you dearly, too, Charlie Harris, but I've been taking care of myself and my tiny rump just fine for many a year. You and Diesel go on home, and don't worry about me."

When Melba was in an obstinate mood, there was not much anyone could do to dissuade her from whatever she meant to do. Evidently Ford knew her well enough to understand that the way I did.

"All right," he said. "But you call us if you need anything." He nodded at each of us in turn before he left.

"Scoot," Melba said. "Don't you even think about hanging around here. Take your poor boy home where it's nice and quiet. He's probably been terrified with all this ruckus going on."

I was already squatting to coax Diesel out from under the desk. He meowed pitifully, and I felt remorse. I should have removed him from the scene earlier, but I got so caught up in everything going on I simply forgot him.

I spoke in a soft, soothing tone. "Come on, boy, let's go home, okay?"

He meowed again, then appeared to consider my words. He wiggled out, stretched, and butted his head against my chin a couple of times. I scratched his head, and he chirped.

"He'll be okay." I stood. "We'll go home now, but you be careful. Promise me."

"I will. You really don't need to worry," she replied. "By the time Penny and his boss in financial affairs get through with Reilly this afternoon, he'll be afraid to squawk at anybody."

"I sure hope so." I gave her a quick peck on the cheek. "Come on, Diesel, we're heading home."

On the sidewalk I checked my watch, and found to my surprise that we had been there not much more than an hour. It had seemed a lot longer.

Diesel trotted happily along, and I was glad to stretch my legs. We reached home a few minutes later, and I released the cat from his harness and leash. As he almost always did, he went straight to the utility room.

I went to the den to retrieve my laptop and brought it back to the kitchen. I could hear the sound of the vacuum in the upstairs hall. Azalea sang as she worked, and I could hear snatches of a gospel song mingled with the wheezing of the machine.

With a glass of Azalea's freshly made iced tea to sustain me, I opened the computer and turned it on. While I waited for it to boot up completely, I thought about what it was I hoped to dig up on the Internet about Oscar.

I decided that I would see what I could find out about Porter Stanley. What was the connection between the two men?

Less than five minutes after I started searching, I discovered that connection, and it was a shocking one.

ELEVEN

||||||||||||||||||||||||||||||||||||||||||||||||

I hadn't expected to find any dirt on Porter Stanley and Oscar Reilly right away, and the fact that I did made me wonder how carefully the college HR department had run a background check on Oscar. I really thought I would have to dig deep to find anything juicy or helpful. Front-page headlines in a suburban Massachusetts newspaper, however, weren't that hard to miss. I decided I should mention this to Penny Sisson. She needed to know that her staff hadn't done a thorough enough job.

The Oscar Reilly who stared out at me from the newspaper photograph sported a black eye. His hands were behind his back, and I suspected from the context of the scene that they were in handcuffs. A uniformed policeman had a hand on Oscar's shoulder. Not more than three feet away, Porter Stanley, also escorted by a man in uniform, looked disheveled and disgruntled but otherwise unmarked.

His hands, tightly clenched, were visible, and his expression as he regarded Oscar chilled me.

After absorbing the details of the visual, I read the article. The Stanleys were a wealthy, influential clan in Massachusetts, according to the paper. Otherwise I doubted this story would have received as much space in the paper. Porter Stanley's sister, Eleanor, was Mrs. Oscar Reilly. Eleanor was reportedly in a nursing facility, having gone there after suffering from the strain of a bitterly contested divorce. I did not collapse from surprise when I read that Eleanor Reilly was divorcing her husband on the grounds of extreme mental cruelty, abuse, and neglect.

The situation in the photograph came about when Porter Stanley and Oscar met at Mrs. Reilly's lawyer's office. After a rancorous discussion during the meeting between the two sides, the dispute continued on the street when the men left the building. Allegedly Oscar, who had to be at least eight inches shorter and a good hundred pounds lighter than his brother-in-law, was the aggressor. The men tussled, and Oscar ended up with a black eye. Witnesses at the scene verified that Oscar threw the first punch.

I checked the date on the news story, and the events it recounted took place seven months ago. I checked for follow-ups to this story and found another article from the same paper. Eleanor Reilly received her divorce, and the prenuptial agreement Oscar agreed to when they married seven years earlier was nullified. The agreement apparently had a clause that made it void if there was evidence of cruelty or neglect.

What a stellar character we had to deal with, I thought. What kind of pathology was at work here? Oscar, at least in my opinion, was a disturbed man. *And not safe to be around*.

On that alarming thought I called Melba immediately. Even armed with her can of air freshener, she might still be in danger of physical harm.

To my relief she answered her office phone after only two rings. "Are you okay?" I tried not to sound panicky. "Where is Oscar?"

"I'm fine," she replied. "He's gone. Got called over to the president's office for a meeting. Why?"

I gave her a quick précis of the news articles. When I finished, she said, "What a scumbag."

"Yes, and apparently one who can be violent," I said. "I really think you should follow Chief Ford's advice and go home. If Oscar comes back to the office, I don't imagine he's going to be in a good mood."

"He's not going to pull any crap with me," Melba retorted. "I'll spray him in the face, and then kick him where it hurts the most if he gets out of line."

Diesel had been quiet, but now he could sense my tension. He meowed and rubbed his head against my leg. I patted him to try to reassure him, but my attention was focused on Melba.

I had to admire my old friend's gutsiness, but I feared she was overconfident. I told her so.

She didn't answer right away. After a few long moments, she said, "I guess you're probably right. If you poke a hornet's nest often enough, you're going to get stung. I'll be out of here in a few minutes."

"Good."

"Look, gotta go, the other line is ringing. I'd better see who it is before I leave."

"Okay. Be careful."

Thankful that she hadn't been stubborn, I put down the phone. I stared at the laptop screen for a moment before I went back to the first article I found. I gazed at the picture of the two men. Why had Porter Stanley sought out his former brother-in-law after the divorce became final? Did Stanley have retribution in mind? I wondered how his poor sister fared after the divorce. I hoped she had recovered well.

There was no mention of children in the articles, so I supposed that meant there were none. The thought of Oscar as a father chilled me.

I shut down the computer and put it aside. Diesel still appeared unsettled, and I devoted a few minutes to reassuring him that everything was fine.

Once the cat settled down again, I found my thoughts reverting back to the subject of Oscar. I could only hope that the meeting he had been called to in the president's office meant that the college was going to take action. If not to fire him outright, at least to remove him from the position as interim director of the library. Given the turmoil that surrounded his brief tenure, Oscar obviously was not the person for the job. Surely the president could see that.

On impulse I reopened the laptop. I searched for the articles I'd found earlier, copied and pasted their links into an e-mail message to Penny Sisson, and sent them to her with a brief message to check them out. I felt a bit like a tattletale, but I didn't want Oscar back in the library. He had to be stopped somehow.

Azalea walked into the kitchen while I was pouring more tea for myself.

"I'm going to the grocery store." Azalea headed into the utility room, where she kept her purse. When she returned, purse over her arm, she said, "Anything special you want? I'm going to make spaghetti and meatballs for your dinner tonight."

"Can't think of anything special," I said. Diesel meowed loudly.

Azalea looked down at him. "I know you're always wanting something special, Mr. Cat. And when did I ever forget to buy your food?" She shook her head. "You spoil that cat rotten, Mr. Charlie."

Diesel meowed again, and I saw Azalea's lips twitch. She pretended most of the time not to be amused by his attempts at conversation, but I knew that secretly she got a kick out of him. I had overheard her chatting to him numerous times when she didn't realize I was nearby. She spoiled him every bit as much as I did. I was wise enough not to point that out, however.

"Well, you know, Azalea, that's what cats are for." I laughed. "And at least he tells you *thank you*, don't you, boy?"

Diesel warbled, and this time Azalea smiled. She shook her head. "Ain't got time to be standing here talking to a cat. I'll be back in about an hour."

Diesel followed her to the back door, and for a moment I thought he planned to go out with her. He sat and watched the door close, though, and stared at it for a moment. He then got up and padded back to me. I rubbed his head, and he purred.

After all the unrest at the library because of Oscar Reilly, I was grateful to be in my quiet home with my devoted feline friend. Now that I was a couple of years past the half-century mark, I appreciated all this even more. I had two wonderful children, a grandchild on the way thanks to my daughter and son-in-law, and a loving partner in Helen Louise.

Don't get maudlin, I told myself mock-seriously. *Time you were up and doing something else.*

But what? I didn't have any matter that needed my immediate attention. The problem of Oscar Reilly seemed to be on its way to a solution, I figured. Diesel and I should be able to go back to the archive tomorrow without interference or unpleasantness. Things could settle back into their nice, predictable routine.

I decided I might as well finish the book I was reading, Sharon Kay Penman's *Lionheart*, about Richard I of England. I loved richly detailed historical fiction, and no one did it better than Penman. Immersing myself in the twelfth century for an hour or two would be a good tonic for the upsets of the past couple of days.

"Let's go upstairs and read," I said to Diesel. He chirped in response. He understood what I meant, and while I read, he would nap on the bed beside me. And if I dozed off, too, well, that would be fine. I would have a late night with Helen Louise probably, and a little snooze now wouldn't hurt.

When my cell phone rang about half an hour later, I was deep in the twelfth century, and it took me a moment to emerge. I picked up the phone, noted that Sean was the caller, and answered.

"Hey, Dad," he said. "Hope you're not too busy at the moment. I need you to come over to the office for a little while."

There was an odd note in his voice, and I couldn't tell whether he was worried about something, or simply nervous.

"No, I'm reading, but I can get back to the book later." I sat up on the side of the bed. "What's going on? Everything okay?"

"Yes, everything's fine," he said. "Don't worry. But I need to talk to you, and I can't get away from the office right this minute."

"I'll be on my way in a few." Before I could continue, he ended the call.

I set the phone down on the bedside table and turned to look at my sleepy cat. "Sean is being mysterious," I told him. "He's up to something, but I have no idea what. We're going to his office, boy, so wake up."

Diesel yawned and stretched while I put on my shoes. I went in the bathroom to brush my hair and freshen up, and a few minutes later we were in the car on the way to downtown Athena.

The law offices of Pendergrast and Harris occupied one floor of a Civil War–era building on the square. I found a parking place in front, and as I was getting Diesel out of the backseat, I noticed a familiar car a couple of spaces away.

"Looks like Laura is here, too, boy," I said. Diesel perked up at the mention of her name. He adored Laura, and she him. I wondered how my boy was going to react, however, when the grandchild arrived. He would have competition for Laura's attention.

We stepped out of the elevator on the second floor, and the office manager, Laquita Henderson, greeted Diesel and me with her usual perky smile. "Hey, there, Mr. Harris. Diesel, you're handsome as ever."

Diesel happily let the attractive young woman scratch his head, and he warbled for her.

"What's all this about?" I asked. "Sean wouldn't tell me anything."

Laquita laughed. "Can't say a word, or I'd be in trouble. Y'all go on into Sean's office, and he'll tell you."

"Okay," I said, feeling suddenly anxious. "Come on, Diesel."

Sean's office lay a few yards down the corridor and faced the square. His door was open, and Diesel and I walked in. There was no sign of Laura, however.

"Hello, Son," I said. "What's all this mystery?"

Sean looked up from his desk, and his expression was enigmatic. "Close the door, Dad, if you don't mind, and then have a seat."

While I complied with his request, he came around from behind his desk and perched on a corner near the chair I chose. He patted Diesel for a moment, then he faced me squarely.

"Alexandra and I are getting married this morning." The words tumbled out. "We found out yesterday she's having a baby, and we decided we should get married right away."

TWELVE

▮▮▮▮▮▮▮▮▮▮▮▮▮▮▮▮▮▮▮▮▮▮▮▮▮▮▮▮▮▮▮▮▮▮

I stared blankly at my son. Two words kept echoing in my brain—*baby* and *married*.

"I know you would have preferred that we were married before there was any sign of a baby." Sean wore a defensive expression I had seen often during his teenage years when he had to admit to behavior or an action he knew I wouldn't condone. Not that it happened all that often, because he had been a mostly well-behaved teenager.

I *was* rather old-fashioned in that way. I would have liked them to be married before they contemplated having a child, but there was no point in repining over it now.

I was going to have another grandchild, not to mention a smart, capable, and beautiful daughter-in-law. That was all that really mattered.

"Congratulations, Son." I stood and smiled at him. "I'm

very happy for you and Alexandra. And Laura and Frank's baby will have a cousin to grow up with."

Diesel trilled and chirped in response to the excitement he felt coming from me. Sean's face broke into a broad grin, and he hugged me tight. "Thanks, Dad," he said, his voice husky.

I thought of his mother and how happy she would be over the news of another grandchild. For a moment my eyes misted over. How I wished she were here to share in the excitement.

Sean released me, and we smiled at each other. I started to ask when the baby was due but decided that could wait. At the moment it would hardly be tactful to inquire.

"I have a favor to ask," Sean said. "Will you be my best man?"

"I'd be honored," I said around the sudden, large lump in my throat. "Where is the wedding taking place?"

"In the conference room," Sean said. "Everyone is waiting for us. Judge Howell is going to perform the ceremony."

"Really? I haven't seen her in a long time. We went to school together, you know," I said as Diesel and I followed Sean from his office and down the hall to the spacious conference room.

The first person I saw when we entered was Alexandra, my soon-to-be daughter-in-law. Her anxious expression disappeared when she saw my beaming face. I moved forward and swept her into a strong embrace.

"Welcome to the family," I said. "I'm so happy for you both."

"Thank you, Charlie," she said. Her eyes sparkled with tears. "Sean and I are so excited. This isn't the way we'd planned things to go, but, well, here we are." She smiled and dabbed at her eyes with a handkerchief. Diesel naturally had to add his congratulations and meowed loudly. Alex laughed and rubbed his head with great affection.

"Isn't it wonderful, Dad?"

I turned to see my beautiful daughter, heavily pregnant, approaching. Her husband, Frank Salisbury, hovered anxiously behind her. He hardly wanted to let her out of his sight, Laura had told me, until the baby came. She still had about two months to go before little Charles Franklin Salisbury entered the world.

We hugged, and I shook Frank's hand. I glanced about to see who else was here. Azalea sat at one end of the table, chatting with the judge, Deborah Howell, with whom I'd gone through elementary school, high school, and college. I was glad that an old friend was performing the ceremony.

There was no sign, however, of Alexandra's father, a near-legendary figure in Mississippi legal circles.

"Where's Q.C.?" I asked Sean.

He laughed and shook his head. "In the Australian outback with a few of his cronies. We tried calling him this morning but he's inaccessible. We thought about waiting until he's home again, but that won't be for another couple of weeks."

Since he had mostly retired from the law practice, Q.C. spent a lot of time traveling these days. He would spend a month or two in Athena, and then he'd be off again on another adventure. After all the years he'd spent working so hard, he deserved the leisure he found in retirement. I envied him a little. I would love to travel to all the places he had been in recent months—Turkey, Greece, Peru, Chile, and now Australia.

"We invited Helen Louise," Sean said. "Unfortunately, she's shorthanded and can't be here."

I felt a sharp pang of disappointment. I knew Helen Louise wouldn't be happy, either, having to miss an occasion like this. One of her part-time workers had probably failed to show up for work, I figured.

Judge Howell approached us. "Hello, Charlie. Great to see you again. I've heard about some of your exploits." She grinned at me, no doubt remembering some of our mutual exploits in elementary school when we both got in trouble for talking too much in class.

I smiled. "It's great to see you too, Debby. You ended up on the right side of the law, I see." I winked at her.

She laughed heartily at that. "I was always late returning my books to the library. I remember how you used to fuss. I should have known you'd become a librarian."

"Of course," I said.

She squeezed my arm affectionately. "Enough reminiscing for now. We can catch up more later. Now it's time for me to marry these two wonderful young people." She beamed at Alex and Sean.

Under the judge's direction, we assembled ourselves properly for the ceremony. Laura served as matron of honor, and I as best man. Frank, Azalea, and Laquita stood in the background.

The actual ceremony was brief, and I watched through misty eyes as my handsome son was joined in wedlock to his beautiful wife. I felt the presence of my late wife, Jackie, hovering at my shoulder. I knew how happy she would be to see this day.

After the vows were complete, Azalea stepped forward and began to sing. Her rich contralto poured forth with "Amazing Grace" and I was stunned at the beauty of it. I had heard her singing and humming around the house, but I had never heard her sing like this. I was moved by it, and by the belief and passion with which she sang. I don't think there was a dry eye among us by the time she finished the final verse.

After the last, haunting note evaporated, we all stood for a moment. Then Sean and Alex thanked her and each kissed her on the cheek. Azalea beamed with pleasure.

As Laura, Frank, and Laquita congratulated the happy couple, I approached Azalea.

"Thank you," I said. "That was beautiful."

"You're welcome," she said with a brief smile. "I pray the Lord will bless them and their child."

"Did you know about this when you left the house earlier?" I asked. "You said you were going to the grocery store."

Azalea shook her head. "They called me after I was at the store. I'll have to go back and get everything."

I nodded. "Thank you again for your song. You made this an even more memorable occasion."

"I wish I could have had more time, and I'd've had something to bring for a reception." She glanced at the conference table, bare of any kind of food or drink.

"I guess they didn't think about a reception," I said. "We can have a nice dinner later to celebrate."

Sean must have overheard me. "We are planning a party, but we want to wait until Q.C. is back in town. So it won't be for at least a couple of weeks."

"Excellent," I said. "I know there are a lot of people who will be happy to celebrate with you and Alex."

I moved on to chat for a few minutes with Debby, who seemed to be enjoying petting and admiring Diesel. He accepted all the attention as his due, and he rewarded his new acolyte with warbles and chirps.

"Where did you ever find this beautiful animal?" Debby asked, and I told her the story of finding Diesel in the shrubbery at the public library.

"I've heard he goes everywhere with you," she said. "You're lucky to have such a steadfast companion."

"Yes, I am," I said. "He came into my life at a time when I needed one. We've been good for each other."

We talked for a few minutes more, then Debby said she was due back in court. The party broke up quickly after that. Frank and Laura both had afternoon classes to teach, and Sean and Alex had client meetings.

After more hugs and congratulations to my son and his wife, I led Diesel out to the car. Once he was in the backseat, I reached in my pocket for my cell phone. I wanted to check on Melba and to let her know the exciting news. I hoped she had followed through on my advice to go home and stay out of Reilly's way.

No cell phone.

I frowned, then patted down the other pants pocket. No phone. I checked my jacket.

Still no phone.

Then I thought about when I'd last had it in my hands,

and I could see myself setting it down on the nightstand after talking to Sean. I was probably so worried by his summons to his office that I completely forgot about it.

I'd call when I got home, I decided as I got behind the wheel. For a moment I thought about swinging by Helen Louise's bistro, but I realized she would be too busy—it was eleven thirty-seven—with the lunch crowd to talk.

On the short drive home I thought about the new grandchild. Would it be another boy, or a girl? I hoped for the latter, since Laura and Frank were having a boy. I would be happy no matter what, as long as both babies were healthy. Laura was due in about two months, and I reckoned Alex was probably due in another six to seven months. I would find out later.

I forgot to ask Sean and Alex whether they would be taking a honeymoon. Probably not until Alex's father returned, I reckoned.

When I turned the corner onto my street, I spotted a familiar car parked in front of my house. What was Melba doing here? I hoped nothing was wrong.

I pulled the car into the garage and let Diesel out. We walked out into the driveway to meet Melba. She had a fierce expression as she approached us.

"Where the heck have you been?" she demanded. "I've been calling your house and your cell phone for the past hour."

I started to explain, but she rushed on before I could get out more than three words.

"You're not going to believe this." She looked as angry as I had ever seen her. "The president didn't fire Reilly, or even put him back in the financial affairs office. Instead, he's reassigning me. To the philosophy and religious studies department. I'm about ready to wring somebody's neck." She paused for a quick breath, then delivered another bombshell. "Reilly's planning to sell off the rare book collection and get rid of the archives, too."

THIRTEEN

▐▌▌▌

I could hardly take in what Melba had said. I had been so sure that the president would decide Reilly wasn't working out. I shook my head.

"Yes, it's true," Melba said.

"I believe you," I replied. "Look, let's go inside and talk about this. I don't know about you, but I need to sit down and try to absorb it."

Diesel had been trying to gain Melba's attention. I knew he was alarmed by her obvious distress, but at the moment she was too agitated to notice him.

"Come on, boy, in the house." I led the way into the garage and unlocked the door to the kitchen. I ushered Melba in, along with the cat, and closed the door after hitting the switch to shut the garage door.

Melba had finally realized that Diesel was beside her. She dropped into a chair by the table and leaned over to hug him. She muttered a few words that I couldn't catch, and Diesel meowed in response. I took my usual spot at the table and waited for Melba to finish communing with Diesel.

When at last she let go of the cat and turned to look at me, I saw that her face was streaked with tears.

"Can I get you a drink?" I thought for a moment. "Sean probably has a few beers in the fridge, and I think there's a bottle of scotch left over from last Christmas."

"Actually, I wouldn't mind some hot coffee," Melba said. "If that's not too much trouble."

"Sounds good to me, too." I got up to make the coffee. "Why don't you tell me how you found out about your being transferred, and Reilly's plans to sell the rare book collection."

"In an e-mail." Melba sounded outraged again. "One that I wasn't even supposed to see, but that idiot Reilly wasn't paying attention when he addressed it. It was supposed to go to a Melissa Gibson, as far as I can tell."

"He probably typed in the first two or three letters of your name and didn't bother to check," I said. "Who is Melissa Gibson, do you know?"

"I searched the college directory, and she works in the financial affairs office," Melba replied. "I don't know her, but I'd be willing to bet she's young, blond, and stacked. That's probably what Reilly wants in the office with him, and not someone who actually knows the job."

I wasn't going to argue with her. For one thing, I figured she was probably right. But mainly I knew she needed to vent, and she was safe with me.

"He was being really indiscreet, if he revealed all these plans to his new administrative assistant."

"Oh, his message to her was just about reporting to the library administration office tomorrow morning."

"Then how did you find out about the plans to sell the rare book collection?" I leaned against the counter while I waited for the coffeemaker to finish its task.

Melba glanced down at Diesel, still sitting beside her chair. She rubbed his head for a moment, and I wondered why she was stalling.

She had a sheepish expression when she looked at me again.

"I was snooping around his desk—that was before I got the e-mail—and I happened to find a folder with some very interesting information in it."

"Like what?" I asked.

"Like the truth about why Peter Vanderkeller quit his job all of a sudden."

I retrieved a couple of mugs from the cabinet and set them by the machine. The coffee should be ready in about two more minutes, I judged. "Why did he quit?" I had wanted to know the answer to that question from the moment I heard Peter had left.

"Because he overcommitted the library budget by almost half a million dollars," Melba said. "I thought he was smarter than that, but I guess the man couldn't balance a checkbook."

"What on earth did he spend the money on?" I asked, stunned.

"I can't remember all the details," Melba said, "because honestly I didn't know what some of it was. But I guess it was electronic stuff for the library. You know, like e-books and databases, that kind of stuff."

I hadn't heard a word about any serious budget issues, and overspending by half a million dollars was definitely serious. I had wondered, like so many others in the library, why the president put a man experienced in finance in charge of the library. Now that decision made more sense.

"Does that mean Reilly was going to try to sell the rare books to make up the deficit?" That was better, I supposed, than wholesale layoffs of library staff. I always hated to see people lose their jobs, but at times harsh measures had to be taken.

"Partly," Melba said. "They're making up some of it with a couple of vacant positions, and taking money from other parts of the budget. Like travel and so on. Cutting part-time student workers, too, and making salaried people fill in." She grimaced. "And moving me to another department, so I can be a drain on their budget instead of the library's."

I didn't know what Melba's salary was, but given the length of time she had worked at the college, she was probably making considerably more than Reilly's friend in the finance office.

"They're probably taking some money from the library's endowment." I poured the coffee and set the mugs on the table. Melba took hers black, but I liked milk and sugar in mine. "Thanks to people like Miss An'gel and Miss Dickce Ducote, the endowment is healthy and can probably stand a hit for a hundred thousand, at least."

"I hadn't thought of that," Melba said, looking slightly relieved. "And speaking of the sisters, can you imagine what they'll have to say if Reilly tries to go through with selling off the rare books and getting rid of the archives?"

I laughed as I stirred the sugar and milk into my coffee. "Yes, I just about can. They won't be happy, and I'll bet Reilly's plan gets canceled." I took a sip of coffee. "I'm not going back there until he's out of the way."

"Why don't you call Miss An'gel and tell her what's going on?" Melba shot me a wicked grin. "That would spice things up real good."

I shook my head. "Tempting, but I am not going to get mixed up any more in this. Miss An'gel and Miss Dickce will find out about it soon enough, and if they come to me with questions, I'll be more than happy to answer them."

"I guess you're right," Melba said. "Sure would love to be there, though, when they talk to you. Miss An'gel is pretty fierce when she gets riled up."

"She is that." I had to grin. "What I'd love to see is Reilly facing both sisters. Now that would be something. Poor, ignorant Yankee would never know what hit him."

Melba hooted. "Nothing deadlier than polite demolition by a Southern steel magnolia. You got that right."

Diesel added to the mirth with a few warbles, and that set Melba and me off again. By the time we both sobered, we were wiping tears from our eyes.

"I know you're not happy, being shunted off to the philosophy department," I said, "but I daresay you won't be there long."

"I darn well better not be." Melba drained her mug and set it aside. "Thanks, Charlie, you've made me feel a lot better. I'm still peeved as all get-out with Reilly, but I just might not run him over if he crosses the street in front of me, thanks to you."

"Good," I replied. "I don't know if I have enough money for bail if you did run him down."

Melba stood. "Reckon I ought to go on home now, get out of your hair." She picked up her purse, then paused as if struck by a thought. "You never did tell me why I had so much trouble getting ahold of you earlier."

"No, I didn't," I said. "I didn't get much of a chance."

She rolled her eyes at that.

"You'd better sit back down," I said. She rolled her eyes again. "Okay, have it your way. I was at a wedding. Sean and Alex got married today."

Melba sank into her chair, her mouth open. "Married? What on earth?" Then her eyes narrowed. "Alex is having a baby, isn't she?"

I nodded. There was no point in dodging the truth.

"Congratulations, Grandpa." Melba got up again and came over to give me a hug. "Two grandchildren, just think of that. Do they know yet whether it's a girl or a boy?"

"No, I don't think Alex is far enough along yet," I said.

"Probably not," Melba said. "Oh, I can't wait to see you with those grandbabies. You're going to spoil them rotten, I know."

Diesel chirped excitedly, as if he understood our conversation. Melba chuckled and scratched his head while he rubbed against her legs. "Diesel can be their godfather. How about that?"

"I wouldn't go that far," I said, though the idea was amusing. "I don't think the parents would go for it. Though Laura might." My daughter really adored my cat.

I showed Melba out the front door and was glad to see

her stride down the walk in her usual confident fashion. She would survive this, as would I.

Diesel and I wandered back into the kitchen, and I heard a key in the lock. Azalea came in with grocery bags in one hand, and I hurried to help her finish unloading the car. That much she allowed me. She insisted on putting away all the groceries, and I had learned long ago not to argue.

We chatted for a moment about the morning's events, and then I remembered my abandoned cell phone. I should retrieve it, in case there were any messages.

Diesel stayed in the kitchen with Azalea while I hurried up to my bedroom. The phone lay right where I'd left it, on the nightstand beside my bed. I checked for voice mail, and sure enough, I had one.

I listened to the message.

"Hello, Charlie, Penny Sisson. I need to talk to you ASAP." She paused, and I thought I detected a sigh. "I'm afraid it's not good news." The message ended.

FOURTEEN

‖‖

I stared at my phone for a moment. I suspected what the bad news was, thanks to Melba's revelations. No doubt I was being let go as part of Reilly's plan to sell off the rare books. I sank down on the bed and thought about that.

I had already told myself I was willing to quit, rather than deal with Reilly any longer. That, however, would have been *my* decision, and I'd thought I would be leaving the rare book collection and the archives intact. With Reilly apparently unchecked, though, I was probably about to be fired, and the collections to which I had devoted several years of work were to be dismantled.

Did I really believe that the rare books and archives would be sacrificed to make up the library budget deficit? No, as I continued to think about it, I didn't believe they would. A significant portion of the archive's contents had been given by families who still wielded influence. In other words, they were alumni with deep pockets, like the Ducotes.

No, Reilly wouldn't succeed with that part of the plan.

But he had succeeded, I had no doubt, in firing me. The president had thrown Melba and me under the bus—perhaps along with a few other library staff—thanks to the combined efforts of Peter Vanderkeller and Oscar Reilly.

Might as well get it over with, I told myself. I returned Penny Sisson's call, and she answered right away. I identified myself and said, "I'm pretty sure I know what your bad news is."

"I'm really sorry, Charlie," Penny said, and I appreciated her sincerely rueful tone. "Your department is being closed, effective immediately. There are no other openings, either, or else you might have been reassigned."

"I understand," I replied. "Frankly, there isn't anywhere else in the library that I'd care to work."

"I don't blame you," Penny said. "And please don't repeat this, but I thought there would be quite a different outcome to the situation that's been brewing in the library."

"I thought there would be, too," I said. "But that's neither here nor there. When can I go in and clean out my office?"

"Would tomorrow morning work for you?" Penny asked. "You'll need to come to my office first. There are a few things we have to go over, and I should have everything ready then. You'll get a small severance package." She paused for a moment. "Then a campus police officer will escort you to your office and stay with you while you pack your things. It's standard procedure."

I bit back the sarcastic comment I wanted to make about

how being treated like a potential criminal who had to be spied on was the cherry on top. Penny wasn't its target anyway. I might sit down in a few days and pen a pointed letter to the president of the college and the board of trustees about all this. I wouldn't go as quietly as Reilly probably hoped I would.

"Yes, tomorrow morning is fine," I said. "How about nine or nine thirty? Would either of those times work for you?"

We agreed on nine thirty, and I ended the call. I set the phone down on the nightstand and flopped backward, my feet still on the floor. I stared at the ceiling. Had I been given to cursing, I would have indulged in an extensive session of it, casting aspersions on the ancestry of Reilly and the college president. Peter Vanderkeller would receive his share, too.

The bed shook as a thirty-six-pound cat landed on it near my head. Diesel stared down at me, looking anxious, and trilled.

"I'm okay, sweet boy, only a little angry," I said. "Nothing to worry about." I pushed myself to a sitting-up position again, and Diesel moved closer, his body now against my side. I put my arm around him, and he rubbed his head against my chest and warbled.

Tomorrow morning, I decided, I should probably leave him at home. I would have a couple of boxes to deal with, and I wouldn't be in the best of moods. Diesel was better off staying with Azalea while I packed up my things. I had a sudden, sickening thought. I hoped I didn't see Reilly tomorrow when I cleared out my office. I might not be able to restrain my occasionally unruly tongue if I did.

I decided I need not explain to Azalea why I would now be home instead of going to work until tomorrow morning. Right now I didn't feel like talking about it with anyone. Helen Louise was the exception to that, but I'd have to wait until tonight to share my news with her.

I caught a glimpse of the bedside clock and realized it was past my usual lunchtime. I didn't feel particularly hungry, but I probably ought to eat something. "Come on, Diesel," I said. "Let's go downstairs and find lunch."

Diesel meowed and jumped to the floor. I remembered to pick up my cell phone this time and stuck it in my pocket before we left the bedroom.

After lunch—a ham and cheese sandwich with a small salad—I decided a nap was in order. I read for about ten minutes, until my eyelids began to droop and the hefty Penman book got heavy. Book set aside, cat sound asleep beside me, I drifted off.

That evening, over the dinner table at Helen Louise's house, I brought her up to date on the situation at the college library. Helen Louise was an alumna of the school, and her expression grew angrier with every sentence.

When I finished, she set down her wineglass, her expression fierce. "I have a good mind to call the president's office tomorrow and tell him I am withdrawing my pledge to the alumni scholarship fund. And I'll tell him exactly why."

I reached across the table to squeeze her hand. "Thank you, love, for your loyalty and support. I'm thinking of writing a letter along the same lines. I've no doubt that when a few others hear about this, they'll express their displeasure, too."

"Like Miss An'gel and Miss Dickce, you mean." Helen Louise grinned. "You know they adore you, don't you? And not just because of Diesel."

Hearing his name, the cat roused from his boiled chicken–induced coma and meowed. Helen Louise and I laughed. She spoiled Diesel badly, insisting on cooking chicken for him when we dined together like this.

"I'm fond of them, too. They have become good friends." I shook my head. "I can only imagine what my parents would say, because they thought the Ducote sisters were royalty. And as we were only the common folk, we didn't mix. They didn't have much chance to get to know one another, even though my dad worked at the bank and they came in often."

"My parents were the same," Helen Louise said. "Funny how that can be in small towns like this. We're supposed to be a classless society, but we're not."

"It all comes down to money, which the Ducotes have always had a gracious plenty of," I said, "while the rest of us had a lot less."

"Things have changed, though," she replied. "Some of the barriers have fallen, or at least lowered." She laughed. "How did we get off on this sociological tangent?"

I shrugged. "Talking about support for the college, I guess. I'm tempted to call the sisters myself, though earlier I told myself I wouldn't do it."

Helen Louise picked up her wineglass and drained it. She poured more for herself and then gestured with the bottle. I shook my head. I still had half a glass, and I felt stuffed from the excellent meal of spinach, cheese, and onion quiche and *salade niçoise*.

She picked up her glass again and stared into it. "I don't imagine you'll have to. My guess is they'll be calling you soon enough. The grapevine in this town is amazingly swift."

"True." I supposed it was the same in every small town in the country, or in any kind of small community. Like a college. A sudden thought struck me. "You know, I hadn't thought about the history department. They will be up in arms against Reilly's plans. The contents are a gold mine for their grad students in Southern history."

"There will be all kinds of allies," Helen Louise said. "Wait until the word has got around. A hornet's nest will have nothing on it." She forked the last bite of quiche on her plate and ate it. When she finished, she said, "Tell me about the wedding. I really hated that I couldn't be there."

"I wish you could have been there, too," I said. "Sean and Alex were disappointed you couldn't come, but they're planning a big party for when her father gets home from Australia."

We chatted for a few minutes more about the wedding. I declined dessert, though I knew it would have been heaven on the tongue. My pants had been feeling a little tight lately, and between Azalea and Helen Louise, my taste buds remained locked in mortal combat with my waistline. The taste buds had been winning more often than not. I heard Stewart's voice in my head.

The gym, Charlie. Come with me and I'll get you started.

One of these days I really ought to pay more attention to Stewart.

Helen Louise had to be up at four the next morning, so Diesel and I reluctantly bade her good night at eight thirty. We were lucky she managed to squeeze in the occasional night like this during the week for dinner together. I always looked forward to Saturday nights, because the bistro was closed on Sundays.

On the short trip home, Diesel and I walked briskly. There was a chill in the air, not unpleasant, but it didn't encourage us to linger. Along the way I thought about what it would be like when Helen Louise and I married. We hadn't actually discussed it, but the time was approaching when we ought to. We'd been comfortable so far with the way things were. Her demanding work schedule meant we didn't have a lot of time together, and I didn't expect that to change with marriage. She loved her business, and I wouldn't ask her to give it up.

There were definitely a number of issues to consider before we took that step. Soon, I realized, we really had to talk.

Once home—quiet and empty except for Diesel and me—we went up to my bedroom. I changed out of my clothes into the worn T-shirt and pajama shorts I favored for sleepwear. I turned down the ringer on my cell phone to a low but still audible setting and picked up my book. Thanks to the nap earlier, I didn't feel that sleepy, so I would be able to get considerably further into the adventures of Richard the Lionheart before I drifted off.

The musical signal of an incoming call on my phone woke me. As I fumbled for the phone, I squinted at the clock. A few minutes after six. The caller ID told me my son was calling.

"Morning, Sean." I yawned. "You're calling really early. Is everything okay?" A terrible thought occurred to me, and I jerked upright on the bed, disturbing Diesel, who meowed sleepily. "Alex is okay, isn't she? She's not sick, I hope."

"No, Dad, Alex is fine, and so is the baby," Sean said. I could hear the barely suppressed irritation in his voice. "I'm afraid I have shocking news. Oscar Reilly was killed sometime last night, and I'm about to head to the county jail to meet Melba. They've taken her in for questioning."

FIFTEEN

||||||||||||||||||||||||||||||||||||

Oh, no, not another murder. I felt sick. Then the last part of what Sean said sank in. "Melba! Why have they taken her in for questioning?"

"That's what I'm going to find out." Sean sounded grumpy, whether with me or the early call to the jail, I didn't know.

"Sorry, of course," I said. "Is there anything I can do?"

"Not at the moment," Sean said. "If they don't hold her, I will bring her to your house. I know she'll want to see you and talk to you about it. I wanted you to be prepared." He broke off. "Look, Dad, I'm pulling up to the jail. I'll call as soon as I can." He ended the call.

I wished I could break him of talking on his cell phone while he drove, but at least he wasn't doing it on a freeway in Houston anymore. I had nightmares about him and Laura talking and driving when we lived there.

My rambling thoughts focused on Melba. Other than the fact that she had been Reilly's administrative assistant, at least until yesterday afternoon, why did they take her in?

An appalling thought popped into my head.

They would take her in if they found some kind of evidence at the scene that suggested she was present.

I refused to believe that my dear friend from childhood had killed Reilly, no matter the provocation. They couldn't arrest her, surely. There couldn't be sufficient evidence.

I realized I had no idea how—or where—he was killed. Frustrated by my lack of knowledge and my inability to do anything constructive to help Melba, I felt like pulling my hair. Poor Diesel picked up on my tension, and talking to him and reassuring him calmed me down as well.

"Our friend Melba's in trouble," I said. "But we'll help her, won't we?"

He recognized Melba's name and meowed in response.

I yawned again. I was tired. I didn't know exactly when I'd fallen asleep last night, but I had read until pretty late. The last time I remembered looking at the clock, it was nearly one.

"Come on, boy, let's wash our faces and then get downstairs for some caffeine. I have a feeling I'm going to need a few gallons of it this morning."

On the way downstairs I recalled my meeting with Penny Sisson. I hadn't remembered it in time to tell Sean I would be out of the house for a while this morning.

As my foot hit the bottom step, I realized that the meeting would have to be put on hold. With Reilly's murder, everything changed. Perhaps I wouldn't lose my job after all.

I chided myself for my lack of compassion while I filled

the coffeemaker with water. A man was dead, and by foul means, and here I was thinking about myself.

A little voice reminded me how much I loathed the dead man, and that false piety over his death was hypocritical. Then I decided I still wasn't awake enough for these kinds of philosophical discussions with myself. I put coffee in the basket and hit the button.

The back door opened, and Azalea walked in. "Good morning, Mr. Charlie. You're up early today." Hearing a loud meow, she looked around to see the cat approaching from the direction of the utility room. "Good morning to you, too, Mr. Cat."

I returned her greeting and then explained why Diesel and I were downstairs before our usual seven or seven thirty. Occasionally eight.

"Lord have mercy, Mr. Charlie." Azalea shook her head. "I reckon you're going to be involved in another murder. You and my daughter."

Azalea's daughter, Kanesha Berry, was chief deputy in the Athena County Sheriff's Department, and their principal homicide investigator. The city had too small a police force to run a homicide investigation, and the sheriff's department stepped in for murder cases. If necessary, they might call in the state cops, the Mississippi Bureau of Investigation.

If the murder occurred on campus, though, the campus police would be involved as well. Talk about complications. Thankfully for me, I didn't have to worry about jurisdiction issues.

Kanesha was a tough, experienced, and smart investigator. I knew I could trust her not to take the easy route and try to railroad Melba if the evidence wasn't convincing. *Whatever it is*, I thought, *it has to be circumstantial, and hopefully Melba will be able to explain it easily.*

"Poor Miss Melba." Azalea pulled an apron from her capacious bag and put it on. She stowed the bag on top of the refrigerator. She had learned early on not to leave it in a more accessible spot if she didn't want a cat trying to climb into it. "With Mr. Sean there being her lawyer, she'll be okay. He's not going to let anything bad happen to her."

"No, he won't," I said, feeling a swell of pride for my capable son. I put my earlier thoughts about her daughter into words. "Kanesha isn't going to prefer charges if the evidence isn't there."

"No, she won't." Azalea and her daughter often butted heads. They were too much alike not to, but you could never get either of them to recognize that fact. Nevertheless, I knew Azalea was fiercely proud of her daughter and her accomplishments. Azalea and her late husband had worked hard to make sure Kanesha had the education and the opportunities they hadn't had, and she had fulfilled their dreams for her.

Except that she wasn't married and hadn't provided any grandchildren. That was a touchy subject, as I knew all too well.

My mind kept flitting all over the place this morning. I needed that caffeine more than I realized. I checked the machine, and it had finished gurgling. I poured myself a cup, added cream and sugar, and had that first heavenly sip. I fancied I could feel my brain start to settle down and focus already.

"Now, you sit on down there." Azalea nodded toward

the table. "I'll get breakfast on right now. You okay to wait for biscuits, or you want toast with your eggs and bacon instead?"

I was torn. I occasionally had dreams about Azalea's biscuits—light, fluffy, dripping with butter and her home-made muscadine jelly. I thought about my too-tight pants and decided dry toast was the better option.

"A couple of scrambled eggs, please," I said, "and three pieces of dry toast. No bacon."

Azalea harrumphed. "Not much of a breakfast to set you up for the day." She shook her head. "But if that's what you want, all right then."

I started to say it wasn't really what I wanted, but if I did, I'd be eating eggs, biscuits, and bacon this morning. I weakened slightly, however. "Maybe biscuits tomorrow instead."

Azalea nodded and turned to preparations for my breakfast. I drank more coffee before I fed Diesel his morning wet food. Then I went out to retrieve the news-paper.

I found it hard to concentrate on the paper. There was no mention of Reilly's murder. The news would have broken too late, but there would be plenty of coverage tomorrow. I wouldn't have to wait that long, though, for details, thanks to Sean. That thought set me to worrying about Melba again, but Azalea soon distracted me with my breakfast.

I thanked her and tucked into my meal. Diesel had watched Azalea's preparations carefully. He was disap-pointed not to smell bacon, I knew. Azalea usually slipped him a few bites when she thought I wasn't looking.

After breakfast I went back upstairs to shower. I took

the cell phone into the bathroom with me and set it on top of the toilet tank. That way I would hear it if Sean or anyone else called.

My shower went uninterrupted, except for an inquisitive feline head that poked around the shower curtain a couple of times. Both times Diesel meowed loudly, as if to ask why I was taking so long. "Silly kitty," I told him.

By the time I'd finished dressing, the bedside clock read seven forty-five. I decided I would call Penny Sisson at home at eight. If our meeting was no longer necessary, there was no point in my going over to the campus. Besides, I needed to wait at home for Sean and Melba. If the layoff plan wasn't affected by Reilly's death, I would arrange to go later in the day to clear out my office.

With those arrangements settled—in my mind, at least—I went back downstairs to the den, where I booted up my laptop to check my e-mail. Diesel left me and headed for the kitchen, no doubt to try to con Azalea out of a treat or two.

I logged into my work e-mail first—at least my account had not been disabled, so that was a good sign. As I expected, there was an announcement from Forrest Wyatt's office about the tragedy that had occurred on campus last night.

The message revealed that the library was the scene of Reilly's murder, and that surprised me. No further information was offered, and I wondered where in the library the crime had taken place. The library was closed today, until the officials investigating the crime had finished with the scene.

In the old days, before the advent of the electronic journals and databases, the closing would have been a major disruption for everyone. Now that so many faculty members and students could access what they needed from their homes and offices, the most significant inconvenience would be to those who came to the library for a quiet place to study.

I thought about calling Helen Louise to share the news with her, but I knew she was too busy to have time to chat on the phone with me. Instead, I focused on reading the rest of my e-mail.

There were two requests for reference assistance with regard to materials in the archive, and another from a person who wanted to examine a copy of an early medical textbook that had belonged to one of Athena's doctors in the 1830s. I thought about how to reply to them and came up with a cautiously worded message that stated the archives and rare books were temporarily unavailable due to unforeseen circumstances. I couldn't offer a definite time frame for availability, and I concluded by saying that I would be in touch as soon as I had more information.

The final new message in my in-box was from Delbert Winston. I did not know him that well, although he did occasionally forward e-mail inquiries from alumni and others who had books they wanted to donate, if the books were of sufficient age to be of value to the rare book collection. We would chat briefly at library meetings, but I really knew little about the man.

Here, though, in my in-box was a message from him saying that he needed to discuss a personal matter with me. *Urgently* was the word he used. *Discuss urgently.* He gave me his cell number and asked me to call whenever I received his e-mail.

I checked the date and time on the message and noted that he had sent it shortly before five this morning.

Was this urgent matter of his connected to Reilly's murder?

I pulled out my phone and punched in his number.

To my aggravation the call went to voice mail immediately. After the beep I told him I'd received his message and gave him my cell number. I concluded with, "Call me at your earliest opportunity."

I checked the time on my phone. Seven minutes past eight. I retrieved a copy of the local phone book from my desk and looked up Penny Sisson's home number.

She answered on the second ring.

"Morning, Penny."

She didn't give me time to say anything. "Charlie, have you heard the news about the murder?" I managed a *yes* before she hurried on. "Isn't this horrible? What if we have a deranged killer wandering the campus? I am not going into the office today. Will that upset your plans?"

"No, not at all," I said. "In fact, I really need to stay home." I couldn't explain why. I wasn't going to be sharing Melba's business with anyone outside the immediate family.

"Thank you," she said. "I just don't think I can face the office today. I'm going to have nightmares because it was such a brutal murder. He wasn't a nice man, but to die like *that*. It's horrible to contemplate."

"Do you know how he died?" I asked.

"You mean you haven't heard?" Penny said, her surprise obvious in her voice. "Oh, Charlie, it was horrendous. The poor student worker who found him had to be taken to the emergency room, she was so upset. She apparently has panic attacks, and finding Reilly like that caused a bad one."

"Finding him like *what*?"

"Crushed to death in the compact shelving in the basement," Penny replied. "Horrible, just horrible."

SIXTEEN

||||||||||||||||||||||||||||||||||||||||||||||||||||

I was so shocked I almost dropped the phone. What a gruesome way to die. Poor Reilly. I felt sick to my stomach and did my best to keep an image from forming in my mind. No wonder the poor student worker was so upset.

"Charlie, are you still there?" Penny's anxious tone brought my brain back into focus.

"Yes, I'm here," I said. "You're right, it is horrible. What on earth was he doing in the basement of the library at that time of night? Does anybody know?"

"No, I haven't heard any other details," Penny said. "The whole thing is truly bizarre. Whoever did it must have hated him terribly to kill him like that."

"Yes, they sure did," I said. "I'd better get off the line now, Penny. I'm expecting another call. You'll let me know when I need to come to your office."

Penny assured me she would be in touch as soon as she had further news about my status at the library, and I bade her good-bye. I set the phone down, and I saw my hand shake. I couldn't help thinking about Reilly's manner of death. I had loathed the man, certainly, but I wouldn't have wished him so brutal an end.

Hatred.

Melba couldn't have done it, I knew with absolute certainty. She might have hated Reilly, but she was not cruel. His death was cruel.

Porter Stanley hated his former brother-in-law, I had little doubt. He seemed a far more likely candidate to have executed Reilly in such a gruesome fashion. Kanesha had better move quickly, though, before Stanley disappeared. Perhaps I ought to call her.

I reached for the phone, and it rang as I touched it. Startled, I almost dropped it. I looked at the caller ID. The number looked vaguely familiar, but I didn't know to whom it belonged.

"Is this Charlie?" the caller said. "This is Delbert Winston."

"Yes, Delbert, this is Charlie," I said. I had forgotten about him. "I called right after I read your e-mail, but you weren't available at the time."

"Sorry about that," he replied. "I really appreciate you calling back so quickly. I guess you've heard that the jerk is dead." He sounded happy about it.

"Yes, I heard," I said. "I also heard that he died in a particularly horrible way. Even he didn't deserve that."

"I'm not going to argue with you about it," Delbert said.

"I don't think you know how nasty he really was. Frankly, I'm surprised somebody didn't take him out years ago. He was twisted."

The distaste in his tone was obvious, and I had to admit to being curious about this strong reaction to the man. Delbert obviously hated Oscar Reilly. Could he be the killer? I had better be cautious in talking to him and not put him off. I might be able to extract useful information from him, information that could help Melba.

"He was not a pleasant man," I said. "He seemed to cause turmoil around him."

"He did, in spades," Delbert said heatedly. "I can't figure out why the hell anybody thought he'd be the right person to run the library while they look for a permanent director."

I wondered how much the high-level library staff, like Delbert, Lisa, and Cassandra, knew about the budget crisis Peter Vanderkeller left behind when he decamped. I didn't want to say anything out of turn, because if they didn't know about it, I didn't want it known that I was the one who told them.

"I suppose it had something to do with his financial background," I said. "Maybe President Wyatt wanted someone with a firm hand on the budget." I thought that was suitably diplomatic enough and didn't give anything away.

Delbert laughed, a short, sharp sound. "So you've heard about the mess good ole Petey left us. I can't believe how idiotic he was. Surely the man had better sense. But I guess he didn't."

"At least he didn't embezzle it," I said. "It was careless

of him to overcommit the budget that way, but I'm sure he had the best intentions."

"He probably did. We all want to make sure the students and faculty have access to the resources they need," Delbert said in tones of great patience. "But at the end of the day, we have only so much money, and we can't spend what we don't have."

"No, I understand that, but the president is going to have to get it sorted out, not us." I decided it was time we got to the point of why he wanted to talk to me. "What is this urgent personal matter you want to discuss with me?"

"Oh, yeah, that." Delbert paused, long enough that I thought I would have to prompt him again. Then he spoke. "You've been involved in murders before, haven't you? I mean, I've heard about you helping the sheriff's department a few times."

"Yes, I have helped a bit," I said. I had a bad feeling about this.

"That's good," he replied. "I mean, that you've got experience. I need help from somebody who knows how to deal with the cops."

"Why?" I asked. "Do you have information about the murder? If that's the case, the best thing you can do is call the sheriff's department and tell them what you know. Or if you don't feel comfortable talking to them, call Martin Ford. He's a good guy, and you can talk to him."

"It's more complicated than that," Delbert said. "Look, this is how it went down. Before I heard about the budget crap, Reilly came to me the first week he was put in charge. He's talking to me about the acquisitions budget, as well as my cataloging budget, asking me all sorts of questions, trying to figure out the process of ordering and paying for resources. I guess because he didn't want to deal with that witch Cassandra. I explained everything as patiently as I could, and he went away." He paused for a long breath. "Then, he comes back a week later, and all of a sudden he's wanting to look at invoices, purchase orders, spreadsheets—all kinds of documentation. So I give him what he asks for, even stuff he should have gotten from Cassandra. He goes away. Then a few days later he's back again, like some damn dog with a bone. This time, though, he tells me he thinks I've been fiddling with the books and that I must have embezzled like a hundred grand out of the acquisitions budget. All because I'm the selector for the history and art history departments, and they have endowed funds that I manage. Cassandra can't stand it because she can't tell me what to do with the money."

With all the controls the college had in place to insure against fraud, I was surprised that Reilly could have found anything suspicious. I said as much to Delbert.

"Right, I know. You have no idea how many hoops I have to go through to get purchase orders and invoices okayed. There's no way I could embezzle anything." He sounded disgusted. "Maybe if I was some high-priced accountant, I could figure out a dodge, but I was a classics major, for crying out loud. What the hell do I know about cooking the books?"

"Yes, I can see your point." I didn't necessarily agree with him but there was no point in my antagonizing him. "He accused you of embezzling. What was your response?"

"I went ballistic," Delbert said. "See, I've got a temper. Most of the time I'm this quiet, mild-mannered guy, gets along with pretty much everybody. But I have a quick fuse, especially when some idiot like Reilly comes along and calls me a criminal. I totally lost it, and I was screaming at him like nothing you've ever heard. And you know what?"

"No, what?" I said, because he was obviously expecting me to.

"The jackass just sat there and stared at me with this superior little smile on his face." Delbert sounded surprised. "I couldn't believe it, and it just made me angrier. I grabbed this brass bookend I have and was about to brain him with it, and then he got up and walked out. I went after him, though I had enough sense to put down the bookend, and I was yelling all kinds of things at him." He paused. "I guess I even said I'd kill him if he ever came back and accused me of anything like that again. So you see why I'm worried, don't you?"

"Did anyone besides Reilly hear you make those threats?" I asked.

"All of technical services," Delbert said. "You've been in our area, you know what it's like. All those cubicles are open, and if you're loud enough, they can hear everything."

"You're worried you could be a suspect in the murder," I said. "I really think you should go to the sheriff's office and make a statement before they have a chance to hear about it from anyone else. I've known Chief Deputy Berry for several years now, and she is tough and determined. She's also principled and intelligent. She's not going to railroad anyone. If you didn't do it, you don't have to worry about it. Just tell her the truth."

There was only silence on the other end. Had I angered

him? I wondered. I wasn't sure what else he expected me to do, other than to give him the benefit of my experience.

"I'll think about it," he finally said. "You won't go to her and tell her about this, will you?"

"Not if you don't want me to," I said. "I will respect your confidence for now, but eventually you will have to talk to her and be straight with her. Just think about it this way. How would you feel if the wrong person is arrested and charged with the murder?"

Delbert laughed, a harsh sound. "I'd just as soon give the guy a medal for getting rid of Reilly. He's no loss to anyone, believe me."

"He may not be, but we can't let a murderer go free," I said. "What if the killer goes after someone else?"

"Why would he do that?" Delbert seemed surprised.

"If the murderer feels threatened somehow, he—or she—might do anything for self-protection."

"I hadn't thought about it that way. Interesting," Delbert said. "But if someone is smart enough, they can keep the killer from finding out what they know."

Something about his tone made me suspicious. "Delbert, if you know anything else about this, I cannot urge you strongly enough—for your own safety—to talk to Kanesha Berry. *As soon as possible.*"

"I'll think about it," he said. "Look, thanks for your advice. I appreciate it." He ended the call.

Did he really know anything that could be dangerous? For his sake I hoped I was misreading the situation.

If I wasn't, however, he could end up in a lot of trouble—or worse. I really ought to talk to Kanesha, I decided. I didn't have to break Delbert's confidence—at least, not yet—but I could emphasize that she really needed to talk to the senior library staff. There was no telling what kind of accusations Reilly might have made against Cassandra or Lisa, for example. He could have subjected them to the same kind of intimidation.

My phone rang and pulled me out of my rumination.

"Hi, Sean. Are you still at the jail? How's Melba?" I asked.

"Yes, I'm still here," he said. "They plan to hold Melba for a while longer."

"Why? Surely they haven't charged her with anything. What's the holdup?"

"They haven't charged her. Yet." Sean sounded grim. "But I think it's only a matter of time."

"Why?" I asked again.

"They have evidence tying her to the scene," Sean said.

"What evidence?"

"A tube of pink lipstick that she says is hers."

SEVENTEEN

||||||||||||||||||||||||||||||||||||||||||||||||||||||||||

"Pink lipstick?" I said, momentarily confused. Then my mind cleared, and I understood the significance.

Sean started to explain, but I cut him off.

"Yes, I know what it means, Son. I was there when Reilly found his car vandalized with the lipstick, and Melba told me about how the lipstick was stolen from her desk."

"That's right," Sean replied. "I'm sure the killer planted the lipstick on the body to implicate Melba."

"And that means the killer also played the prank on Reilly."

"More than likely yes, or the killer stole the lipstick from the prankster. We can't overlook that possibility."

"No, you're right," I said. "I should have thought of that."

"I imagine you would have," Sean said, a touch wryly. "Look, Dad, I have more to do here, then I'll be going to the office. I may call you later to discuss this. Would you be able to come to the office?"

"Sure," I said. "I don't have a job to go to at the moment, so I'm free."

"You'll have to tell me about that later. Bye."

I was thankful my son was there to help Melba. In situations like this, he remained cool, always watching out for his client. Melba couldn't be in better hands.

I hated for her to languish in police custody, though. I knew how galling it must be to her, and I wished there were more I could do to help her. I would have to stick my nose into this, though I knew Sean would worry, and Kanesha might be furious.

I decided I would call Kanesha, even though she was in the midst of this investigation. I speed-dialed her cell.

"I know you're swamped," I said the moment she answered. I rushed on before she could respond. "Look, you know as well as I do that Melba didn't kill Oscar Reilly. She would never do such a thing. There are other much more likely suspects. In particular, there's Reilly's ex-brother-in-law, Porter Stanley. You'd better track him down before he disappears."

"Thank you, Charlie, you're always helpful." Kanesha did not sound grateful, but at least she didn't sound furious, either. "I was planning to get around to you later today. For your information, I am aware of Mr. Stanley's existence, and I am trying to track him down. Will you be at home today, or at the archive?"

"Home, unless I'm with Sean at his office," I said. She was obviously in a hurry to get me off the line, so I would explain about my job later.

"All right. I'll check with you later." She ended the call.

I set the phone aside and thought about my options. Despite what I had told Sean and Kanesha, I was thinking about leaving home and heading for the library. Then I remembered that it was closed for the day. That frustrated me, because I itched to *do* something. Talking to people in the library would be relatively easy. I couldn't go knocking at their doors at home and expect them to invite me in to talk about why they might have a reason to kill Oscar Reilly.

Diesel padded into the room and meowed. I patted the sofa and indicated that he should join me. He came closer and climbed up beside me, resting his head on my leg. He stared up at me, then twisted his body until he lay on his back. That was a signal that he needed his chest and belly rubbed. He didn't do this often, and I hastened to fulfill his wish.

He purred as I stroked and scratched. No doubt he had a bellyful of treats from Azalea to add to his contentment.

As always, taking time to focus on Diesel helped me calm myself and order my thought processes. He was a remarkable tonic at times, I thought affectionately. Better than anything my doctor could prescribe.

I hoped Kanesha would be able to locate Porter Stanley soon. He was my favorite suspect. He had seemed menacing to me, and I didn't imagine he'd had Reilly's best interests in mind when he tracked him down here in Athena.

Had Stanley come here intending to kill Reilly?

If he had, surely he would have been more unobtrusive about it. He wasn't exactly a man who could fade into a crowd, not with his height and those broad shoulders. If he had been in the library last night, there ought to be witnesses who could place him there. Students could be oblivious when they were studying, but there ought to be at least one or two who would have noticed him.

Delbert Winston, on the other hand, was exactly the kind of bland, nondescript man who *could* be overlooked. Average height, an ordinary face, neither handsome nor homely, bland coloring, bland clothing, and so on. Until I had known the man for a couple of years, I had trouble remembering who he was when I saw him around the library.

I couldn't remember if there was a security camera in the basement. There ought to be, of course, but that didn't mean one existed. All the sports facilities and the scientific laboratories on campus had them, but the library was rather farther down the priority list when it came to expenses like security cameras and monitoring systems.

I ought to mention that to Miss An'gel and Miss Dickce. They were avid supporters of academic programs at the college, and I knew the welfare and security of students, staff, and faculty were important to them. Yes, I really should talk to them about it.

Now was as good a time as any, I decided, and picked up my phone.

Miss An'gel answered after three rings. "Charlie, what on earth is going on at the college? Dickce and I have been sitting here talking about it. Do you know any of the details?"

Diesel's keen ears detected the voice of one of his pals,

and he warbled loudly. He wanted to say hello to Miss An'gel. I told her that before I attempted to answer her question.

"Tell him I said *hello* back. And tell him Endora and Peanut are looking forward to seeing him again soon."

Diesel had accompanied me a couple of times to Riverhill, the sisters' magnificent antebellum home, and he had made friends with the Abyssinian cat, Endora, and energetic Labradoodle, Peanut, the sisters adopted several months ago. He also adored the sisters' young ward, Benjy Stephens, now a freshman at Athena.

"He would love to come see you all, I know," I told her. "Now, back to your question." I filled her in on what I knew and, after a moment's hesitation, told her about Melba as well. She knew Melba and had a high regard for her, and I knew she would be concerned for her.

"Dickce, you'll never believe this," she said when I finished. I heard her sharing some of the details with her younger sister. Then she spoke into the phone again. "How gruesome. He must have been a terrible person for someone to hate him that much."

"I suppose so," I said. "I didn't care for him, I can tell you that much." I might as well tell her about Reilly's plans for the library. I gave her a quick rundown, and as I expected, she was outraged.

"I don't know what Forrest was thinking," she said. "I've got a good mind to call him up and tell him if he goes through with any such thing, he can count on never seeing another dollar from me and Sister."

"Don't be hasty, Miss An'gel," I said, though I had to

admit this was exactly the reaction I had hoped for. "Now that Reilly's gone, I'm sure the president will rethink his plans for the archive. The publicity around all this isn't going to be good for the college."

"No, it isn't," she agreed. "I think a meeting of the board of trustees is in order, and I'm going to call Forrest right away. Dickce happens to be president of the board this year. Did you know that?"

"No, I didn't," I said. "That's excellent news."

"Don't you worry about the archive, or your job there," Miss An'gel said. "The board will sort out the issues with the budget. Now, you tell Melba that Sister and I will be praying for her, and if she needs anything, anything at all, she should let us know."

By that, I knew Miss An'gel meant that she and her sister would happily give Melba the money, if she needed it, to pay any legal fees.

"I'll thank you on her behalf," I said. "I know she will appreciate your kindness."

"You call me the minute you hear anything more," Miss An'gel said, and I promised I would before we said good-bye.

I put the phone aside, feeling rather smug. "It's good to know people who can get things done," I told Diesel. He meowed as if he agreed.

I also felt a bit callous, but there was nothing I could do for the dead man. Kanesha would see justice done on his behalf. The living were more important, and the library and its staff needed help to recover, not only from the ghastly murder, but from the budget crisis also.

The doorbell rang, and Diesel climbed down from the sofa and scampered out the door. He loved visitors and usually reached the door before either Azalea or I could.

As I stepped into the hall, I saw Azalea at the door, the cat right by her side. She opened the door and remained in front of it. I couldn't see who the visitor was until I reached them.

Lisa Krause, her face blotchy from crying, stood on the doorstep. Azalea urged her to come in, but Lisa didn't respond until she saw me.

"Charlie, I'm so worried," she said. "I'm sorry to keep showing up on your doorstep like this, but I didn't know who else to turn to."

"You come right on in here, child." Azalea gently took Lisa's arm and pulled her in. "Come on into the kitchen, and I'll make you something to drink. Coffee? Or hot tea?"

"Thank you, ma'am," Lisa said. "Hot tea would be great."

Azalea led the young woman into the kitchen and got her seated at the table, then busied herself filling the kettle with water and putting it on to boil.

I took a seat across from Lisa. She looked pitiful. I had never seen her upset like this, but she was obviously distressed.

"I'm happy to do what I can to help you," I told her. Diesel had gone to sit by her, and I knew he would be rubbing his head against her leg in an attempt to comfort her. "Tell me what's wrong."

Lisa's glance flicked to Azalea and back to me.

"It's okay," I said. "Azalea will help, too."

"Thank you," Lisa replied. "I'm so scared, Charlie, I

don't know what to do." She choked back a sob. "I've been terrified ever since I heard the news about the murder."

"What has terrified you?" I asked. "I can't believe you killed the man. Did you?"

"No," Lisa said, obviously fighting hard to retain some composure. "But I may be the reason he's dead."

EIGHTEEN

||||||||||||||||||||||||||||||||||||||||||||||||||||||||

"Here you go now." Azalea set a mug of hot tea in front of Lisa. "You want anything to go in it?"

"Thank you," Lisa said. "If you have milk or cream, and a little sugar, that would be great."

Azalea nodded and retrieved a carton of heavy cream from the fridge, and I found the sugar bowl and a spoon for her. I waited until Lisa had prepared her tea to her liking and had a couple of sips before I questioned her about her dramatic claim.

"How could you be the reason that Reilly was murdered?" I asked gently. "I really don't understand."

Lisa stared into her tea. "I've been dating one of the assistant football coaches, Brent Tucker. They call him Tuck." She smiled briefly. "Tuck the Truck, because of the way he used to barrel down the field, knocking other players out of the way."

I did indeed know Tuck the Truck, although not person-ally. He had played collegiate ball at Athena, then gone on to a brief stint in the NFL before serious injuries ended his career. As I recalled, he was about six foot five and weighed nearly three hundred pounds. Not as massive as Porter Stanley, but still a big guy.

"Yes, I know who he is," I said. "Are you afraid your boyfriend is responsible? What did he have against Reilly?"

"Brent is really protective of me, you see," Lisa replied.

When she failed to continue, I prompted her. "And?"

Lisa paled, and her hands tightened around her mug. "I told you how Reilly accused me of lying. Well, that wasn't the whole story." She paused for a sip of tea. "He, well, he touched me and said he was sure everything would be okay if I cooperated with him."

If Reilly hadn't already been dead, I think I would have gone after him myself. I loathed men who tried to take advantage of women in such a sleazy fashion. Lisa was young enough—barely—to be my daughter, and my pro-tective instincts came to the fore.

I took a moment to master my temper before I spoke. In the meantime, Diesel meowed and rubbed his head against Lisa's leg in a determined fashion, and I could see that his attentions helped her keep her composure, at least for the moment.

"You told your boyfriend about what Reilly did," I said. Lisa nodded.

"When?"

"Last night, around nine thirty." Lisa gazed at me, terror in her eyes. "Brent went crazy. I'd never seen him like that. He put his fist through the wall in my apartment. He swore he was going to find Reilly and rip his head off. He stormed out of the apartment. I went after him, telling him not to do anything stupid, but he wouldn't listen. He jumped in his truck and drove off. I haven't seen or talked to him since." She burst into tears, and Azalea, who had been standing near the stove, came quickly to her side and bent to wrap her arms around Lisa.

After a couple of minutes, Lisa pulled away. She looked up into Azalea's concerned face and thanked her. Azalea patted her on the shoulder and resumed her position by the stove.

"Lisa, I'm so sorry you've been through all this. Reilly was a despicable man for subjecting you to that."

She nodded. "I was going to talk to HR about it when I filed my complaint. I never should have told Brent, but I had no idea he would react so violently." Her eyes filled with tears again. "Charlie, what should I do? I'm so worried about Brent and what he may have done."

"My best advice is to talk to the officer in charge of the investigation, Kanesha Berry," I said. "She's Azalea's daughter, I don't know whether you knew that."

"No, I didn't." Lisa frowned at Azalea. "No offense, but if I had known that before, I might not have talked so freely."

Azalea fixed Lisa with her unflinchingly forthright gaze. "I don't go running to my daughter with every little thing I hear." She snatched up a dishrag and marched into the laundry room.

"Oh, dear," Lisa said, gazing after her. "I've offended her." Diesel warbled loudly, and Lisa grimaced. "Sounds like he's not happy, either."

"Yes, you have offended her," I said. "Diesel is reacting to the tension he feels. I understand that you're distraught over the situation, and I repeat, my best advice is to talk to Kanesha. Right away. If your boyfriend is that violent, you might need protection from him. I'm not saying he murdered Reilly, but his reaction to what you told him concerns me."

Lisa stared at me. "Oh my Lord, I never thought about that. I don't think Brent would hurt *me*."

"I would hope not," I said. "I don't think you should take any chances. He ought to understand, if he's innocent, why you went to the sheriff's department."

"I don't suppose you would go with me," Lisa said, entreating me with her eyes. "I'm nervous about going on my own."

"Kanesha is planning to come here at some point before too long," I said. "Why don't you stay here? You can talk to her here, instead of downtown. I might have to leave for a while, but Azalea will look after you."

"I'd better apologize to her first, though," Lisa said. "Thank you, Charlie, I will stay here if you don't mind. I don't feel safe now, going back to my apartment alone."

Diesel meowed, and Lisa patted his head. "Thank you, sweet kitty." She pushed back her chair. "I'm going to apologize." She headed for the utility room, from whence I could hear sounds of the washing machine in operation.

Have mercy, what a mess. Another suspect in the murder, and definitely one much more convincing than poor Melba. After a moment's thought, I pulled out my cell phone and started composing a text message to Kanesha.

**Come soon as you can to my house. Have
someone here who may have vital info.**

I hit the Send icon and held the phone, anxiously watching the screen for a reply. I waited for two long minutes before Kanesha responded.

There in about ten.

Feeling much relief, I put the phone down on the table. Lisa walked back into the kitchen, Diesel at her heels.

"I apologized, and she accepted," Lisa said. "I wish that deputy would get here soon."

"I heard from her a moment ago," I said. "She'll be here in about ten minutes."

"Good." Lisa picked up her mug from the table. "Okay if I help myself to more tea?"

"Certainly." I went to the fridge to retrieve a can of diet soda. I was in the mood for more caffeine, but I wanted it cold.

Back at the table, I regarded Lisa with concern. She appeared calm now, and I hoped she would remain that way once Kanesha arrived.

"Deputy Berry can be stern and look like she's annoyed when you're talking to her," I said. "That's simply her way. You can trust her, because she's fair and won't jump to conclusions. Do you understand?"

Lisa nodded. "Thanks for telling me, otherwise I might have been freaked out." She sipped her tea. "I'm pretty nervous, actually. I've never had to talk to an officer of the law like this."

"It will be okay," I said. "Don't hold back. Tell her everything." I didn't know whether it had occurred to Lisa yet that she herself could be a viable suspect in the murder. Reilly's harassment of her could be considered a strong motive.

My phone rang, and I saw that Sean was calling. "Excuse me a moment. I need to take this." I scooped up the phone and walked into the hallway to answer it. Diesel followed, watching me closely.

"Hi, Son, what's the latest?"

"I'm in the office," Sean replied. "Can you come now?"

"I need to stay home for a while," I said. "Kanesha is on her way, and I have one of my fellow librarians here with me. She needs to talk to Kanesha, and it could be important. I can't say anything more at the moment, but this could be a big help to Melba."

"Okay, Dad," he said. "I should have known you'd be a magnet for anyone involved in this mess." He didn't sound critical, more slightly amused. "Give me a call as soon as you're done with Kanesha."

"Will do," I said. "How is Melba holding up?"

"Fine." Sean chuckled. "She, of course, knows everybody at the jail, and they're treating her more like a guest than a potential murder suspect."

"Good for her," I said. "She'll be out of there soon, I hope."

"Doing my best," Sean said and ended the call.

I had made it halfway to the kitchen when the doorbell rang, and Diesel and I turned around to admit Kanesha.

"Come on in," I said.

She stepped inside. "So who is it you've got here?" She

patted Diesel's head, and he chirped for her. She was no longer standoffish with him, and he had grown comfortable with her, having seen her so often. I preferred not to think of the reasons *why* he had seen her so often.

"Lisa Krause, a librarian at the college. She has a story that could have a bearing on the murder."

Kanesha nodded and headed for the kitchen.

I followed closely. "Your mother is here, by the way," I said in an undertone. She nodded again.

Lisa rose from the table as we approached. I performed a hasty introduction, noting my coworker's expression of apprehension.

"I understand you have information for me, Ms. Krause," Kanesha said.

"Yes, Deputy," Lisa replied.

"Perhaps you'd prefer somewhere more private?" I said.

Kanesha responded with a brisk nod. "That would be best, I think, unless Ms. Krause is okay with you being present."

Lisa hesitated.

"I'm okay either way," I said. "Whatever you feel more comfortable with."

"Thank you," Lisa said. "I think I'd like to talk to Deputy Berry on my own."

"Of course." Frankly I was a bit surprised by her choice, but I really didn't need to hear her story again. "Why don't you go into the living room? You'll have privacy there."

"Thank you," Kanesha said. "Ms. Krause, if you'll come with me."

Lisa followed Kanesha out of the kitchen. Diesel started after Lisa, but I called him back. Kanesha had grown accustomed to his presence, but I didn't think she would want him along this time.

Diesel meowed at me, as if in protest.

"I know you'd like to keep an eye on Lisa," I told him, "but she'll be fine without you." At least, I hoped she would. Kanesha didn't always cope well with weepy females.

Azalea walked in from the utility room. "That Kanesha at the door?"

"Yes, she and Lisa are in the living room, talking," I said.

"Good. That child needs to hand her burden to somebody stronger." She shook her head. "She just asking for trouble, being with a man got that kind of temper. I'll be praying he don't hurt her."

"Me, too," I said. "I think maybe I'll suggest to Lisa that she might want to stay with a friend until the investigation is done."

"That's a good idea," Azalea said. "That child don't need to be on her own, just sitting there brooding on her troubles."

The ringing of the house phone broke into our conversation. I got up from the kitchen table to answer it.

"Good afternoon, Charlie Harris speaking."

"Good afternoon, Mr. Harris. Would you hold for a moment? I have President Wyatt on the phone for you."

"Certainly." Why was the college president calling me?

"Charlie, how are you?" Wyatt's bass rumbled through the line.

"I'm fine, Forrest, how are you?"

"Tolerable, Charlie, tolerable."

He always said that, I realized.

"What can I do for you?" I asked.

"I'm glad you asked," he said. "As I am sure you are aware, there have been some problems in the library since Vanderkeller left so abruptly. I thought we had found someone able enough to steer the ship until we found a permanent replacement, but that obviously did not work out. And now we find ourselves dealing with a murder investigation."

I began to feel uneasy. I had an idea now why Forrest wanted to talk to me.

"Yes, the library is not a happy place right now," I replied.

"No, it is not, and I deeply regret my error in judgment." Forrest did not mince words. One of the things I admired about him was his willingness to own up to mistakes. He didn't shift the blame for bad decisions onto others. Fortunately for the college, he had made few errors over the seventeen years of his tenure.

"To put it bluntly, Charlie," he said, "I need a new interim director for the library. The search for a permanent head is ongoing, and we have some excellent early candidates. But it will be at least another four months before we can bring someone on board. If this latest development doesn't put off potential candidates, that is." He paused. "However, we will forge ahead. I have just come from a meeting of our board of trustees. Your name cropped up in our discussions about finding a new interim, and I know you have been a library director before."

"Not exactly a director." I hastened to make this clear,

although I didn't think it would make the slightest bit of difference to Forrest. "I was a branch manager in the public library system for nearly fifteen years, but I wasn't head of the whole system."

"The point is, you have the administrative and managerial experience we need," Forrest went on as if I hadn't spoken. "I am calling on you, Charlie, to act as interim director for us. I hope I can count on you and your love for your alma mater to help us out when we need a man with your abilities."

Neatly played, I thought. If I declined now, I would feel like a jerk. I sighed. "Very well, Forrest. I will accept the job."

"Good man."

"There is one condition, however," I said.

"I think I know what it is." Forrest chuckled. "You want to bring that giant cat of yours to work with you. Well, that's fine with me. As I remember, he's a well-behaved boy, and I know the staff all love him."

"Yes, that's it." If Forrest had been opposed to my having Diesel with me, I might have found the courage to decline the temporary position. Our canny president, however, was obviously determined to leave me no room for wiggling out of the spot I was in.

"Excellent, excellent. If possible, could you be in the office first thing tomorrow morning? There are a number of issues to address."

"Yes, that's fine," I said. *I'd better lay in a large stock of headache pills first, though.*

"Excellent," Forrest repeated. "I appreciate this tremendously, Charlie. I will be talking with you again soon. I would like you to take an active part in the search for a permanent director."

"I'll be happy to do that," I said.

Forrest ended the conversation, and I put the phone down, still in a daze.

NINETEEN

||||||||||||||||||||||||||||||||||||||||||||||||||

"What's wrong, Mr. Charlie? You look like a man that's looking trouble right straight in the face." Azalea regarded me with concern.

Diesel meowed and put a paw on my thigh. I patted his head and replied to Azalea, "I'm okay. That was the president of the college. He wants me to take over as director of the library until they find a person for the position."

"Don't see anything so terrible about that," Azalea said. "They must think a mighty lot of you to want you to do that." She sniffed. "Somebody there's got some sense."

"Thank you, Azalea, I appreciate that." I shook my head. "I hadn't expected this. There will be quite a few headaches with the job, even though it will be temporary."

"How temporary, you don't mind my asking?"

"No more than three or four months, I'm hoping. If it's

any longer than that, I may be bald by the time I'm done."
I smiled, yet I was serious. There were significant challenges ahead, and I hoped I was up to the task of leading my fellow librarians through it. Having Melba would be a huge help because she had been administrative assistant to the library director for many years. If there was anything she didn't know about the day-to-day activities of the director's job, it wouldn't be something I'd have to worry over.

Provided, of course, that Melba isn't in jail.

That unpleasant thought brought me up short. I had forgotten for the moment that Melba was in a difficult position right now. *Well, Sean will just have to get her out of it.*

Diesel tapped my thigh with his large paw again and meowed. "How would you like to go to the library five days a week? Think you would like that?"

The cat stared at me for a moment, as if he were considering the question. Then he warbled loudly, and I took that as an affirmative.

"What about the public library?" Azalea asked. "You going to have to give that up for a while, I reckon."

"You're right," I said. "I'd better call Teresa Farmer right now and let her know I won't be able to volunteer for several months." I felt a sharp pang. I enjoyed my Friday volunteer shifts at the Athena Public Library, and Diesel loved going there and spending time with his friends among the staff and the patrons. There would be a lot of disappointed faces when Diesel didn't turn up on Fridays. I doubted they would miss me nearly as much. I had to smile at that thought.

Before I could call Teresa, however, Kanesha walked into the kitchen. "I'm going to have to postpone our talk until later today," she said after greeting her mother. "I need to act on the information Ms. Krause has given me, and that has to take priority."

"No problem," I said.

"When you going to let Miss Melba go?" Azalea asked. "You know she didn't kill that man, even if he needed it."

Kanesha glared at her mother. "Mama, I am not going to argue with you. I am doing my job, and I'll do it as I see fit."

Azalea glared right back at her. "I know that, Miss Chief Deputy. I also know you're smart enough not to go chasing down the wrong street after somebody'd never hurt no one like that."

"Mama." Kanesha packed those two syllables with a mixture of exasperation and affection. "If you must know, we'll be releasing Melba soon as I get back to the department. I can't say why, but although she remains a person of interest, she is not an official suspect. Satisfied?"

Azalea sniffed. "Knew you'd have to see sense eventually."

Kanesha's poker face did her proud in the midst of such maternal provocation. I was thrilled to hear the news about Melba, and at the same time I was trying hard not to laugh at the interchange between the two women. It wasn't really funny, I supposed, but seeing the immovable object meet the irresistible force, so to speak, had a certain entertainment value.

Kanesha turned to me, and I put on my best bland expression.

"Miss Krause will be coming to the department shortly to make a formal statement. Thank you for your help in getting her to talk to me." She nodded in turn at me and her mother. "I'll check in with you later."

She left the kitchen, and moments later I heard the front door open and close. Right after that Lisa came in, her shoulders slumped and her eyes downcast.

"Are you all right, child?" Azalea asked. "Would you like more tea?"

"No, thank you." Lisa raised her head and smiled at Azalea. She turned to me. "Thank you, too, Charlie. You were right. I had to tell Deputy Berry everything. I'm going to keep praying that Brent isn't responsible."

"Do you have a friend you can stay with for a couple of nights?" I asked. "I really don't think you should stay by yourself in your apartment."

Lisa looked startled. "I guess I could stay with Cassandra. I'll have to think about it."

"Please do," Azalea said.

"I will. Thank you both again for everything." She bent to rub Diesel's head. "You, too, Mr. Kitty. You are the sweetest thing ever. I wish I had your twin brother at home." She straightened. "Guess I'd better go on down to the sheriff's department and get it over with."

"That's best, I think." I rose to escort her to the front door, and Diesel came with us. Lisa gave him one last pat on the head, then surprised me with a quick hug before she hurried down the walk to the street and her car.

I realized I hadn't mentioned to her that I was going to be her boss for a while, but that could wait until tomorrow. I imagined Forrest Wyatt would send out some kind of college-wide announcement soon. Given the situation, no doubt he would do his best to allay the fears of everyone on campus.

Time to call Sean, I reminded myself. My phone wasn't in my pocket, and I recalled I'd put it down in a stupor after my conversation with Forrest Wyatt.

"Come on, Diesel, we're going to see Sean," I said. The cat gave an indifferent warble as he accompanied me to the kitchen. He liked Sean, but my son didn't shower him with the same amount of attention that Laura did.

After a quick conversation with Sean, Diesel and I got in my car and headed downtown to the law office. The cat seemed to enjoy riding in the car. He gazed out the window at the passing sights, as much as his harness and safety rig would allow.

Laquita greeted us when we walked in and sent us straight on to Sean's office. The door stood ajar, but I knocked anyway. The back of Sean's chair faced us, and I could see long legs that ended in cowboy boots propped up on the credenza behind his desk.

At my knock the legs came down and the chair turned. Sean had a phone stuck to his ear. "Fine. Yes, first of next week." He put down the phone. "Hey, Dad, come on in. You, too, Diesel."

I made myself comfortable in one of the pair of chairs in front of his desk, and Diesel stretched out on the lushly carpeted floor beside me. He yawned and closed his eyes.

"Kanesha left the house not long ago, and she said Melba was going to be released soon."

Sean nodded. "Yes, they informed me. She should be on her way home now."

I frowned. "Shouldn't you be with her? How is she getting home?"

"Right now I imagine all she wants to do is get home, have a hot shower, maybe followed by a nap," Sean said. "As to how she's getting home, she has her pick of escorts among the deputies. They'll be falling over themselves to be the one to drive her." He grinned. "How come you never fell prey to her charms?"

I snorted with laughter. "Because I've known her ever since she was a snotty-nosed, pigtailed little pest of a girl who bossed everyone around like factory foreman. She's a dear friend, but I'd no sooner get romantically involved with her than I would a, well, I don't know what." I threw my hands up. "I just know we're better off as friends."

Sean regarded me, one eyebrow arched, as if he didn't believe me. He didn't respond to my disclaimer, however.

"Other than the lipstick they found with the body," Sean said, "they have no evidence that Melba was at the scene of the crime. She says she was at home watching television all evening. Went to bed around ten thirty, alone, and didn't go near the main library building last night. I believe her. I can't see that she had a particularly strong motive to kill Reilly."

"No, she didn't, and she would never subject even a jerk like Reilly to that kind of appalling death." I grimaced at the thought of the man's death by crushing. Those compact, automated shelves would have been relentless.

"There is some evidence he might have been unconscious when the shelves were activated," Sean said. "It's possible he didn't know what was happening."

"For his sake, I hope he didn't," I said. Then the full meaning of Sean's statement penetrated my image-clogged brain. "What kind of evidence?"

Sean made a moue of distaste. "I haven't seen the crime scene photos yet, but I'm given to understand by a reliable source that the head, unlike the rest of his body, somehow escaped crushing. Preliminary examination revealed he'd been struck fairly hard in the face. His nose was broken."

I tried not to imagine how Reilly's head had escaped crushing, but I knew there were gaps left on the shelves for the times when more volumes needed to be added to a particular range. Somehow he had fallen so that his head was in one of those gaps. That was the only explanation that occurred to me. For a moment I thought I would throw up, I felt so queasy.

"Dad, are you okay? You're really pale." Sean sounded alarmed. "Q.C. has brandy in his office. Should I get you some? Or whiskey?"

I shook my head. "No, I'll be okay. My vivid imagination got the better of me for a moment."

"Sorry, I probably shouldn't have told you," Sean said. He looked upset. "I didn't realize it would have this effect on you."

"Really, Son, I'll be okay. The queasiness is passing. Actually, if you have a can of diet soda, that would be good."

Sean jumped up from behind his desk and disappeared into the hallway. He was back in less than thirty seconds with a cold can. He popped the top and handed it to me. I had a healthy swallow and felt immediately better. It was probably all psychological, because I doubted the diet drink had that kind of medicinal efficacy. Either way, real or imagined, it did the trick.

"Thanks." I took a deep breath. "The part about the broken nose is really interesting. There's a possibility Reilly was attacked by a violently jealous young man whose girlfriend Reilly harassed."

"How do you know that?" Sean frowned. "This is the first I've heard of it."

Since Lisa Krause was giving a statement to the sheriff's department, I knew Sean would have the information at some point. I might as well tell him now as further indication that Melba had significant competition as a murder suspect. I filled him in on Lisa Krause's story.

When I'd finished, Sean said, "I remember him. Tuck the Truck, I mean. He once ran thirty-seven yards the wrong way and scored a touchdown for the opposing team." He laughed. "Not the brightest athlete on the field." Then he sobered. "He's certainly big enough to have done that kind of damage to Reilly's face without even trying to hit him very hard. But if he's got a violent temper, well, he could break a guy's neck with a really hard hit."

I thought about that for a moment. "If he did hit Reilly really hard and killed him, do you think maybe he panicked and put the body in the compact shelving to cover up what he'd done?"

TWENTY

||||||||||||||||||||||||||||||||||||||||||||||||

"That's a plausible scenario," Sean said.

"But how can we explain the lipstick?" I frowned. "Unless Brent Tucker was responsible for the prank on Reilly's car, too."

"How could he have gotten hold of Melba's lipstick?" Sean asked.

"From his girlfriend. Lisa had the opportunity," I replied. "But if that's the case, it means she was a party to the prank. It's not something I would have expected of her."

"How well do you really know her, Dad?"

I thought about that for a moment. "Probably not that well," I had to admit. "We don't work in the same building, but I often see her when I have occasion to go to the main building." I paused for a moment. "Starting tomorrow, though, I may be seeing her on a daily basis."

"Why?" Sean asked.

I told him about my new position as interim director of the library. To my surprise, Sean seemed really pleased by the news.

"I think that's great," he said. "I have to say, I've thought for a while now you need more to occupy your time than a part-time job and volunteer work. You need more stimulation. You're not as energetic as you used to be, before you moved back here."

"As long as I had a wife and two children to support," I replied, slightly nettled, "I was happy to be energetic. I loved my work, but once you and your sister were out on your own, and then with your mother gone, well, I was happy to slow down a bit. I think I worked hard enough over the years that I earned the right to semi-retire if I want to."

"You did, Dad." Sean ran a hand over his head, a gesture that usually meant he was embarrassed. "You earned the right to do what you want. I didn't mean for you to think I don't respect that. You and Mom always worked hard, and you instilled your work ethic in Laura and me." He paused, as if considering his words with care. "It's just that Laura and I worry about you sometimes, the way you keep getting mixed up in these murders. I guess we both think that if you had more to keep you busy, you might not get involved in these things."

"I don't go looking for dead bodies, you know," I said tartly.

Sean gave me a sheepish grin. "No, I know you don't, but nevertheless, you do somehow keep stumbling over them."

"And as long as I do, I can't help but do what I can to

make sure an innocent person, like Melba, isn't wrongfully accused." That sounded pompous, even to me. "Well, you know what I mean."

Sean laughed. "Yes, I do. You're a good man, Charlie Harris. Now forget what I said, and let's get back to talking about the murder."

"Fine with me," I muttered. Diesel warbled loudly. He had picked up on the sudden tension between Sean and me, minor though it was. A few head scratches reassured him.

"Brent Tucker sounds like a much more viable suspect than Melba," Sean said. "There's also the former brother-in-law, Stanley."

"He could certainly have struck Reilly hard enough to kill," I said. "He could also have decided to make use of the compact shelving. I wonder if the killer thought it might be taken for an accidental death."

"If he did, or she did," Sean said, "then it was a pretty big gamble. How could someone die accidentally that way?"

I considered the question. The shelves moved steadily together, but not that fast. A reasonably agile person could probably escape if two of them suddenly started moving toward each other. A clumsy person who tripped, on the other hand, could end up dead.

But what would have triggered the mechanism to move the shelves? That had to be done manually. I didn't think the shelves would move spontaneously, even by accident. I put my thoughts into words for Sean.

"I suppose it could have been a freak accident," he said. "But I think the chances of that are almost nil. In this case, the killer deliberately caused the shelves to close in."

"Yes." I drank more of the diet soda to quell my rebellious stomach. "While you were at the sheriff's department, did you hear anything about the attempts to track down Stanley?"

"No," Sean replied. "I'm sure they'll find him, though. A guy that size can't hide out for long. He's too noticeable."

"That's true," I said.

Sean consulted a paper on his desk. "Tell me about your encounter with Reilly and his vandalized car."

I gave him a detailed account of the incident, and he scribbled a few notes. "Thanks," he said when I'd finished. "I need to talk to the campus cop. What's his name again?"

"Martin Ford," I said, and Sean wrote that down.

"One thing I don't understand is what Reilly was doing at the library last night," I said.

"Meeting someone," Sean suggested. "That's the best explanation I can come up with. The question is *who*. Also, was Reilly lured to that part of the library with the intent to murder him by using the compact shelving? Or did the killer simply take advantage of the means at hand? Premeditated, or opportunistic?"

I shrugged. I had no idea.

"Are you familiar with that area of the library?"

"I've been down there a few times," I said.

"I haven't seen it," Sean said. "Describe it for me."

I thought for a moment, trying to visualize the space. It had been more than a year since I'd had reason to go into the basement.

"It's really just a storage area," I said. "Unless things have changed in the past year, there are no study areas down there. Only shelves and shelves of older bound journals.

Once upon a time there were carrels and tables there, but about ten years ago the library started running out of space on the shelves on the other floors. They decided to convert the basement to storage."

"Is it easily accessible to everyone?" Sean asked.

"Yes, basically. Library staff will go down to retrieve items for patrons, but patrons can easily do it themselves." I paused. "There have been a few incidents over the years of, shall we say, amorous activities down there, but that kind of thing happens in other parts of the library as well."

"Really? Pretty risky behavior." Sean shook his head.

"Yes, it is," I said, "but that kind of thing happens more often than people realize. Even in a public library in the daytime." I recalled an incident in the branch library in Houston where I worked for many years, in which an overly enthusiastic couple were caught going at it in one of the restrooms. Thankfully by an adult, and not a minor.

"Okay, to put this discussion back on track, the basement might have been chosen because the killer wanted privacy for a meeting with Reilly." Sean leaned back in his chair and stared at the ceiling. "Seems to me the killer would have to be someone familiar with the library. That would let Porter Stanley off the hook, unless he had spent time exploring the library."

"I'll find out tomorrow," I said. "I can make a few inquiries. If he was roaming around the library, someone will have noticed him."

"Good idea," Sean said. "But be careful, Dad. If the killer is one of the library staff, you don't want to provoke him or her into attacking you."

"I'll be careful," I said. "Speaking of library staff, though, reminds me that there's another potential suspect."

Sean sat forward and picked up his pen. "Who is that?"

I explained who Delbert Winston was and his role at the library. Then I related what Delbert had told me about his run-in with Reilly. "I think it would be difficult for Delbert actually to embezzle money from the library," I said, "but if he *was* embezzling, and Reilly figured it out, he would certainly have a motive."

"Plus he's been working in that library for years, right?" Sean laid down his pen.

"At least fifteen, I think, maybe more. I can check tomorrow."

"Any other librarians with a grievance against Reilly?"

I nodded. "Cassandra Brownley. She is, to put it tactfully, a difficult woman. She didn't get along all that well with Peter Vanderkeller, so it's no surprise she wasn't getting along with Reilly." I told Sean about the scene I'd witnessed between Cassandra and the dead man. "There's no telling what he might have accused her of. If he sexually harassed Lisa, he might have tried it with Cassandra, too. She may be unpleasant, but she's attractive."

"We have five suspects then," Sean said. "Porter Stanley, Brent Tucker, Lisa Krause, Delbert Winston, and Cassandra Brownley. Anybody I'm missing?"

"Other than Melba and me, no, I don't think so," I said.

"You?" Sean said. "Why would you include yourself on the list?"

"I wouldn't necessarily include myself," I said, "but someone else might. I've ended up with the man's job, haven't I? Not to mention the fact that Reilly gave me grief about bringing Diesel to work with me. That putative someone might argue that I wanted the job pretty badly, was really angry about being overlooked, and then got rid of Reilly so I could replace him."

Sean considered that for a moment. "I grant you that could be a potential motive, but how could you count on being chosen for the spot? Why would the president select a part-time staff member for such a position in the first place?"

I shrugged. "I'm not saying it's entirely logical, because I have never expressed any interest whatsoever in being director of the library. But someone else who wanted the position might consider me a rival. I do have a lot of management experience, after all. Even though it's in a public library setting, not an academic one."

Sean looked grim. "If the killer went after Reilly because he or she wanted the job, then you could be a target, Dad. Have you considered that?"

"The possibility had occurred to me, yes." It was one of the reasons I wasn't that keen on accepting the job, but Forrest Wyatt had manipulated me too neatly for me to refuse.

"I don't like this," Sean said.

"I'm not thrilled about it, either," I replied. "I'm banking on Kanesha finding the killer quickly. I don't want anyone else to get hurt, or killed."

Diesel, once again sensing the sudden tension, butted his head against my thigh and meowed loudly. Sean gave the cat an irritated look, but I ignored that and concentrated on soothing Diesel. His intervention broke the tension, though, and Sean relaxed a bit.

"Is there anything else you'd like to discuss with me?" I asked.

"Not at the moment," Sean said.

"How is Alex doing?" I asked.

"She's doing great," Sean replied. "Only some minor morning sickness, but not that bad."

"That's good. Your mother had a more severe case of it with you. Not so much with Laura."

We chatted for a few more minutes about Alex and pregnancy in general. I was pleased to see my son so excited about his wife and child.

"Okay, Diesel, I guess we'd better head back home." I rose from the chair. The cat stood and stretched. "You know where I'll be tomorrow."

Sean nodded. "Be careful, Dad."

"I will." I left him once again pondering his notes.

Diesel and I paused to chat briefly with Laquita before heading to the car. She told me she was planning a baby shower for Alex and Sean and promised to let me know when the arrangements were fixed.

On the drive home I thought about presents for this second grandchild. Laura had already raided the attic at my house for the baby crib and nursery furniture my wife and I had kept and that I had moved with me when I came back to Athena. Sean and Alex's baby would need a crib, and I planned to shop for one this weekend.

Occupied by those happy thoughts, I almost missed a car parked on the street in front of my house. The occupant was Porter Stanley. My hands trembled on the wheel as I pulled into the garage. I shut off the car, hit the button to close the garage door, and pulled out my cell phone to dial 911.

TWENTY-ONE

||||||||||||||||||||||||||||||||||||||||||||||||||||||||||||||||||||||||||||||

While I got Diesel out of the car and into the house, I talked to the 911 operator. I made sure the kitchen door was locked and bolted, then I went to the living room so I could peer out the window. The 911 operator stayed on the line, and when I reached the window, I spotted a police car turning onto the street at the end of the block.

I glanced at the spot where Porter Stanley was parked and was stunned to see the car gone.

He must have driven off within seconds after I pulled into the garage. I relayed this information to the operator, who in turn, I supposed, shared it with the police department. I ended the call and watched as the police car parked in the spot vacated by Stanley.

Two officers climbed out, both young-looking men, one heavyset, the other lanky. I opened the door, making sure Diesel stayed inside, and then closed the door behind me.

"Afternoon, sir," the heavyset cop said. "Everything okay now?" He and the other officer stopped a couple of feet away and regarded me blandly.

"Yes, Officer, thanks." I shrugged. "Stanley must have driven off right after I pulled into the garage. I'm sorry for the false alarm, but at least we know he's still in town."

"You told the operator this guy is wanted in connection with the murder at the college," the lanky one said. I peered at their nameplates but couldn't decipher them. Did I need glasses? I wondered.

"Yes, that's right," I replied. From behind me came scratching and wailing noises. Diesel wasn't happy that I'd left him inside.

"What's that noise?" the first cop said.

"My cat." I smiled. "He's not happy that I've left him inside."

"You're the guy with that real big cat, aren't you?" The second one grinned. "I've heard about you. I sure would like to see that big cat."

"Sure." I opened the door, and Diesel stepped out, still meowing. Both cops stepped back, and one of them whistled. Diesel stared at the cops, looking interested but unsure whether to approach them.

"That is a big cat," the first officer said. "Looks more like a bobcat than a house cat."

I explained about Diesel's breed and stressed the fact that he was actually much larger than the average Maine Coon. "He's quite gentle," I said. "He might look ferocious because of his size, but he's not."

On cue, or so it seemed, Diesel warbled for them, and they both grinned. Then the first one nudged the second one and said, "Well, if everything's okay, sir, we'll be going. We'll let the sheriff's department know you spotted this guy. In the meantime, if he comes back, call 911 right away."

"Thank you, Officers," I said. Diesel chirped as they turned and headed back to their patrol car. "Come on, boy, back inside."

I felt both foolish and relieved. The fact that Stanley was gone by the time they arrived might have led them to conclude he hadn't been there at all. On reflection, I decided I was glad they hadn't dismissed me as a crank.

Diesel went off to the utility room, and I went around the whole first floor of the house to check every door and window. Then I went up to the second floor to check those windows. Probably an overreaction, but I didn't want to take any chances.

I was glad Azalea had gone for the day, because if Stanley did show up again, I didn't want her to be at risk. The man frightened me, and the sooner Kanesha rounded him up, the better.

Diesel met me in the kitchen. I glanced at the clock. Too early yet for dinner, though for some reason I felt hungry. I checked Diesel's food and added crunchies to his bowl. While he munched happily on the dry food, I went back to the kitchen and peeled a banana. I felt virtuous in having that, rather than a slice of Azalea's freshly made lemon icebox pie that I spotted in the fridge.

Phone in one hand and banana in the other, I went back to the living room to check the street.

No sign of Porter Stanley. I pulled a chair near the

window and got comfortable. I decided I would keep watch for the next hour or so. After that, I wasn't sure what I'd do. I didn't really want to spend the rest of the afternoon and evening staring out at the street, much less all night.

Diesel joined me a few minutes later and sprawled out on the floor beside my chair. He was soon asleep.

Finally, while I sat there watching, it occurred to me to ask myself, *Why is Porter Stanley interested in me?*

I had no answer to that.

Another question popped into my head: *What, if anything, did Reilly tell Porter about me?*

Again, I had no answer.

My phone rang, and it startled me so badly I dropped it on the floor. The phone missed the cat by a few inches, but Diesel was so frightened by the sound he scrambled up and shot out of the room like a sprinter in the hundred meters.

The phone didn't appear to be broken, but it had stopped ringing. I checked the recent calls and recognized Melba's number. I called her, and after a couple of rings, she answered.

"Saw you tried to call me," I said. "I dropped the phone, and by the time I picked it up, it was too late."

"I was leaving you a message," Melba said. "Glad I don't have to wait to talk to you."

"How are you doing?"

Diesel came slinking back into the living room, alert for any more surprises.

"Okay, I guess. First thing I did when I got home was take a shower. Just felt like I had to." Melba laughed.

"Something about that jailhouse air. It seemed to me my clothes and my hair smelled funny."

"I'm so sorry they put you through this," I said. "I know you didn't kill that man."

"I sure as heck didn't," she said. "He wasn't worth it, even though he was a sorry excuse for a human being. I'll tell you another thing, I wouldn't go down in that basement for love nor money. It's too dang spooky down there."

"I imagine at night it probably is. The lighting isn't that good. We ought to look into that." I'd have to write that down, otherwise I would forget by morning.

"What do you mean, *we* ought to look into it?" Melba said. "That's a strange choice of words. I guess it means you're not laid off, though, and I won't be transferred."

"No, you'll be back at your desk in the morning, as long as you feel up to it. Do you?"

"Yes" was the prompt reply.

"I'm going to be there with you, but in the director's office." I waited for that to sink in.

"Charlie." She practically shrieked my name. "You're going to be the interim director? Ain't that a hoot?" She laughed. "How did they wrangle you into it?"

"Forrest Wyatt made me an offer I couldn't refuse," I said.

"Loyalty to your alma mater in its time of need. Right?"

I chuckled. "Got it in one."

"He's good, you got to give him that."

"I do, believe me, I do." I sighed. "I'm grateful you'll be there with me so I don't make a mess of things."

"Don't be ridiculous," Melba retorted. "You wouldn't

make a mess of things. Although you'll do better with me there." She giggled.

"Look, there's something I have to tell you. When I came home from Sean's office a little while ago, Porter Stanley was sitting in his car, parked on the street near my house."

Melba gasped. "What did you do?"

I gave her the rundown. "I'm sitting at the window right now, keeping watch. I think you should be on the alert, too. I have no idea why he's interested in me, but he could be watching you, too."

"He tries to break in on me," Melba said, "he might get his fool head blown off. Don't you worry about me. I can take care of myself."

"Good," I said, "but be careful."

"I'm surprised he's still in town," Melba said. "I figured he'd've hightailed it out of here the minute he killed Reilly. Him hanging around doesn't make any sense."

"If he did kill Reilly—and there are other suspects, which I'll tell you about in a minute—then he must want something badly enough to hang around. I have no idea what it could be, though."

"Me neither," she replied. "What's this about other suspects?"

After my quick summary of suspects and motives, Melba said, "Lord, that man caused a lot of hurt and trouble right off the bat. You have to wonder how he got hired, because you can bet he got up to the same kind of mess where he worked before."

"He probably did, but maybe he was always really good

at covering his tracks," I said. "Plus employers can't tell you any of the bad stuff because it makes them liable to a lawsuit."

"True," she said. "But there's ways of not saying things to get your message across. Somebody needs to have a talk with Penny. Either she or one of her coworkers would have checked his references."

"It's kind of moot now, but I did send Penny the articles I found about Reilly." I said. "Unless a victim from his past came here after him. Other than his ex-brother-in-law, that is."

"Gives you a headache, doesn't it? Thinking about all this and trying to make sense of the mess he caused."

"That it does. Hang on, I'm getting another call." The beeping in my ear startled me.

"No problem. I'll see you in the morning. Don't be late." She clicked off.

"Hello," I said.

"You have time to talk?" Kanesha Berry asked.

"I sure do. Can you come by? Or do you mean on the phone?"

"Phone," she replied. "Porter Stanley showed up at your house earlier, I understand."

I told my story yet again.

"Any idea what he's after?" she asked.

"Not a clue," I said. "I only met the man once, and all he seemed interested in was Reilly. If he's the killer, why is he still in town? I thought that, with Reilly out of the picture, he'd be long gone."

"Exactly what I wanted to ask him," she said. "Among other things. He was hanging around town because there was something here he wanted, and he was willing to risk arrest to get it."

Her choice of words puzzled me. "You kept saying *was*. Why?"

"Because he's dead. I'm at the motel where he was staying. We got the call about ten minutes ago."

TWENTY-TWO

My hand tightened on the phone. The casual way in which Kanesha informed me of this second murder was unsettling. "Not something I would have expected," I said.

"Puts an interesting twist on the case, that's for sure." She paused. "I'd give a lot to know exactly why he came to town looking for Reilly. It's got to have something to do with both killings."

"Wish I could help you on that," I said.

"Until we can solve this case, you'd better keep your head down and your nose to yourself."

"Have you been talking to my son?" I said half-jestingly. "I don't go out of my way looking for these situations, you know."

"Uh-huh," she replied. "Gotta go, but I may have more questions for you later." She ended the call.

I hadn't had a chance to tell her about my temporary promotion. She would find out soon enough.

I called Melba again. She had to hear the latest.

"Hey, Charlie, what's up?"

"I've got news. That was Kanesha calling me, and she told me that Porter Stanley is dead. Murdered."

Melba gasped. "Lord have mercy, what is going on?" She paused. "You know what this means, don't you?"

"Unfortunately," I said. "One of our coworkers is a murderer."

"Yeah, and right now I'm not all that anxious to get back to work. I don't like the idea of being in that office by myself when you're gone to meetings. Which you will be doing a lot of, by the way."

"The joys of management," I said. "Meetings, and meetings about meetings. I'm going to call Forrest Wyatt and tell him I think we need a security guard on duty in the building until this case is solved. The main library has security, and we should, too."

"Good," Melba said, "otherwise I'll be bringing my own security to work with me."

I didn't relish the idea of Melba's bringing her gun to work, but I doubted she would listen if I tried to talk her out of it.

"I'm hoping it won't come to that," I said. "I'm sure Forrest will agree that we need a person on duty. I'm going to call him right now."

"Okay, let me know how it goes."

Before I could call Forrest, however, I had to look up the number. I loved the fact that I didn't have to go searching for a campus directory. I could call one up, right on my phone, in only a few seconds.

Once I found it, I clicked on it, and moments later, the phone started ringing. Forrest's assistant answered quickly. I identified myself, and she said she would put me through.

"Afternoon, Charlie, lucky you caught me. I was about to head to a meeting with the deans. What can I do for you?"

I might get in trouble with Kanesha later for doing it, but I told Forrest about the second murder. He uttered a couple of curse words when I'd finished.

"They need to wrap this up quickly," he said. "The whole campus will be in an uproar, and we'll have parents here demanding answers and taking their kids home."

"The situation is tricky," I said. "Additional security might reassure everyone."

"I'll talk to Marty Ford. He'll arrange it, and I'm sure the board of trustees will okay the added expense."

"Great," I said. "I would appreciate it if I could have one of those added security officers in the library admin building. There's just Melba Gilley and me there, you know, and I'll probably be out of the building frequently. Melba doesn't like the idea of being there by herself."

"No, of course not," Forrest said. "Marty will take care of it. Thanks for letting me know what's going on, Charlie. I'd better run now, the deans are waiting."

I thanked him and ended the call. I wondered whether it had occurred to him yet, now that Reilly's former brother-in-law was dead and obviously no longer a suspect, that one of his employees was a murderer.

Insistent meows recalled my attention to the feline at

my feet. I patted his head. "We don't have to keep watch anymore," I told him. "That big scary man isn't going to bother us now." He chirped happily in response.

I stood and put the chair back in its usual spot. "Come on, boy, let's go see what Azalea left for dinner."

What Azalea left was a roast with potatoes and carrots. No roast for Diesel, though, because there were onions and probably garlic in it. I put the roast in the oven to warm and made a salad to go with my meal. I found a small container of boiled chicken in the fridge with *Mr. Cat* written on the lid with an indelible marker. I warmed the chicken in the microwave and doled it out while I ate my own meal.

Diesel purred happily over his chicken and let me enjoy my own dinner mostly in peace. While we ate, I thought about the new job. I was not eager for it, but I would do my best for the library and its staff while I was at the helm.

I realized that one benefit of the temporary position was that I could go around the library and ask questions under the guise of familiarizing myself with its day-to-day operations. I would have the opportunity to observe my coworkers and watch for any suspicious behavior. The library held the key to the murders, I had decided.

Instead of reading that evening, I spent time on the phone, first bringing Sean up to date on the new developments in the case, and then making notes and writing down questions for my first few days on the job. By the time I'd finished, my shoulders ached, as did my head. I went upstairs, took a painkiller, and got ready for bed. After a chat with Helen Louise, filling her in on the latest news, I turned out the light and promptly fell asleep.

Only to be awakened a few hours later by the ringing of my phone. I grabbed the phone and checked the screen. I was too befuddled to recognize the number, though it seemed vaguely familiar.

"Charlie, sorry to disturb you at this hour. Martin Ford here."

Why was the chief of campus police calling me at—I peered at the bedside clock—two fourteen in the morning?

I asked him that.

"There's been a break-in at the library administration building. One of my men saw a light in the office and went to check it out. By the time he got inside, though, whoever it was had gone. There's damage to the director's office and Melba's as well."

Had I been a cursing man, I would have let loose with a few choice epithets right then. As it was, I did express the hope—mentally—that whoever broke in developed a painful rash in the tenderest parts of his or her anatomy.

"Do you need me to come there?" I asked. Behind me, Diesel stirred and emitted a sleepy, interrogatory meow or two.

"I hate to drag you out in the middle of the night like this," Ford replied, "but I think you'd better come. How soon can you be here?"

"Give me about fifteen minutes," I said. "I'll have Diesel with me." I didn't give him time to respond to that. I ended the call.

"Come on, boy, we're going to the office." I rubbed his head, yawned, and started pulling off my pajama shorts and T-shirt.

Seventeen minutes later Diesel and I pulled up in front of the library administration building. A couple of campus patrol cars were parked nearby, and I saw an officer waiting at the door for us.

I greeted the officer, who nodded and opened the door. Diesel followed me in, and we went straight to Melba's office. Marty Ford waited there, along with another officer.

Ford extended his hand, and I shook it. He again apologized for dragging me out of bed, but I waved that away. I stared, appalled, at the mess in the office.

The intruder had gone through her desk, no doubt after forcing the lock, and pulled out the entire contents of every drawer. At least, that's what it looked like. Papers, folders, pens, boxes of paper clips and rubber bands, staples and a stapler, and other office supplies lay scattered on the top of the desk and on the floor.

The filing cabinets—four of them—had also been emptied. Melba would have a fit. It would take hours, if not days, to refile it all.

"Have any idea what the guy was looking for?" Ford asked after a few moments.

I shook my head. "No idea whatsoever. Is the director's office in the same condition?"

"Pretty much," Ford said. "Come have a look."

We stepped around papers and other items on the floor after I put Diesel in a chair near the window and told him to stay there. I stood inside the other office and surveyed the same chaos I'd seen in Melba's space, with the addition of empty shelves and books strewn on the floor. I hoped vaguely that none of them had been damaged. None was particularly valuable, as far as I knew, but I hated to see good books ruined.

"Can you tell whether anything is missing?" Ford asked.

"No, sorry," I said. "I was in this office frequently while Peter Vanderkeller was director, but not so much recently. Perhaps once I've had time to put everything back, I might see that something is missing. But for now, no."

"All right," Ford said. "I'd appreciate it, if you come across anything odd, that you let me know."

"Certainly," I said. "Is someone going to look for fingerprints? Although surely the intruder was smart enough to wear gloves."

"Probably was," Ford replied. "We'll check, or rather the sheriff's department will. I haven't called them. I wanted to talk to you first." He turned to the officer with him, who so far hadn't uttered a word. "Call them now." The man nodded and stepped into the other room, pulling out a cell phone as he did so.

"How did the intruder get in?" I asked, somewhat belatedly.

"With a key," Ford replied. "There are no signs of a break-in anywhere. Do you know who has keys to this building?"

I thought about that moment. "The director has a key, of course. I suppose the killer could have Reilly's key. Other than the custodial staff, there's just me and Melba."

"I'll check with the sheriff's department on Reilly's key," Ford said. "You or Melba haven't lost yours recently, by any chance?"

"I haven't, and Melba hasn't said anything to me if she

did," I replied. "So the killer probably has Reilly's key. Assuming that the intruder and the killer are one and the same."

"Have to be," Ford said.

"Probably. Do you need me to stay?"

Ford considered that for a moment. "No, I can tell the deputies who respond what you've told me. You will probably get a visit from Chief Deputy Berry in the morning anyway."

"I'm sure I will," I said. "I'd better remember to call Melba first thing in the morning." I laughed. "Later this morning, that is, and warn her. She'd have a heart attack if she walked in on this unaware."

"Thanks for coming over," Ford said, and I took that as my cue to collect the cat and go home.

In the car on the short ride back to the house, I told Diesel we would have a lot of work to do getting the office back in order. He meowed in response, as if to say he'd be glad to help.

Back in bed, the lights off, I thought about the chaos I'd seen. What on earth had the intruder been looking for? Whatever it was, it was important to the solution of the murders, I felt sure. Otherwise, why take the risk of getting caught?

I didn't like the idea of the killer having a key to get into the building. Perhaps I should ask to have the locks changed immediately. Maybe Ford would see to that without my even asking. He probably would, I decided, and closed my eyes. Sleep came more easily than expected, and when the alarm went off at six thirty, I was deep in dreamland.

TWENTY-THREE

||||||||||||||||||||||||||||||||||||||||||||||||||||||||||||||||||||||||||||||||||

"I'd better see if Azalea would have time to take a few things to the cleaners for me." I glanced down at the cat peering into the closet with me. "I haven't worn some of these suits in several years." I sighed. "I don't look forward to wearing a suit to work every day."

Diesel meowed.

"If I'm going to be rubbing shoulders with the presidents and vice presidents in charge of this, that, and the other, not to mention the odd dean or two—and a couple of them are really odd—I'll have to dress the part." The prospect did not appeal, but I had agreed to do the job, and therefore I had to look the part. "I hope some of them still fit."

Diesel warbled as if to say he had doubts that they would.

"You're right about that," I said. "The jackets will be fine. I may need a girdle to get into the pants, though."

Diesel meowed twice. I thought he might be getting tired of standing in front of the closet with me. I'd been at this for a good ten minutes now. I pulled out three suits and laid them on the bed. The cat promptly hopped on the bed to sniff at them, and when I came back from the bathroom moments later, he was stretched out atop them.

"Off, Diesel," I said. He considered me for a moment, then slowly stood and stretched before he stepped off the suits. I gathered them up and told him to come with me. Time we were heading to the office.

Downstairs, after a brief conversation with Azalea about the suits, I loaded Diesel into the car and off we went. We were expecting thunderstorms on and off throughout the day, so there would be no pleasant stroll to and from work. I hoped the dark skies and increasing winds were not an omen for the task ahead.

By agreement, Melba waited in the parking lot behind the building until we arrived a few minutes before eight. I knew she was apprehensive about entering the building, and I couldn't blame her. She hadn't taken the news of the break-in well, even though I assured her we would have a campus police officer in the building with us all day. That was the fruit of another early morning phone conversation with Forrest Wyatt.

We entered through the back door, and when we walked into the front hallway, sure enough, there was a campus policeman sitting in a chair near the front door. We greeted him, and then Melba braced herself for her first sight of the chaos in her office. She stared at the mess for about half a minute while Diesel and I waited, then she shook her head and without a word walked over to her desk and set down her purse.

She turned to me, her expression hard. "Give me a few minutes to make some coffee and get my computer up and running. I'll check your schedule to see whether you have any meetings, and then I'll start on this mess."

"Okay, whatever you think best," I said. "I already know of one meeting. Forrest Wyatt and I are meeting with the library staff at nine thirty. Until then Diesel and I will be trying to sort out the mess in the other office."

"In *your* office," she said with a slight smile. "Better get used to that, because it's going to be yours for a while."

I responded with a rueful grin. "You're right. We'll be sorting out the mess in *my* office. Come on, boy." I headed toward my door. Diesel, however, had other plans. He went to Melba and meowed.

"I'm okay, sweet boy," she said. "Why don't you come with me and help me make the coffee?" He meowed again.

"Okay, you two," I said. "Looks like you have your own assistant." I watched as the two of them walked out of the room. Having Diesel around would help cheer Melba up, I knew.

I stepped around the papers strewn over the floor as best I could and worked my way into my office. I set my briefcase down in a chair near the door, pulled off my jacket and hung it on the back of the chair, and surveyed the room, trying to decide where to start.

About forty-five minutes and one cup of coffee later, I had managed to get things tidied away. Books were back on the shelves, and papers stacked neatly on the desk. Melba and I would have to go through them later to get them properly sorted, but at least they were off the floor.

I made notes as questions occurred to me, and I called Forrest's office and spoke with his assistant about gaining access to Reilly's work e-mail. I knew our campus IT department wouldn't make it happen without the proper authorization, and the sooner that happened, the better. I had to know what Reilly had been doing during his brief tenure as interim director.

Plus it might shed light on his murder.

That, too, I acknowledged to myself. I was sure the sheriff's department would be seeking access to Reilly's e-mails and work files also.

Kanesha Berry told me so when she showed up about twenty minutes before my meeting with Forrest and the library staff. She had with her another deputy and a person from campus IT, and they were going to copy all the files from Reilly's computer, she informed me.

That was also when she dropped the bombshell about Reilly's keys, found with his body. I was surprised by the news. "Then where did the intruder get the key to this building? There must be another key floating around that we don't know about."

"Yes," Kanesha said. "Chief Ford is looking into that." She glanced over at the desk, where the campus IT staffer was working on the computer. "This may take some time. Sorry to hold you up, but if there's anything pertinent to the investigation on that computer, I have to have it."

"It's not a problem," I said. "I have a meeting at nine thirty over in the main library building, and that may last an hour. Forrest Wyatt and I are talking to the library staff about the situation." I checked my watch. "That's in twelve minutes. I might as well head on over." I picked up my jacket and briefcase. "I'll leave you to it. If you need anything, let Melba know."

Kanesha nodded, still intent on the activity at the computer.

I spoke briefly with Melba and her feline assistant before I departed for the meeting. I knew Diesel would be happy with Melba. I might take him with me to future staff meetings, but for this first one I thought it inappropriate. I didn't think Forrest would appreciate being upstaged by a cat, and I also knew that tension would be running high in the meeting. Diesel would find that distressing.

The campus police presence at the main library was obvious, and I hoped the library staff, faculty, and students found that reassuring. The sooner things got back to normal here, the better.

On my way to the meeting room at the rear of the first floor, I stopped along the way to say hello to the few staff on duty. Not everyone could attend the meeting, because there had to be personnel on duty. The library was open, and the students were there in force, studying and making use of the computers.

When I walked into the meeting room, the buzz of chatter suddenly stilled, and I felt for a moment like an intruder. Expectant faces examined me, and I summoned up a confident and, I hoped, reassuring smile as I strode to the front of the room. Forrest hadn't arrived yet, so it was up to me to take charge of the meeting.

"Good morning, everyone." I set my briefcase on the floor behind me. "You're all probably as surprised as I am to find me standing here. I know President Wyatt e-mailed all of you to explain that I will be serving as interim director, and I hope you all had a chance to read that message thoroughly."

I paused for a moment and scanned the crowd. I didn't sense any hostility in the room, only curiosity and a little apprehension.

"President Wyatt will talk to you about the tragic event that occurred here, and I know he will address your concerns about safety and security. I'm sure you've noticed the increased presence of campus police, and that will continue until the investigation into the murder is closed. Chief Ford and his department will be working hard to make sure the library is a safe place for all of us, staff, students, and faculty."

I glanced over at the door to see Forrest entering the room. "I'll yield the floor now to President Wyatt."

Forrest strode confidently to the front of the room and shared a grave smile with the assembled staff. I stepped to one side and leaned against the wall. Forrest was a masterful speaker with an authoritative manner. I had often thought that, had he chosen another path, he would have made an outstanding preacher.

He reiterated what I had said and gave the staff an update on the investigation. He took pains to reassure them that he and Chief Ford were determined to keep the campus safe and told them to talk to me or to the campus police about anything that concerned them.

He fielded a few questions, but for the most part the staff seemed comfortable with what he told them. The one exception was Cassandra Brownley, who, predictably, scowled the whole time and looked skeptical at every statement.

"Chief Ford is working closely with the Athena County Sheriff's Department and the officer in charge of the investigation," Forrest said. "I trust that you will all cooperate fully with Chief Deputy Berry and her officers. They have an important task to perform, and your cooperation will ensure that it is done efficiently and swiftly. Are there any last questions?"

Delbert Winston raised a hand, and after a nod from Forrest, he stood. "Is anything going to be done about lighting in the basement? We've been asking for more lighting down there for years, and surely now that would be a priority."

Forrest nodded. "Excellent point. Yes, I'm happy to tell you that our physical facilities department will be taking care of that. Their work will cause some disruptions, but I know you will all be patient until the work is complete. I don't have a completion date yet, but as soon as I do, I will communicate with your interim director." He nodded toward me.

"Let me say how pleased I am that Charlie has agreed to serve as interim director until we find a permanent director. I'm sure you all are aware of his years of experience as a manager, and of the fine job he has done recently with our rare books and archives. I hope you will give him your full support to ensure the smooth running of one of Athena College's great assets."

With that, he thanked them for their attention and departed.

I stepped forward again. "I won't keep you much longer. I know we all have busy schedules. I just want to say how proud I am to be working with you all, and that I will do my best for you and the library. If at any time you're concerned about anything, I hope you will come talk to me."

Lisa Krause stood. "We're with you, Charlie." She glanced around the room. "I think I speak for all of us when I say we're happy to have someone who actually knows how to run a library in charge."

That brought a round of enthusiastic applause, and I did my best not to blush. This kind of attention always made me squirm.

"Thank you all," I said. "I appreciate your support. I'd like to ask the department heads to remain with me for a few minutes, but everyone else is free to go."

They began to file out quickly, until only Lisa Krause, Delbert Winston, and Cassandra Brownley remained with me. I pulled out a chair and turned it to face them. Normally there would have been a fourth department head, for serials and electronic resources, but that position was vacant. These three people constituted my management team, and I hoped we could work well together. Only Cassandra really concerned me, because she was always difficult about everything.

I had been aware of her baleful gaze the entire time I spoke to the staff, and I braced myself for whatever it was she was practically bursting to say to me.

"Cassandra, do you have any concerns you'd like to share?" I asked.

She stood, pushing back her chair so hard it knocked over another one. *"Public librarian."* She managed to load both venom and contempt into those two words. "What do *you* know about running an academic library?" She stalked out of the room without waiting for a response.

TWENTY-FOUR

||||||||||||||||||||||||||||||||||||||||||||||||||||||||||||||||||||||||||||||

Cassandra's unpleasant behavior disconcerted me. I'd had no idea of the depth of her animosity toward me, nor did I understand the reason for it.

Lisa and Delbert exchanged an uneasy glance. Lisa said, "She's bitter, Charlie. She's been here for twenty years and, in her mind anyway, she keeps getting passed over for promotion. Apparently she applied for the director's job when Peter was hired and obviously didn't get it. Then, a few years ago, when Peter decided to appoint an associate director, he hired from outside. She never forgave him for that."

"When the associate director left"—Delbert took up the thread—"the year after you came, I think it was, Charlie, she thought Peter would promote her then. But he decided not to fill the position because of budget issues.

Of course, when Peter left so suddenly, she thought she'd be named the interim director."

"She's been nursing these grievances for years," Lisa said. "I don't think it's really personal. She wouldn't be happy with anybody in the position, because it's not her who's in it." She shook her head. "The problem is, she can't see that she isn't being promoted because she doesn't have the right people skills to be a manager at that level."

"We've had problems with turnover in her department for years," Delbert said. "Her staff doesn't like her, and she's rude to them all the time."

"If she's so unhappy here, why hasn't she looked for another job?" I asked. "She might stand a better chance elsewhere."

Delbert emitted a short bark of laughter. "She has looked, even gone for a few interviews, but nobody else will hire her. Can you imagine that she's any more pleasant when she interviews than she is on a daily basis here?" He grimaced. "She just doesn't get it."

"Thank you for the background information," I said. "I'm going to have to talk to her about her behavior, and it's good to know the history. Now, on to other matters. I need to get up to speed on what's going on in your departments. What I'd like is to have a meeting with each of you, separately, to go over your budgets, any personnel issues you might have, and discuss any concerns you and your staff have. I want to understand the workflow in your areas, too, so information on that will be helpful. This is the end of the week, and I'm not expecting you to pull everything together today. How about Wednesday?"

"That's fine with me," Lisa said. Delbert nodded.

"Excellent," I said. "If you will, e-mail Melba and set up a time. I don't know offhand what my schedule might be for Wednesday, but she will get it sorted out. Now, before we get back to work, is there anything you'd like to ask?"

"How detailed do you want the budget information to be?" Delbert asked. "I mean, I've got spreadsheets like you wouldn't believe, thanks to Reilly, who wanted the same information presented seventeen different ways." He snorted. "I think he did it just to be difficult."

Lisa nodded. "I've never spent so much time on a budget in my life."

Was Reilly being purposely difficult? I wondered. Or was he hoping to find discrepancies, evidence of financial malfeasance? I kept those thoughts to myself when I answered.

"I'd like to see your most recent figures, with expenses to date for the year, plus, let's say, the last three years. Can you pull that together by Wednesday?"

Both Lisa and Delbert nodded.

"Thanks very much." I rose. "I know that, with your help, we'll get through the next few months in good fashion. I'll be on the search committee for the new director, and I'm hopeful we'll find someone outstanding."

"That would be a nice change," Delbert said. "See you later." He loped off, and Lisa, after a quick smile, followed him out of the room.

I stared at the wall for a moment. I didn't relish my next task, but I couldn't put it off. I had to talk to Cassandra and let her know I was not going to tolerate her behavior. I had dealt with recalcitrant employees before, and though

I didn't like confrontations, I also wouldn't shrink from one, especially in cases like this.

I picked up my briefcase and wended my way through the public areas to the staff-only section in the southeast corner of the building. The librarians' offices formed a row against the outside wall. The wall of each office facing the common area was floor-to-ceiling glass, and that allowed the occupants to see the activity in the staff cubicles and work areas. I spotted Cassandra, phone to her ear, and I headed for her office. I smiled and greeted staff members as I passed.

I knocked on Cassandra's closed door, then opened it without waiting for an invitation to enter. I was determined to have the upper hand and keep it. If this action put her off balance, all the better.

Cassandra glared when I walked in.

"I'll have to call you back," she said, then hung up the phone.

I stopped in front of her desk and stared down at her.

"Forrest Wyatt asked me to serve as interim director of this library," I said. "I agreed to do it, and however long I hold this position, I expect complete cooperation from every single staff member in the library. I will not tolerate anything else, and I will not tolerate the kind of behavior you exhibited a few minutes ago. If there are any further incidents like that, then you and I will be sitting down with Penny Sisson in HR and deciding what action to take. I will be going through all the personnel files and examining performance appraisals, staff turnover, and budgets in minute detail. I will not tolerate any obstacles."

Cassandra looked shell-shocked, and I had to wonder

whether anyone had ever stood up to her bullying behavior.
I doubted Peter had. He shrank from confrontation much
more than I did and was inclined to let problems fester
until they became worse. I wasn't fond of confrontation,
either, but in my management roles in Houston I'd had to
be tough on occasion.

"I will be meeting with you on Wednesday to go over
your budget, your staff, and any ongoing issues in your
department that need attention. Please e-mail Melba to
arrange a time. I don't know yet what my schedule for that
day will be, but I expect to see your appointment with me
on it by the end of the day. Is that clear?"

Cassandra nodded, then opened her mouth to speak.

"I don't believe there's anything else I have to say at the
moment, and I know you have work that needs attention,
so I will let you get on with it. Have a good day." With that,
I turned and walked out of her office.

I realized I had forgotten to close her door behind me
when I went in, and obviously some of the staff in nearby
cubicles had overheard everything. I was aggravated with
myself for the lapse, but also amused to see the miming
of applause from several people as I walked by.

During the time it took for me to wend my way through
the library and back to my office in the other building, I
worked on cooling my temper down. I despised bullying
in any form, and that's what Cassandra was basically: a
bully. She used her rudeness and blatant contempt for other
people to bulldoze her way through things. When she
didn't get what she wanted, she had no idea why she didn't
get it. I had dealt with her kind before in the workplace,
and they had all moved on. I could be unbelievably

stubborn over some things, and this was one of them. She would not persist in this behavior. She would either learn to behave properly and professionally, or she could find a job elsewhere.

Back in the office, I found Melba filing and Diesel lolling on the carpet near her. "How's it going?" I asked. There was no sign of Kanesha and her department. The campus policeman remained on duty near the front door, though.

Diesel chirped happily at the sight of me and got up to come rub against my legs. I scratched his head, and he meowed in pleasure.

"Not bad," Melba said. "Fortunately the idiot got interrupted before he could dump *all* the files on the floor, only about a third of them." She waved a hand to indicate the cleared floor. "I've got most of them sorted, and I'm filing them. I should be done by lunchtime."

"Good," I said. "I'm going to be working on the files in my office."

"No need." Melba smiled. "I started in there and got everything sorted and filed. I printed a copy of your schedule for today and next week, and it's on your desk. The IT person has set things up so you can access all the files you need, and given you access to Peter's and Reilly's e-mail accounts."

"I'll be drowning in information," I said wryly. "Speaking of which, I'd like to take a look at the personnel files we have on the department heads." I told her about the meetings I wanted set up for next week.

"You're in luck," she said. "Those files were in the group that the idiot didn't get to. I'll pull them and bring them in to you in a minute. There's fresh coffee, if you'd like some."

"Thanks," I said. "I could use some caffeine." I set down my briefcase and was about to head to the kitchen for coffee when Melba stopped me.

"No, you go on and get to work. You've got a lot to do," she said with a smile. "I'll bring you some coffee."

"That would be great. You really are the best." I knew better than to argue with her. "Come on, Diesel, we'd better get to work." I picked up the briefcase and, with the cat beside me, strode into my office.

Melba had indeed worked wonders while I was in the library staff meeting. The pile of papers I'd left on the desk was gone, filed expertly, and the bookshelves looked neat and more orderly than I'd left them. Diesel crawled under the desk and stretched out near my feet while I got comfortable at the computer and started looking through e-mail.

Melba came in a couple of minutes later with my coffee, and I decided I should tell her about my meeting with Cassandra. She chuckled when I finished recounting the one-sided conversation.

"Good for you," she said. "It's about dang time somebody told that witch off. Peter never would do anything about her." She sniffed. "She should have been fired years ago, but nobody would stand up to her."

"I don't know whether it will do any good," I said after a sip of coffee. "I told her I expected to see an appointment with her on my calendar by the end of the day. Let me know if she doesn't comply. I'm not going to let up on her."

"Will do," Melba said. "I'll be back in a minute with those files."

I decided I had better e-mail Penny Sisson about the confrontation with Cassandra. Better to have it documented, because I wouldn't put it past Cassandra to file a complaint with HR against me. I also wanted staff turnover information from HR, and I would compare that to what the department heads gave me.

I spent about ten minutes composing my message to Penny, during which time Melba came in and deposited three files on my desk. I nodded my thanks and kept working on the e-mail. I read it through a couple of times, tweaked it a little, and finally sent it.

A glance at the printed schedule Melba provided made me happy. No meetings the rest of the day today. On Monday morning, however, I was scheduled to meet with the president and the deans of the various schools for two hours. After that, I had a meeting with the vice president in charge of finance, no doubt to discuss the budget and the efforts to get it back on track. The rest of the afternoon was clear. There were a few meetings the rest of the week, but Wednesday was blank. No problem about meeting with the department heads in one-on-ones then.

In light of my Monday schedule I decided I had better spend the rest of the morning reviewing the budget. Dealing with budgets had never been anything I enjoyed, but they were a necessary evil.

By the time the lunch hour rolled around, I had a headache and blurry vision. Diesel had remained mostly quiet while I worked. Occasionally he went to Melba's office but he spent a fair amount of time asleep under the desk by my feet.

When I told him we were going home for lunch, he perked up and meowed. "I agree," I said. I left my briefcase. I had no plans to make this a working lunch.

I stopped to tell Melba we were headed out.

"I'll be going in a few minutes myself," she said. "I'll make sure the offices are locked. See you in about an hour."

Diesel and I headed down the hall to the back of the building. Though the skies outside remained gray and the wind had picked up a bit, there was no rain yet. Diesel ambled toward the car ahead of me, and I glanced at it and stopped as if stuck to the pavement.

The windshield was shattered.

TWENTY-FIVE

||||||||||||||||||||||||||||||||||||||||||||||||||||||||||||||

My blood pressure went through the roof, and it was a wonder I didn't stroke out on the spot. Once the cloud of fury began to dissipate from my brain, I realized Diesel was trilling anxiously. I needed to calm down for his sake as well as my own. I drew a couple of deep breaths and rubbed the cat's head and along his spine. Diesel quieted, and my heart rate slowed to a more normal pace.

Was the shattered windshield a sign from the murderer? Or had someone with a grudge done it for spite? And by *someone with a grudge*, I meant Cassandra Brownley.

I pulled out my cell phone and punched in the number for the campus police. I explained the situation tersely and requested that Chief Ford come if at all possible. I couldn't stop staring at my car. The unnecessary expense of repairing it annoyed me, but the intent behind it both enraged and frightened me.

Was this a sign that I was the killer's next target?

I stumbled back to the rear stoop and sat down. Diesel climbed up beside me and regarded me with concern. I put an arm around him and snuggled him close. I was suddenly afraid for him as well, because he could easily be a target in a campaign against me.

What was behind it? My brain kept circling back to that one question, but I could find no clear answer.

A campus police car pulled into the lot and parked near me. Chief Ford climbed out along with another officer. The subordinate went to look at my car while Ford came up to me and Diesel.

"Are you all right?" he asked. "Your face is a bit red. Should I call emergency services?"

"No, I'll be okay. My face is red because I'm furious." I set Diesel gently aside and stood. "I'm trying to figure out what's behind this." I quickly related the morning's events, including my confrontation with Cassandra. "Something I did or said must have made whoever did this angry, or perhaps afraid."

"I apologize," Ford said. "I should have put an officer on duty here, and I will now. Too late to stop this." He waved a hand toward my car.

"You couldn't have known," I said. "I certainly wasn't expecting anything like this." Diesel meowed in agreement.

Ford smiled briefly at the cat. "Excuse me a moment while I go have a look at the damage."

I resumed my seat on the stoop, and Diesel hunched up against me. I concentrated on keeping him calm and felt my blood pressure dropping to normal levels. I began to review the morning's events, trying to find a hint to the motive for the damage.

I hoped it would turn out to be nothing more than a fit of pique on Cassandra's part, taking out on my poor car what she couldn't take out on me directly. That would be a pain to deal with, but it was better than knowing that it was a warning from the killer.

My stomach rumbled, and I realized how hungry I was. Stress often had this effect on me. I glanced at the sky. The clouds had receded somewhat, and the sun was trying to break through. Perhaps we could walk home and then back again without getting wet.

Ford returned to where I waited. "There's a big rock in the driver's seat," he said. "Looks like it came from one of the flower beds around the main library building. We'll get it tested for trace evidence, and if we're lucky, we'll find something to identify the prankster with."

"Do you think that's all it was?" I asked. "And not a warning?"

Ford shrugged. "Hard to say, but I'd advise you to be on your guard until the murder investigation is complete. Do you have an alarm system at home?"

"Yes," I said, "but I don't use it unless I'm going to be gone overnight and the house will be empty. Most of the time there is someone in the house even when I'm not."

"Better use it even when you're at home for now," he said. "I will check on the whereabouts of the senior members of the library staff you mentioned." He pulled out a notebook and repeated their names as he jotted them down.

As he did so, I remembered there was another potential suspect, one I had forgotten about till now. "What about

Brent Tucker? He could have done it for Lisa's sake, or at her request because I advised her to come clean with you about everything."

Ford shook his head. "I don't think he's guilty of this, at least. Last I heard, he was sitting in the DeSoto County jail for DUI and attempting to assault an officer. He might have made bail and be out by now. I'll check on that."

"Do you need me any longer?" I rose from the stoop. "Diesel and I were headed home for lunch when I discovered the broken windshield. While I'm there, I can arrange for repairs."

"Sure," Ford said. "We'll be finished with it in a few minutes, and I'll have an officer on duty. You go on home and get something to eat."

"Thanks," I said. "Come on, Diesel. Let's go home." I picked up the leash, and the cat set off in the correct direction. He knew exactly where we were headed.

I tried to keep my mind blank on the walk home. If I thought too much about the situation, I would get angry all over again. I needed to remain calm, not only for my health, but in order to figure this out. I did make a couple of decisions while we walked, though.

One was to inform Azalea of the potential danger and to suggest that she not come to the house until the case was done. I'd never forgive myself if anything happened to her, and I knew Aunt Dottie would haunt me without mercy the rest of my life if anything did. Whether Azalea would agree with me was a matter beyond my control. I knew who had the upper hand.

The second decision was to call Sean. I knew he would be alarmed and would probably try to talk me into resigning from my temporary position. Laura would do the same, no doubt. I didn't want to cause either of them to worry, not when they both had their families to think about. Besides, that stubborn part of me that I couldn't ignore wouldn't allow me to tuck tail and run.

Azalea greeted us at the front door. "I was expecting y'all earlier," she said. "I put your food in the oven to warm." She bustled off to the kitchen while I removed Diesel's leash. I left the harness on because we wouldn't be here that long. He scampered off toward the utility room while I hung the leash on the hall tree.

By the time I reached the kitchen, Azalea had my food on the table. Today's lunch consisted of a baked chicken breast, mashed potatoes and brown gravy, green beans, and two rolls—homemade, naturally—to be washed down with Azalea's wonderful sweet tea.

I knew that eating and enjoying my meal would help keep Azalea in a slightly more tractable mood, so I delayed telling her about what happened to my car until I was nearly done. She sneaked Diesel some bits of chicken while I ate.

Azalea's eyes narrowed as I talked, and when I'd finished, she said, "So wicked. Why some people have to go around destroying what good people like you work for I surely don't know. The Lord have mercy on their soul."

I nodded. "The problem is, you see, I'm not sure exactly why I was targeted like this. It could be simply spite because I had a run-in with one of the library staff today. Or it could be something a lot worse. The killer could be warning me to back off."

"I see," she said. "Then I guess in that case you're gonna

want me not to come to work until my daughter lays hands on the murderer."

Feeling relieved that she understood, I said, "Yes. There's no telling what the killer might do, or who he might target."

Azalea snorted. "Not going to send me running to hide under my bed. I got a shotgun at home, belonged to my husband, and I know how to use it. Anybody tries to harm me or anything in Miss Dottie's house is gonna end up talking to Saint Peter quicker than he ever thought about."

I should have known she would react this way, and I also knew there was not a thing I could do or say to dissuade her. As always, I was touched by her loyalty to my late aunt and her home. But I worried nevertheless.

"Promise me you'll be careful," I said. "I'm going to show you again how to set the alarm for the outside doors and the windows, and I want you to keep the alarm on whenever you're here. Especially when you're here alone."

For a moment I thought she would protest, but then she nodded. We spent a few minutes going over the workings of the alarm, and then I dug out the phone book to look up the number for the nearest glass company.

Ten minutes later I had completed arrangements to have my windshield replaced. I didn't bother to call my insurance agent because the amount quoted for replacement and installation was under my deductible.

Finally, I called Sean. At the last minute, I wavered on telling him what had happened over the phone. "Would you have time to drop by my office sometime this afternoon? I have a few things I'd like to discuss with you."

"Let me see," he said. "Yeah, I can come by around

four, if that's okay. I should be done here at the office by then."

"That's fine," I said. "See you then." I ended the call and stuck the phone in my pocket. "Okay, Diesel, time to go back to work. Thanks for the delicious lunch, Azalea. I was starving."

After reminding her to set the alarm once we left, Diesel and I headed back to the office.

The windshield repairman was due by two, and it was a few minutes after one thirty now. I cast an anxious glance at the sky. The clouds looked threatening again. Perhaps I should try to find plastic or a tarp to cover the breakage with. I didn't want the inside of the car soaked.

I picked up the pace, and Diesel trotted along with me. We both could use the exercise, though I didn't want to push either of us too hard. We arrived at the library administration building in record time, but instead of going in the front, we continued along the sidewalk to the back parking lot.

As promised, Chief Ford had an officer on duty, an obvious presence in the police car parked in the lot close to the street. I approached my car and was surprised and gratified to see the windshield already covered with a tarp. Ford or perhaps Melba must have arranged it.

I acknowledged the officer in the patrol car, and Diesel and I entered the building through the back door. A new officer was on duty by the front door. We stopped to say hello, then heeded Melba's summons to come into her office.

"Chief Ford told me what happened to your car," she said. "I'll tell you right now, if it weren't for the campus police on guard duty here and outside, I'd be home locked up like Fort Knox."

"I can't blame you," I said. "Chief Ford advised me to use my alarm system at home, and I'm going to. Can't take any chances until this thing is settled."

"No, we can't." Melba shivered. "I got a guy I know in physical facilities to cover your windshield. It was looking like rain, and I didn't know when you would get it repaired."

I told her the arrangements I had made earlier. I handed her my car keys. "If the repairman needs them, would you mind giving them to him? When he's done, I'll write him a check."

"I'll take care of it," she said. "You go on. I know you're anxious to get back to work."

"Thanks." I looked down at the cat, standing next to Melba and rubbing against her legs. "I think he may want to stay with you for a while."

"That's fine with me." She patted his head. "He can be my extra guard-kitty." Diesel meowed, and we both smiled.

In my office I shed my jacket and went to work at the computer. I found the master budget spreadsheets for the current and past three fiscal years and began going through them, looking for anything suspicious or unusual.

The only time during the next three hours that I wasn't going through budgets was the few minutes I spent writing a check to the glass company. I thanked the repairman, stretched my shoulders, arms, and neck for a moment, and was soon back at the computer.

Finally, I had to quit. My shoulders and my head ached, and my eyes felt like I had sprung the socket muscles. I leaned back in the chair and closed my eyes. Cells of numbers danced in my tired brain.

After all that intense concentration, I hadn't found anything that stood out as questionable. Every line item looked okay—other than the overages okayed by Peter Vanderkeller, that is. I didn't see how Peter's mistakes in judgment were connected to this, other than the fact that his abrupt resignation and disappearance had made it necessary for another person to take over. That person being the first murder victim was only tangentially related, surely.

I would go through it all again, though, before I was completely satisfied. Still, I was reluctantly coming to the conclusion that the motive for Reilly's murder had nothing to do with the library's finances.

TWENTY-SIX

||||||||||||||||||||||||||||||||||||||||||||||||||||||||||||||

Sean's knock on my open door broke through my reverie. "Hey, Dad, sorry I'm late. Last-minute stuff at the office." He advanced into the room and took one of the chairs in front of my desk.

"I didn't even realize you were late." I massaged the back of my neck as I regarded him. "I was so engrossed in budget spreadsheets I lost all track of time."

"Having fun?" he said. "I hate spreadsheets."

"I'm not fond of them myself," I replied. "They're a necessary evil with budgets, along with financial statements. I've gone through a number of those as well."

"Time for a break, then." Sean crossed one booted foot over a leg and smiled at me. "What was it you wanted to talk to me about? I wouldn't hurry you, except Alex and I are having dinner with a law school classmate of hers and the classmate's partner."

I doubted the coming conversation would go well, but I couldn't put it off any longer. "You're not going to be happy about this," I warned my son before I told him about the broken windshield.

He listened without comment until I'd finished, although his expression revealed his concern.

"When I told you I thought this job would be good for you," he finally said, "I never considered you might be a target. That's serious, and I don't like it."

"I don't, either," I said. "But to consider all the angles, it could be Cassandra Brownley getting back at me because I told her she basically had to behave properly or else find herself another job."

"Does she have a history of vindictive or spiteful acts against persons who have annoyed her in the past?"

"I don't know," I said slowly. "Not that I've heard of, but I know someone who probably will know." I started to get up from my desk, but Sean indicated that I should remain where I was.

He got up and went through to Melba's office. She, along with Diesel, returned with Sean. Diesel padded around to head-butt my knees while Sean pulled out a chair for Melba and then resumed his seat.

"What's up?" Melba said. "Sean said you wanted to consult me."

I nodded. "Cassandra Brownley. Do know of any instances in the past when she has been vindictive toward anyone who has thwarted or challenged her in any way?"

"You think she smashed your windshield because you confronted her?" Melba nodded. "Yes, I can see where that would get her hopping mad. She's the librarian that's been at the library the longest, and she likes to think she knows everything. Let me see." She paused to consider my question.

Sean and I waited patiently. Diesel rubbed against my legs and meowed when I stopped patting his head. He quieted when I gave him more attention.

Melba nodded as if to confirm something to herself. Finally she spoke. "Yes, I can think of two incidents when she did something nasty. Not that anyone could ever prove it was her, but nobody else had a reason to do what she did."

"What happened?" Sean asked.

"In the first instance—and this happened, oh, maybe fifteen years ago—" Melba said, "a new librarian, pretty girl right out of library school, hadn't been at the library long, corrected Cassandra on something in a meeting with all the librarians. From what I heard, she did it really tactfully, but Cassandra didn't take it well." Melba grimaced. "She's always right about everything and can't stand it if you prove her wrong. Pompous know-it-all witch."

"What did she do?" I asked.

"This girl, I think her name was Betsy Fox, was terrified of spiders. Bugs of any kind, really. Well, she came into her office real early one morning—it was winter, and nobody else was there yet—and when she turned on the light, all she could see was bugs everywhere. Poor girl ran out screaming, tripped over a chair, and broke her leg and her arm."

"They surely weren't real bugs," Sean said.

"No," Melba said. "Plastic, but they looked real enough to poor Betsy, and there must have been two hundred of them in her office."

"They never figured out who did it?" I asked.

"Nope, they sure didn't, although everybody knew it was Cassandra," Melba said. "Once Betsy recovered from the broken arm and leg, she found a job in another state."

"Can't say that I blame her," Sean said. "Although frankly I think more should have been done to prove the identity of the prankster."

"They really did try," Melba said. "But Cassandra is pretty smart, I have to admit. She pulled it off, and nobody could prove it." She frowned. "I should have thought of them sooner, but I guess I was just so caught up in my feuding with Reilly that they slipped my mind."

"You said there were two incidents. What was the other one?" I asked.

"This one happened about five years ago," Melba said. "Same kind of thing. One of the male reference librarians got into an argument with Cassandra over these books he wanted to order for the library, and Cassandra wouldn't approve them. Told him they were not relevant, and she wasn't going to waste the library's money. He about had a stroke, from what I heard. He had a PhD in whatever the subject was, and I reckon he knew better about those books than Miss Know-It-All." Melba snorted. "He went over her head, and Peter backed him up."

"What did she do to get back at him?" Sean asked. "Although I'm not sure I want to hear the answer."

"He had a sweet tooth like you wouldn't believe," Melba said. "Looked like a fishing pole on legs, but he was always eating some kind of chocolate. He also had a bad habit of helping himself to other people's candy without asking." She grinned. "I know I shouldn't laugh, but it was kinda funny."

I had an idea where this was going, and yes, it had its humorous aspects, but it was also dangerous.

Melba continued the story. "He found a box of chocolates that supposedly came from one of the library vendors. It didn't have anybody's name on it, and he took it for himself. Must have eaten half the two-pound box, and then after a while he lit out for the bathroom. Stayed in there for the next two hours is what I heard. Finally had to go to the hospital to be checked out."

"And again, everyone suspected Cassandra," Sean said, "but no one could prove it."

"Exactly," Melba said.

"Did he get another job, too?" I asked.

"Three months later, he was gone," Melba said. "I heard he threatened to run Cassandra down in the street if she ever got near his car, but that was probably just talk."

"Sounds like this woman is vicious when she's crossed." Sean frowned. "Besides your windshield, Dad, what were the pranks aimed at Reilly?"

"The petroleum jelly and *Oscar the Grouch* in pink lipstick on his windshield, and the letters allegedly from him, firing all three department heads."

"They're not the same," Sean said. "At least, not as physically harmful as the other pranks. Unless she's changed her methods, I'm not sure she's responsible for these current shenanigans."

"It would take a psychologist to sort it out," Melba said. "But for my money, the woman is a lunatic. I think smashing a windshield is in line with the other tricks she pulled. Maybe not those letters and Reilly's car, but putting a big rock through a windshield is vicious to me."

"You may have a point," I said. "There is a difference, perhaps subtle, but it's there."

"In that case, are you thinking Cassandra's responsible for your car? And that the murderer pulled the other pranks?" Sean asked. "I suppose you could make a case for that line of thinking."

"I don't know," I said. "I'd certainly rather have it simply be Cassandra getting back at me than the killer trying to warn me off. But who knows?" My headache was worse now, and I needed pain relief. "Maybe Cassandra *is* the murderer. It would make things less complicated."

"It sure would," Melba said. "And I wouldn't put anything past her."

"I think you should tell both Chief Ford and Kanesha what you told us," Sean said to Melba. "It may have no bearing on the case, but they need to know anything that could possibly be related."

Melba nodded. "You're right. I'll call the campus police office. If I talk to Marty Ford, he can relay everything to Kanesha."

"That's fine. Do you both feel reasonably secure working here with the campus police on guard duty?" Sean asked. "If you don't, Dad needs to talk to the president about shutting this office down until the murder investigation is complete."

"I'm fine, as long as they're here," Melba said, and I agreed.

"Besides," I said, "I don't like the idea of tucking my tail and barricading myself at home behind the security system."

"I'm going to be Laura for a moment," Sean said,

"because I know exactly what she'd say to you, Dad. *Discretion is the better part of valor.*"

I shook my head. "Close, but not right." I quoted the line properly, "'The better part of valor is discretion, in the which better part I have sav'd my life.'" I paused to dredge the memory banks further. "*Henry the Fourth, Part One,* act five, scene four. I'm pretty sure that's where it's from. Falstaff saved his life by pretending to be dead."

Sean grinned in defeat. "I was always more a Chaucer man myself anyway. I could never match you and Laura when it came to Shakespeare." He paused, and his sober expression returned. "All quoting aside, the fact is you could both be in the killer's sights, and I would like to keep you around for a while longer."

Melba reached over and squeezed his arm. "I'm not planning on going anywhere anytime soon. But like Charlie said, I'm not tucking my tail, either. We'll be fine."

Sean threw up his hands. "I'm not going to argue any longer." He stood. "I'd better get going. Alex is waiting." He gave Melba a quick hug and said good-bye to me and Diesel, then he was out the door.

I checked my watch. Four thirty-seven. "Do you think that buddy of yours in accounts payable is still in her office?"

"Probably," Melba said. "She's a strict by-the-clock kind of person. She doesn't get off until five, and so she's not going to leave a minute sooner."

"Good," I said. "Would you mind e-mailing her and asking her to pull—on Monday, of course—all library invoices from vendors for the past couple of years? I'll go over in the afternoon"—I checked the printed schedule

Melba gave me earlier—"around two, to look at them. That should give her enough time, don't you think?"

"It ought to. She's efficient like all get-out." Melba frowned. "But why don't you just ask to see the files they keep in the library? They'll have duplicates of everything, because they have to create the purchase orders and then send everything to accounts payable."

"I thought of that, but I think it would cause less anxiety if I go through accounts payable for what I need. Right now I don't want to stir things up any more than I have to."

"Good idea. We don't want Miss K-I-A getting more riled up than she probably already is. She's liable to burn down the building if she gets too pissed off." Melba giggled.

"Don't even think about such things," I said in what I hoped was a repressive tone. Though repressive tones rarely had any effect on Melba, as I knew all too well.

Melba stood. "I'm going to be packing up to go home soon. How late are you planning to work today?"

"I won't be much longer myself. I'd thought about coming in tomorrow but then I realized I could probably access most of what I need through the campus network from home. Especially now that they've got me set up to see all of Peter's and Reilly's files." I rubbed my forehead. "Besides, I've got a headache, and sitting here staring at the screen for another hour or so isn't going to help."

"I'll get you something for that." Melba left my office at a fast pace and returned before I could do much besides gather up the personnel files and stuff them in my briefcase. I scooped up a few pens from Reilly's desk drawer and stuck them in as well. I couldn't seem to keep them in my desk at home because various residents kept helping themselves to any I put there.

Melba handed me a cup of water and two aspirin. "These will do the trick."

I dutifully popped them in my mouth and washed them down with the water. I returned the cup and thanked her. "I'm going to check for last-minute e-mails, and then I'll be ready to go."

"I'll be ready when you are," she said.

Diesel, who had been remarkably quiet until now, decided to join the conversation. He treated us to a combination of chirps and warbles, and I supposed he was telling us that he, too, would be ready to go. He was starving and upon the point of utter collapse, due to severe malnutrition, and I had better get him home quickly if I didn't want an expired feline on my hands and my conscience.

That's how I interpreted the various sounds he made, anyway, based on my past experience during mornings when I did not get out of bed soon enough to tend to his dietary requirements.

Melba laughed along with me as the feline version of a diatribe came to an end. I patted his head and assured him we wouldn't be long.

I was relieved to see no new e-mails. I checked my briefcase to be sure I had put in it all I wanted to take home, put Diesel's leash on, and grabbed my jacket. I paused to lock the door, and then Melba and I were ready to go.

The repairman appeared to have done the installation of the new windshield properly. Rain began to fall lightly as I was getting Diesel into the car, and I was thankful to have the glass in place.

The downpour grew slightly heavier, and I turned on the wipers and the headlights. The sky had grown darker. I'd be glad to get home before the weather got any worse.

I slowed the car as we neared the house, preparatory to making the left turn into the driveway. My heart thudded painfully in my chest when I saw not one, but two sheriff's department cars parked on the street in front of my house.

TWENTY-SEVEN

IIIIIIIIIIIIIIIIIIIIIIIIIIIIIIIIIIIIIIIIIIIIIIIIIIIIIIIIIIIIIIIIIIIII

Why didn't someone call me? My hands trembled on the wheel as I steered the car into the garage. *I should have been firmer with Azalea and convinced her to take time off.* I was so rattled I almost left Diesel in the car. Only several loud meows stopped me from abandoning him in the garage. I was desperate to get inside to find out what had happened.

Diesel shot inside the moment the door opened wide enough. I stumbled on the threshold but caught myself before I went sprawling on the floor. My chest heaved as I righted myself and stared into four startled faces. My housekeeper occupied one chair, and Kanesha, Stewart Delacorte, and Haskell Bates occupied the others.

"Thank the Lord you're okay, Azalea." I managed to squeeze the words out. "What happened? Did someone try to break in?"

"Have mercy, Mr. Charlie, what's the matter with you?" Azalea replied over the barking of a dog. I spotted Stewart's poodle, Dante, wiggling ecstatically as he tried to lick his buddy Diesel's face. Diesel swatted at him but failed to convince him the attentions were not appreciated.

"I saw the patrol cars outside, and I figured there had been some kind of emergency," I said. Stewart and his partner, Haskell, exchanged glances while Kanesha frowned at me. "But nothing happened, I guess."

"That's correct," Kanesha said. "I came by to check on my mother, and Stewart and Bates stopped by to see you."

I leaned against the refrigerator and drew deep breaths. My pulse rated dropped back to normal, and I felt like an idiot. "I'm glad nothing's wrong."

Diesel, accompanied by the happy poodle, disappeared into the utility room. I pulled out the chair next to Kanesha and sat. "Nice to see you, Stewart," I said. "You, too, Haskell. We don't get to see much of you these days."

"I keep telling Haskell he ought to give up that tiny apartment of his and move in here with me." Stewart grimaced at his boyfriend. "There's plenty of room, even for his ginormous boot collection, but he keeps resisting."

Haskell frowned. I knew he didn't like discussing personal matters in front of others. He was so reserved he would make a clam seem chatty.

"It would be fine with me," I said. "There's more room on the third floor if you'd like extra space. Justin uses only the one bedroom, and the other two are empty. Plenty of closet space."

"Thank you," Haskell said. "I will keep that in mind." He shot Stewart a glance that seemed to promise an argument once the two were alone together. Stewart appeared not in the least worried, though. He grinned back at Haskell. I had no doubt Stewart would eventually get his way.

I turned to Kanesha. "How's the investigation progressing? Did Chief Ford get in touch with you about what happened to my car?"

Stewart responded before Kanesha could answer me. "What happened to your car? Did somebody hit you?"

"No, I got a great big rock through the windshield. Deliberately."

Stewart frowned, but this time Kanesha spoke first. "Yes, I heard about it. To answer your first question, yes, the investigation is progressing."

I waited to hear more details but she didn't continue. "That's all you're going to say?" I asked.

"That's all you need to know," she replied coolly as she rose. "Make sure you keep using the alarm system, you and Mama both." She looked at Bates for a moment. "It might be a good idea if you did stay here a few nights, Bates. You're off this weekend, too."

Haskell frowned. "Is that an order, ma'am?" He didn't appear happy at being forced into this particular corner.

"No, it's not," Kanesha said. "But I would take it as a personal favor if you would stay here, at least until the investigation is complete. I would feel a lot better about the security of this house with you on the premises."

Thus she boxed him up and tied the bow as neatly as Forrest Wyatt had done with me. There was no way he could refuse now without looking like a completely selfish jerk. I felt sympathy for him, but I was relieved as well.

"All right, ma'am," he said.

Stewart grinned and leaned over to whisper in Haskell's ear. To my amusement, and Haskell's no doubt chagrin, he blushed. He nodded and kept his gaze averted from the rest of us for a moment.

"Thank you, Haskell. I really would feel a lot safer having you in the house the next few days," I said.

Diesel and Dante came back into the room. The poodle had calmed down a little. He was no longer hopping around Diesel, but he continued to gaze adoringly at his friend. Diesel ignored him and headed straight for Stewart.

"See, Haskell, Dante is thrilled to be spending time with Diesel," Stewart said as he rubbed the cat's head. "And Diesel is *so* happy to see his uncle Stewart, too, aren't you, boy?"

Diesel recognized his cue and meowed and chirped in response. I saw one corner of Haskell's mouth twitch. Even he wasn't completely immune to Diesel.

"If there's gonna be two more men for dinner," Azalea announced, "I got me some cooking to do." She shot pointed glances at Kanesha and me. "You got time to stay and eat?" This last was addressed to her daughter. "Be ready in about thirty minutes."

Kanesha shook her head. "Thank you, Mama, but I'm due back at the department. Time to check on a few things. Charlie, would you mind seeing me out?" She nodded at Stewart and Haskell and headed out of the kitchen.

I hurried to catch up with her. I wondered what she wanted, after saying to me a few minutes ago she had nothing to share concerning the investigation.

"What is it?" I asked when she stopped at the front door.

"I couldn't talk in front of my mother and Stewart." She frowned at me. "It's bad enough I'm talking to you about a murder case."

"I see. I can understand that."

"I know how nosy you are." Kanesha crossed her arms. "You'll be trying to find things out like you always do, and I figure I might as well get some benefit out of it. As long as you do not put yourself or anyone else—*particularly my mother*—in harm's way by doing so. Do you understand me?"

"Yes, of course," I said. We'd had similar conversations before, and I had no idea why she felt she had to repeat her usual admonitions.

"All right. I'm trying hard to figure out what the motive is for Reilly's murder. In the case of his brother-in-law, I figure it's because he knew something, maybe saw something, and the killer got spooked. Took him out as a precaution." She looked grim. "But with Reilly I can't get a handle on why he was killed. So I'm asking you, have you come across anything that could constitute a motive?"

"Not yet," I said. "I spent several hours today going over the library's budgets for the last few years. I figure there might be a connection to money somehow, since that was supposed to be Reilly's area of expertise. I'm meeting with President Wyatt and the board on Monday, and I may get more details about any financial issues then. In the meantime it wouldn't hurt if you got in touch with Wyatt or the vice president for finance, Wayne Taylor. You might find out something pertinent from them."

"Sounds good. Anything else?"

"I'm meeting with the department heads, Lisa Krause,

Delbert Winston, and Cassandra Brownley, on Wednesday. I know Lisa has talked to you, but what about Delbert? I urged him to, after he came to me and insisted on telling me his story. He had a motive, certainly. Cassandra, I'm not sure about. She's a difficult woman, but I'll do my best with her. I know she was really angry with Reilly over some matter, but then she's angry with just about everybody." I relayed the scene I'd witnessed two days ago when Cassandra stormed out of Reilly's office.

"Thanks for the information," Kanesha said. "I have talked to Mr. Winston, so I'm aware of his potential motive. Can you think of anyone else, besides the three department heads, who had any reason to want to get rid of Reilly?"

"Not unless there is someone in the financial affairs department he got on the wrong side of, I can't think of anyone."

She nodded and reached for the doorknob, but before she could open the door, I spoke. "Can you answer one question for me?"

Kanesha eyed me warily, her hand still on the knob. "Maybe. What is it?"

"What's the status of Brent Tucker? Chief Ford told me about his being arrested in DeSoto County."

"He was released on bond this morning," Kanesha said. "So if you're wondering whether he could be the one who smashed your windshield, the answer is *yes*."

"What about the murders? Was he already in jail when the second murder occurred?" If he had been locked up, I reasoned, at the time of Stanley's death, he probably hadn't killed Reilly, either.

"We have only an approximate time of death for

Stanley," Kanesha said. "A window of about three hours at the moment. It's possible that Mr. Tucker murdered both men. Now, is that all?"

I knew better than to press my luck any further. "Yes, thanks."

She nodded. "Stay safe." She opened the door and stepped out. I closed it behind her.

Haskell Bates passed by me as I entered the kitchen, and moments later I heard the front door open and close again. Stewart, still at the table, watching the antics of cat and dog as they played nearby, said, "Haskell's making a run to his place to retrieve a few necessities. He'll be back in time for dinner."

"Good," I said. "He surely wouldn't want to miss whatever that is you're cooking, Azalea. It smells wonderful. What is it?"

"Meat sauce." Azalea stirred the pot on the stove. "Mr. Stewart's recipe."

"It may be my recipe," Stewart said, "but you make it better than anyone, even me." He smiled when Azalea turned around to thank him.

"I do add a little something extra," she said before she turned back to the stove.

"And you won't tell me what it is," Stewart replied in a mock-severe tone. "I've guessed everything from allspice to wormwood, but she won't ever tell me if I'm right. You're a hard woman, Azalea Berry, but I adore you anyway."

"You get on with your fool self." Azalea waved a hand in Stewart's direction without turning around. "Why don't you set the table, do something useful."

"Yes, ma'am," Stewart said and grinned at me. He and Azalea picked at each other like this all the time.

"While you do that," I said, "I'm going to run upstairs and change out of my monkey suit into more comfortable clothes."

Stewart eyed me critically. "You do look handsome in a suit, Charlie. It doesn't take much imagination to see where that gorgeous son of yours gets his looks, Grandpa." He winked.

"Thank you." I rewarded him with a courtly dip of the head. Chuckling, I headed upstairs to change.

Halfway up I realized I had left my briefcase in the car. I would retrieve it after dinner, I decided. I had no plans to work this evening. Upward I went.

Downstairs again a quarter of an hour later, I discovered Azalea on the point of departure. The food was ready, and we could serve ourselves. Stewart was assuring her that he would personally see to the cleaning of the kitchen.

"I'll supervise," I said, and Azalea smiled.

"You need me to come in tomorrow, Mr. Charlie? I don't mind. I could turn out one of those bedrooms upstairs, get it ready."

"No, that's not necessary," I said, and Stewart echoed me.

"I'm going to have to work on Haskell a bit more before he'll be willing to live here permanently," Stewart said. "There will be time enough for that once I've convinced him."

"All right then," Azalea said. "Have a blessed evening, and enjoy your meal."

I escorted her to her car, which was parked in the driveway, and for once she didn't argue. It was already dark outside, thanks to the storm clouds. Although the street-lights did illuminate the street decently, they were far enough apart to allow shadows in some places. Shadows made me uneasy at times like this.

I waited and watched till Azalea's taillights disappeared down the street before I turned to go back inside. No car followed her, and I relaxed. She should be safe at home, especially with that shotgun of her late husband's.

Because I wasn't paying attention, I caught my foot on the welcome mat, and I stumbled sideways a couple of inches. Something buzzed right by my head and struck the door just as I put my hand on the knob.

TWENTY-EIGHT

I twisted the knob and pushed at the same time so I could dive inside. I slid a couple of feet on the polished wood.

"Charlie, are you all right?" Stewart hurried toward me.

"Stay back," I said as I propelled myself around behind the door, scrambling like a crab. "Someone shot at me." I slammed the door shut and then slowly got to my feet away from the windows on either side of the door.

Stewart halted several feet away and pulled out his phone. Moments later he was speaking to the 911 operator. While he talked to the operator, I turned off the lights in the hall and the one over the front door outside. Then I peered cautiously through the blinds at the yard and the street. Everything appeared as usual. No one wielding a gun, no cars driving by. I engaged the locks on the door.

The faint noise of a siren reached my ears. I went to the stairs and sat on the third tread. My chest still heaved from the exertions and the adrenaline. Diesel and Dante ran into the room, and the cat came right to me. He meowed, and I rubbed his head. Dante danced around Stewart's feet and barked until Stewart shushed him.

The sound of the siren had grown increasingly louder, and now I could see the play of the flashing lights against the blinds. Stewart ended the call with 911 and went to slip the lights back on. He had the door open before the Athena police officers were halfway up the walk. Right on their heels came Haskell Bates, a large canvas bag in one hand and a suitcase in the other. He had changed out of his uniform into civilian clothes.

I spent the next twenty minutes talking to the police officers while Stewart and Haskell kept Diesel and Dante out of the way. Finally, Haskell stepped forward to assure them that he would communicate with the sheriff's department, who would investigate further because of the connection of this incident to the ongoing murder investigation. The city cops didn't argue. The police department and the sheriff's department worked well together, and in cases like this, they didn't waste time over jurisdictional matters.

Before they left, however, the older of the two policemen examined the door and found the bullet embedded in the thick oak. It had entered the door a good inch above my head.

"You were lucky, Mr. Harris," he said. "Good thing you stumbled at just the right time."

In the background I heard Haskell talking on his cell, and I wondered how long it would be before his colleagues arrived to examine the door.

"Yes, sometimes being clumsy has its rewards, I guess." I smiled. "Thank you, Officers, for responding so quickly."

I ushered them out, and then Stewart, Haskell, and I, along with two hopeful four-legged friends, moved to the kitchen for our delayed meal.

While we ate—and Diesel and Dante both begged for food—Stewart, Haskell, and I discussed the incident. Stewart opened a bottle of red wine, and we toasted my lucky escape. My blood pressure was settling back to normal, and I thanked the Lord for my clumsiness at the right moment.

"Although," I said, "I can't help thinking that there was more than luck involved in this."

"What do you mean?" Stewart asked. "If you hadn't stumbled when you did, well." He grimaced.

"Either the shooter isn't a good marksman," Haskell said, "or he never intended to kill Charlie. Maybe frighten him or only wound him."

I nodded. "That's what I was thinking, after the first rush of sheer terror subsided." I had a sip of my wine. "Otherwise, why did the shooter wait until I was about to come into the house to fire? I was a lot closer to the street for a couple of minutes, and surely if he wanted to kill me, he had a better chance of succeeding then, instead of when I was at the door, an additional fifty or sixty feet away."

Diesel tapped my leg with a large paw, and I gave him a bit of buttered bread. No garlic, only bread and butter. He chirped in thanks as he attacked his tidbit.

"I see what you mean," Stewart said.

The doorbell rang, and Haskell stood. "That will be

Chief Deputy Berry. I'll go." He walked briskly from the room.

I had time for the last bite of pasta and meat sauce and a final sip of my wine before Haskell came back with Kanesha.

"Were you hurt?" she asked.

"Maybe a bruise or two from hitting the floor," I said. My knees would be complaining before long. "Nothing serious, though."

Kanesha nodded. "Tell me what happened."

I complied with her request, and when I'd finished, she didn't respond right away. Finally she said, "I wonder if the shooter was aiming to kill you or only frighten you."

"We were discussing that before you arrived." I repeated the gist of the conversation.

"Hard to say, really, but it seems to me more like a threat rather than an intent to kill." Kanesha looked at Haskell. "Where were you?"

He regarded her with his usual stony expression. "I ran home to pick up a few things. I was gone less than half an hour."

Kanesha shrugged and turned back to me. "I'll check on the whereabouts of the suspects, try to find out what they were doing when this happened."

"Is your mother okay?" I asked.

"She's fine. The police are keeping an eye on her house. Melba Gilley's, too, just in case. They should have the bullet out by now. I have to go. Y'all be careful." She turned and walked out. Haskell followed her.

"She's in a bad mood," Stewart said. "She can't stand

it when things like this happen. She's definitely got control issues."

"That's probably one of the things that makes her so good at her job." I had a few control issues myself, and I could sympathize with Kanesha. "I hope she gets this sorted out soon. I don't like feeling I'm in a state of siege, practically."

Stewart got up from the table and started clearing. Dante pranced around, still begging for food, but Stewart told him firmly the food was all gone. Diesel tapped my leg again. I had saved one last bite of bread and butter for him, and he accepted it happily before Stewart took my plate away.

I got up and put my wineglass in the sink. Two servings of wine were my limit. Stewart and Haskell were welcome to the rest of the bottle.

Haskell returned, stony expression still intact, and poured himself more wine after he resumed his seat. "They're gone." He drank down half the wine in his glass and set it aside.

Interesting dynamics, I thought as I resumed my seat. Was Kanesha really angry with him because he wasn't present when the attack took place? If so, it wasn't fair. He couldn't have known. I started to say something, then thought better of it. Haskell was intensely private, and I didn't want to offend him. His relationship with his boss was his business, not mine.

Stewart came over to him and laid a hand on his shoulder. Haskell looked up at him, and Stewart smiled. Haskell returned the smile briefly, and I could see the set of his shoulders change to a more relaxed position.

I pretended to be busy giving Diesel attention, lest Haskell realize I had seen the interaction.

"Seems like there isn't much progress in this case." Stewart sat across from Haskell and refilled his wineglass. "Any luck in tracing the gun that was used in the second murder?"

"We've identified the type of bullet used," Haskell said. "But since this state doesn't require registration of firearms, for the most part, it doesn't do a lot of good. Unless the suspects voluntarily reveal their firearms, we can't do much."

"Unless you can get a search warrant," Stewart said.

Haskell nodded. "And even with a search warrant, they can conceal the weapons somewhere else. We pretty much have to find the weapons on them. In a lot of cases, that's what happens, especially in domestic violence situations. Something like this, however, is much harder."

"That's discouraging," I said.

"The way it is," Haskell replied with a shrug. "How about you show me how your alarm system works? Long as I'm going to be here a few days, I'd better know how to set it and turn it off."

"I can show you," Stewart said. "You haven't changed the code lately, have you, Charlie?"

"No, it's still the same." The six-digit code I used was my late mother's birthday.

Stewart rattled it off, and I nodded. "That's it."

I stood. "Since you're going to take care of that, I guess Diesel and I will head upstairs. I'll bid you both good night."

They both said *good night* in return, and I was halfway

up the stairs, Diesel at my side, when I remembered my briefcase. This time I did turn around and go down the stairs. When I walked into the kitchen, Stewart was standing behind Haskell, still in his chair, massaging the deputy's neck and shoulders.

"Sorry," I said, "I forgot that I needed to get my briefcase out of the car. It'll only take a moment."

The two men nodded, and I hurried past them to the door. I flipped on the switch for the garage light and went to the car. I grabbed the briefcase and hurried back inside, turning off the light and locking the back door. "Good night again," I said.

"See you in the morning," Stewart called after me. He told Dante to stay, otherwise I think the poodle would have followed me upstairs for more playtime with Diesel.

I found my sweet boy on the bed when I got upstairs. He was already stretched out, no doubt tired from all the attention from his small and enthusiastic canine friend.

I put the briefcase on top of the chest of drawers and proceeded to change into my comfortable pajama shorts and T-shirt. I had about a hundred and fifty pages left in *Lionheart*, and I planned to read until it was time to call Helen Louise around ten.

A quarter of a frustrating hour later, however, I discovered that not even Penman's masterful storytelling could keep my mind from jumping back and forth from the twelfth century to the present. Reluctantly I set the book aside, marked my place, and let my mind focus on the events of the day. Particularly on the terrifying event of the evening.

Had the shot been an attempt at murder? Or simply intimidation?

What was the point of intimidation? To keep me from going back to the library and perhaps reneging on my acceptance of the temporary position?

What good would that do, other than simply to delay the inevitable? At some point, the job would be filled, and the new library director would no doubt be asking the same questions about the budget that I would. If there were indeed problems with the budget other than those caused by Peter Vanderkeller, that is.

I hadn't found anything in my studying of the figures today, but that didn't mean there wasn't a problem concealed in them. I might have to dig deeper—a lot deeper—to find evidence of any malfeasance, if it was there.

I considered the other unanswered questions.

Why had Porter Stanley come to Athena in search of Reilly?

How did the intruder get into the library administration offices without a key?

Was there a connection between Stanley's appearance and Reilly's murder? Or only coincidence?

Hard luck on Stanley if it were the latter. Had he simply been in the wrong place at the wrong time? In other words, had he happened to witness Reilly's murder?

Were the pranks against Reilly the work of the murderer? Or were murderer and prankster two different people?

After lying there a few minutes and going round and round over these questions, I decided I ought to write them all down. I often thought better, and more clearly, when I wrote things down.

I got out of bed to retrieve a notepad and pen from the briefcase. I settled back against my pillows and began to record my questions. When I'd finished, I read through them again. Diesel never stirred the entire time. *He really must be tired*, I thought.

I tapped the pen against the pad while I went over the questions yet again. As I did so, I noticed that the cap looked odd. I held it under the bedside light to examine it, and I realized that the cap contained a detachable part. I pulled it out and discovered that it was a thumb drive.

How clever, and how useful. Then I noticed the pen bore the logo of one of the library's longtime vendors. Vendors often gave away promotional items like pens, thumb drives, notebooks, and so on. This was the first of its kind that I had seen. It wasn't mine, so it had to be one of the ones from the director's desk.

I looked at my list of questions again and ran down them. I tapped the pen against the paper a few more times. Then I stared at the cap of the pen. I pulled out the thumb drive and looked at it in sudden wonder.

Could this be what the intruder had been searching for?

TWENTY-NINE

I suddenly thought of Edgar Allen Poe's story "The Purloined Letter." Was the answer as simple as that?

One way to find out. Telling Diesel I would be back in a few minutes, I hurried downstairs to retrieve my laptop from the den. Quiet reigned on the first floor, with only a couple of lights on, and I figured Stewart and Haskell must be in Stewart's rooms on the third floor. I scooped up the laptop and huffed my way back to my bedroom.

I had to sit on the bed for a minute to catch my breath. Diesel watched me, one eye open, then he yawned and went back to sleep.

Propped up in bed, I booted up the laptop, and when it was ready, I inserted the thumb drive. When the window popped up, asking what I wanted to do with the drive, I clicked on the option to view its files.

There were several folders listed, along with a few files

not in folders. The folder names were dates preceded by the letters *FY*, and I figured that indicated fiscal years. I clicked on the first one, for two years past, and viewed a long list of files; some documents, others obviously spreadsheets. I scanned the names of these, and they corresponded with what I had already seen on the desktop computer in the director's office.

Maybe this thumb drive was simply an ordinary backup, for the convenience of working offline perhaps. Otherwise the college network kept backups of everything, and there wasn't much need for storage like this in the normal way of things.

I examined one of the spreadsheets that consisted of the library's master budget for two fiscal years before. It looked fine to me, but I would have to compare it to the file on the college network.

I logged in to the network and then accessed the files linked to the account. It took me a few moments to find the directory I wanted, and then I had to scan the file names to find the right spreadsheet. I opened it, and then I went back and forth between the two.

After a couple of minutes of this, I concluded the files were exactly the same. The same number of line items, the same figures in each. The file on the thumb drive was only a copy.

I did a random check of three other files, and all turned out the same. Copies.

I stared at the screen. Was I wasting my time on this?

I examined the thumb drive's directory more closely. I noticed a folder named *Assets*. I didn't remember seeing a similar folder on the network drive, so I clicked on it.

The resulting list contained more spreadsheet files, a few word-processed documents, a number of PDFs, and several pictures. I clicked on the pictures first, and to my amazement I found myself staring at the picture of a ring.

This surely didn't belong to the library. I knew there was no jewelry among the archival collections, other than a few military service medals donated by several families whose ancestors had attended the college before the Civil War.

The ring looked expensive. The large center stone appeared to be a cabochon-cut sapphire surrounded by diamonds. The diamonds were not small, either. It was a gorgeous piece, and I wondered to whom it belonged.

The next picture revealed a sapphire and diamond necklace, with matching earrings. The sapphires, though smaller in the necklace and earrings, were also *en cabochon* to match the ring. I counted at least forty diamonds among the three pieces, and I had no doubt this set was extremely valuable. The remaining four pictures revealed two bracelets, both emerald and diamond, three emerald rings with diamonds, and a handful of gemstones.

The styles of some of the pieces looked old, and I speculated that most of them were antiques. How old, though, I couldn't say.

Was this what the intruder sought? These pictures of expensive jewelry?

Where were the real items? I wondered. If they had been in Reilly's office, had the intruder found them?

Could they have been the reason Porter Stanley came looking for his former brother-in-law?

My head was awhirl from all the questions. I had no answers, either. I realized what I had to do, however.

I picked up my phone and speed-dialed Kanesha's cell. The call went immediately to voice mail, and I left an impatient message for her to call me ASAP, that I had found what could be important evidence.

After that, I copied the contents of the thumb drive onto my laptop. Kanesha might not like it, but I had a hunch I might find other useful information somewhere in the drive's contents.

I looked through the pictures of the jewelry again. I had an idea they might belong to Reilly's ex-wife. Her family was wealthy, I recalled, and these pieces could have been handed down. If Reilly had stolen them, I could understand why Stanley had come after his former brother-in-law. Of course, he could have reported the theft to the police and turned it over to them, but maybe for some reason he had decided to handle it himself. I suspected Stanley had borne Reilly a healthy grudge and would have taken satisfaction in forcing the jerk to return the jewels to their rightful owner.

Had Reilly returned them to Stanley? Was that where the two had gone, to retrieve the jewels after I left them together in Reilly's office?

My phone rang. Kanesha, I saw from the caller ID.

As usual, she wasted no time on formalities. "What's this important evidence you've found?"

I explained about the thumb drive and its contents. "Do you think this jewelry has anything to do with the murders?"

"It's related," Kanesha said. "I just heard from the police in Massachusetts. After his death was reported, Stanley's sister told them she discovered that her most valuable jewelry—all family heirlooms—had disappeared. The family suspected Reilly, and Stanley came here to find him and retrieve the jewels."

"Did you find them with Stanley?" I asked.

"No," Kanesha said. "I'm pretty sure the killer has them. Whether they were the reason Stanley was killed, that I don't know. It could simply have been luck on the murderer's part to find them on the victim."

"If you can find the jewels, you find the murderer."

"Yes," Kanesha said.

"Are you going to come by and get the thumb drive tonight?"

"I can't, but I'm going to send someone. Expect him there in about fifteen minutes, twenty at the most." She paused. "I presume you've already copied the contents."

"Yes," I said, not completely surprised by her question.

"I figured you had," she said. "If you find anything else pertinent, let me know."

"Will do."

I put the phone down, powered down the laptop, and got up to set it on the chest of drawers with my briefcase. I removed the thumb drive, replaced it in the cap of the pen, and then went downstairs to wait for the deputy to arrive.

This time Diesel accompanied me, but while I turned off the alarm, he ambled into the utility room. After a few moments I heard the sounds of litter being scratched. Next came quiet for about five seconds, and then the sounds of a cat eating dry food. With the house so still around us, it was amusing to hear Diesel attending to his basic needs.

He finished and came to sit by my chair in the kitchen about five minutes before the doorbell rang. He chattered to me, alternating warbles and chirps with the occasional meow, and I wondered what story he was telling me. He had these moods when he gabbed like an effusive teenager, and I answered back as I considered appropriate. Anyone who observed this behavior in me would think I needed immediate psychiatric intervention, but another human with a talkative cat would no doubt understand perfectly.

The doorbell cut the conversation short. I checked through the peephole before I opened the door. I wanted to be certain there was a person in uniform on the other side before I opened it.

There was, and I did. The deputy accepted the pen, thanked me, and then departed. I reset the alarm, and we headed for the stairs. When we reached the second-floor landing, I glanced up to see Haskell peering at me over the railing from near the top of the stairs to the third floor.

"Everything okay?" he asked.

"Yes, just one of your fellow deputies coming by to pick up something. I'll tell you all about it in the morning."

"Right." The head vanished, and Diesel and I continued into my bedroom.

I eyed the laptop and considered turning it on again and having another look at the contents of the thumb drive. But the day had been long enough, and it was nearly time to call Helen Louise. I would have time tomorrow to dig into those files.

I debated whether to tell Helen Louise about the smashed windshield and the gunshot tonight, because I didn't want her to get upset and not be able to get the rest she needed. She had enough on her mind without worrying about me. Then I realized how furious she would be if I *didn't* tell her tonight and she heard about it from someone else first, so I decided I had better.

Right after I told her about both incidents, I stressed the security measures we were taking, and she was relieved to hear that Haskell would be staying in the house for a few days.

"As long as you don't do anything risky," she finally said, "you should be safe."

"I don't plan to do anything risky," I replied.

"I know." She yawned. "Sorry, honey, I'm about wiped out. Promise me you'll be extra special careful until Kanesha and her officers have the killer behind bars."

"I will, love, I will. You go to sleep, and I'll do the same."

We exchanged a few more words, then ended the call. I soon dropped off to sleep and slept soundly until morning.

Diesel and I had our usual Saturday lunch date at Helen Louise's place, and I ate a lighter breakfast than the one Azalea made for me during the week. Cereal, yogurt, and a couple of bananas. I felt virtuous for now, but that wouldn't last past lunch, not with the thought of one of Helen Louise's delicious pastries for dessert.

I was at work in the den, cat at my side, by the time I heard Stewart and Haskell downstairs. I left them to their breakfast in peace, though Dante came in search of Diesel right away. The two of them played on the floor while I worked my way through the folders and files I had copied last night from the thumb drive.

Other than the pictures of the jewels, I found nothing out of the ordinary. Spreadsheet after dreary spreadsheet, and one folder full of PDFs and scans of invoices. I took an occasional break to let my eyes rest and to rub my neck and shoulders, but I was determined to wade through as much of these documents as possible today.

Diesel and I had a welcome break with Helen Louise. He scarfed down the boiled chicken she provided, while I enjoyed one of her delicious quiches and a salad. The bistro was busy, and Helen Louise didn't have much time to chat, but at least we got to spend a little time together. She spent most of the time adjuring me to be careful and not put myself—or Diesel—in harm's way again.

"See you tomorrow, love. I promise I'll be extra careful." I gave her a quick kiss before Diesel and I left. She blew kisses after both of us.

The house was quiet when Diesel and I returned. I attended to the alarm, and Diesel visited the utility room. Stewart's car was here, and I supposed he and Haskell were upstairs. I headed straight for the den to resume work on those files.

First, however, I decided to check my work schedule for the coming week. I wanted to see if Lisa, Delbert, and Cassandra had made appointments as I had requested. If they had communicated with Melba, the appointments would be on my calendar.

I logged in to the college network and opened my e-mail. I scanned the messages, but there was nothing urgent. I clicked on the calendar and examined it. I focused on Wednesday. I saw appointments with Lisa and Delbert, but none for Cassandra.

She was obviously determined to defy me. I had told her to make an appointment through Melba before the end of the day, and she hadn't done so.

I wasn't going to put up with this.

All right then, Ms. Brownley. Time for a little hardball.

I composed an e-mail to her that wasted no words. I also copied Penny Sisson on it. The message read:

> You have failed to make the appointment for Wednesday as I requested. I will expect you in my office at nine o'clock Monday morning, and I will request that a representative from Human Resources join us to discuss your insubordinate and unprofessional behavior.

I signed it simply, Charles Harris, Interim Director, and sent it. I sent a follow-up to Penny to explain why the message was necessary and to request her presence at the meeting.

Cassandra could always claim she hadn't seen the message, I realized, so I looked up her office number and called it. I left her the exact same message on her voice mail.

The challenge had been issued, and I was curious to see what she would do.

Would there be another incident like the smashed windshield? A bullet fired in my direction? Or perhaps something worse?

I had better be on my guard.

THIRTY

||||||||||||||||||||||||||||||||||

The following day, Sunday, passed quietly, at least in terms of the murder investigation. Diesel and I had a leisurely morning with Stewart, Dante, and Haskell. Stewart insisted on cooking breakfast, and I didn't argue. He made us bacon and cheddar omelets, one of my favorites. He made sure to fry extra bacon for Diesel and Dante. Everyone stepped away from the breakfast table thoroughly satisfied.

I thought about opening the laptop and doing a bit of work, but then decided I deserved a day off, especially after the last several days.

We had a delightful potluck family luncheon and had to put the leaf in the table to accommodate the four couples. Haskell appeared a bit uncomfortable at first, but my children and their spouses soon made him feel like a part of the family. Sean and Laura had accepted Stewart almost as an uncle. I tended to look on him as the younger brother

I'd never had, and since Haskell appeared to be in the picture for the long run, he became part of the family, too. Diesel and Dante were beside themselves with so many hands willing to stroke and scratch and hand out tidbits.

I looked at Helen Louise at the other end of the table and thought how beautiful she was, and how amazingly lucky I was that this exceptional woman cared for me as much as I cared for her. She caught me looking and smiled. We shared the moment while the conversation flowed around us.

After lunch, with the table clear and the kitchen clean, my children and their spouses departed. Stewart and Haskell headed upstairs with Dante, leaving Helen Louise and me to ourselves. With Diesel, too, of course.

We snuggled on the sofa in the den and chatted. Diesel lay beside Helen Louise with his head in her lap. I kept the conversation away from anything to do with work, either hers or mine. Instead we talked about a trip we hoped to take in mid-May. Neither of us had been to Italy, and we planned to see Florence, Siena, and Rome.

Late in the afternoon Helen Louise reluctantly took her leave. She had to plan her menus for the coming week, and Diesel and I walked her to her car on the street. We nodded at the policeman sitting in the car near hers, and I was thankful for the extra security.

Once Helen Louise was under way, Diesel and I hurried back into the house. I had debated calling off today's lunch, but none of the family would hear of it. They all insisted on coming as usual. I prayed for a quiet day, and a quiet day we had.

I only hoped it wouldn't be the calm before the storm.

* * *

Diesel and I made it into the office on the dot of eight thirty. Melba was there before us. After we exchanged greetings, I told her about the situation with Cassandra Brownley.

"Let me check my e-mail," Melba said. "She might have e-mailed me after we left the office on Friday."

I was willing to bet she hadn't. She certainly hadn't replied to my e-mail from the weekend. I had checked this morning before breakfast, and again a few minutes ago, on my phone.

"Did you get a response from your friend in accounts payable? I really need to see those files this afternoon."

"I'll check that, too," Melba said. "I'll get the coffee started and be right back."

I nodded. Diesel accompanied Melba to make the coffee, and I unlocked my office door and turned on the lights. I halfway expected to find it in shambles or filled with bugs, either live or plastic, but everything appeared to be as I had left it on Friday afternoon.

Once my computer was awake and I could log on, I checked e-mail again. Still no response from Cassandra. I checked for voice mail on the office phone, but there was none. I glanced at my watch—eight thirty-nine. I opened my briefcase and pulled out my own thumb drive, onto which I had copied from my laptop all those files I'd found on Reilly's thumb drive. I had decided earlier I didn't want to lug my laptop to work and back.

Melba appeared in the doorway. "No e-mail from Cassandra, but Margie Flaxdale, my friend in accounts payable, did e-mail back to say she would have the files ready for you to look at. You won't be able to remove them from their offices, but you can look at them there."

"Thanks for checking," I said. "Have a seat for a moment. I need to bring you up to date on a few things."

Diesel came around the desk to meow at me. I was sure he wondered why we were here, instead of in the archive office. The window here didn't have the wide sill he was accustomed to upstairs.

"You'll have to find a new place to nap for a while," I told him. "We're going to be in this office for at least a couple of months."

He meowed again, as if to express his displeasure, and then walked back around to the desk to stretch out on the floor by Melba.

She grinned at the cat. "What's been going on?"

I filled her in on the weekend's events, and she paled when I told her about the gunshot.

"Lunatic," she said. "Thank the Lord you weren't hurt."

We discussed the incident a few minutes longer, and then I noticed the time. Four minutes before nine. I mentioned it to Melba, and she rose.

"I'll keep an eye out for her," she said before she walked back into her office.

Moments later I heard another person speak to Melba, but it didn't sound like Cassandra. Then Penny Sisson walked into my office.

"Good morning, Charlie," she said.

I returned the greeting and asked her to have a seat. "Thank you for coming, but as you can see, Ms. Brownley has not shown up."

"No, she hasn't," Penny responded. "She called me fifteen minutes ago to inform me that she was ill and would not be at work this week, nor the first part of next week. Her physician has put her on complete bed rest for the next seven to ten days."

To judge by Penny's stony expression, she was not pleased with Cassandra's delaying tactics. Diesel lightened that expression, however, by greeting Penny with a meow and a rub against her legs. Penny patted him and smiled.

"I reminded her, of course," Penny went on, "that she would have to have a note from the doctor before she would be allowed to return to work after an extended period of sick leave, and she assured me she would have one."

I shook my head. "If she is really ill—which I doubt—I am truly sorry. But this gamesmanship of hers is trying what little patience I have left."

"I understand how you feel," Penny said. "After I received your e-mail to her, I did some digging in her personnel file. Some of this you can find out yourself by looking at annual reviews of her performance, so I will share that with you now. During the time she has been here, she has had several of these episodes that required bed rest. These episodes appear to have always coincided with times that she was in conflict with her supervisor."

"I see." I thought for a moment. "Tell me realistically, Penny, do we have any firm ground for firing her? We can't keep tolerating behavior like this, although she's evidently gotten away with it for years."

"I would be happy to see her gone," Penny said, "because she has caused trouble for years. Unfortunately, the documentation we have isn't strong enough for us to be able to fire her for cause. Now, if we could find proof, for example, that she was behind any of the recent incidents, well, we would certainly have cause."

"And the police might have cause to haul her off to jail, too." I grinned. "I'll talk with Chief Deputy Berry and Chief Ford about this, try to find out whether they have any evidence for who pulled those pranks, including smashing my windshield."

"Good plan," Penny said. "Let me know if you find out anything." She rose to leave. "I'm so sorry you're having to deal with her, Charlie, on top of everything else. Hopefully some good will come out of it."

I rose and came around to see her out. "Thanks, Penny. We'll get through it somehow. I appreciate your help tremendously."

Diesel followed Penny into Melba's office, and I returned to my desk. I had a meeting with the president and the deans of all the schools at ten, and I wanted to be prepared. I scanned the agenda that Forrest's secretary had sent and reread an e-mail from Forrest outlining what he wanted me to present.

I left the office ten minutes before ten, admonishing Diesel to be a good boy. He wanted to come with me, but I didn't think it appropriate to take him along. Until the college found a permanent library director, I would have to leave him in Melba's care frequently. I knew I could trust her to look after him, but I really couldn't make him understand why he couldn't go with me.

My head ached by the time the meeting with the president and the deans had finished. I had just enough time to make a restroom stop and buy a can of diet soda from a vending machine before I met with the vice president in charge of finance. That meeting lasted only forty-five minutes, to my great relief. I came out of it with a clear understanding of the library's finances, and we discussed the measures necessary to get the budget back on track after Peter's disastrous overspending. I walked back to my office already tired and ready to go home for the day, but I had another meeting ahead of me.

Diesel greeted me with a series of meows and trills, all of which told me how disgusted he was with having been left behind. Melba smiled while she listened to me repeat several times, "I'm sorry, Diesel."

When he lapsed into silence and smugly began to lick a front paw, I told Melba we were going home for a quick lunch. I had to be back in time for my two o'clock meeting with her friend in accounts payable.

"I'm going to lunch, too," she said. "I'll be back in time to watch over Mr. Chatty here for you."

"Thanks," I said. "You're the best."

She grinned. "I know."

I had to make it a working lunch, although the thought of it annoyed me. I took my salad and sandwich to the den, where I powered up the laptop and logged in to the college network. I needed to catch up on e-mail. My first task was to compose a message to Kanesha and Marty Ford about Cassandra. The woman's behavior was more than merely annoying. I also found it suspicious, despite her history. I had a hunch there was more to it this time than simply stonewalling her supervisor. If I couldn't get through to her, perhaps Kanesha or Marty Ford could. Personally, I would love to watch Kanesha interrogate Cassandra. Ms.

Brownley was a tough nut, but Chief Deputy Berry had cracked far tougher.

At three minutes to two, I knocked on the office door of Melba's friend, Margie Flaxdale. A petite brunette, sixty-ish and attractive, Ms. Flaxdale regarded me with a reserved expression from behind her desk.

"Yes?" she said.

"Charlie Harris," I replied and stepped into the room. "I'm here to go through those library purchase orders and invoices."

She nodded and pointed to a table in the corner. I saw three stacks of files, each about eight inches high. My heart sank. I'd never get through all those this afternoon.

"I will remind you that you cannot remove any of those files from this department," she said, her tone admonitory. I felt like a third-grader being told not to talk in class.

"Certainly, I understand the rules." I couldn't hold back the note of frost in my words. The woman was a bit too officious for my taste.

She merely nodded. I went to the table, pulled out the chair, and attacked the closest pile of file folders. One of the spreadsheets I had found consisted of a ten-year history of the library's major resource purchases—electronic journal collections, databases, and print resources. I was particularly interested in the current fiscal year and Peter Vanderkeller's sudden overspending. There was something about it that bothered me, and I hadn't been able to figure out exactly what.

The first pile of folders contained purchase orders and

invoices from two fiscal years ago. I hunted through the piles and located those for the current year. I went through them, noting Peter's signature on them. His handwriting had certainly deteriorated, I thought. His scrawl on these invoices was nearly illegible.

I realized I couldn't really accomplish what I wanted sitting there. I needed copies that I could take to my office. This was a huge task and could take days. I closed the file and returned it to the stack.

I stood abruptly. "Thank you, Ms. Flaxdale. I appreciate your help."

She looked startled. "That didn't take long."

"No, it didn't. I have what I need," I replied. I thanked her again and walked out of her office. I headed for the main library building. Despite my earlier intention to avoid going through the department head's files there, in order not to arouse suspicion, I decided I had no choice. If I did alarm someone, that might not be a bad thing.

THIRTY-ONE

In the main library building I made straight for the staff area at the rear of the building. The files I wanted would most likely be in Cassandra's office. As head of collection development and acquisitions, she was responsible for overseeing the purchase order and invoicing processes for library resources.

I greeted staff members as I passed through the public areas and continued into the technical services area. I saw Delbert Winston in his office, and the staff members appeared busy at their desks.

Cassandra's door was locked, and I approached the ranking staff person in her department, Terrie Hall, and asked her if she had a key.

"No, sir," she said, looking somewhat taken aback. "Delbert has one, though. It's the same key that opens all the librarians' doors."

I thanked her and walked over to Delbert's office. He had his back to me, evidently focused on his computer. I knocked on the door and said, "Good afternoon." He started and swiveled in his chair to face me.

He blinked. "Oh, hi there, Charlie. What brings you here?"

"I need some files from Cassandra's office. Can you let me in?"

He looked alarmed. "She doesn't like anyone going in her office. She'll have a fit. Are you sure you have to get in there?"

The woman apparently had everyone among the library staff cowed. Except me, that is.

"Yes, I am sure. Please unlock the door. I will deal with Cassandra."

He shrugged. "If you insist." He rose from his desk and pulled a key ring from his pocket. I stood aside as he exited his office and walked the few paces to Cassandra's door.

I glanced at Terrie Hall, whose cubicle was nearby, and saw that she was on the phone. She cast a nervous glance at me, then turned her back and continued her conversation. I frowned. I didn't know why, but I had the feeling she was talking to Cassandra.

"There you are." Delbert opened the door with a flourish and stood back.

"Thank you," I said. I advanced into the office and shut the door. Delbert lingered outside a moment before moving away.

Cassandra's desk was bare of everything except her computer, keyboard, mouse, and mouse pad. Her desk drawers were locked, as were her filing cabinets.

I went to the door, opened it, and approached Terrie

Hall's desk. "Ms. Hall, do you have keys to Ms. Brownley's cabinets?"

She stared at me, her eyes wide.

"I hope you do," I said in a pleasant tone. "Otherwise I will have to call the physical facilities department and ask them to send someone here to force the locks. I'd really rather not damage college property, but I will if there's no other way."

She nodded. "Yes, sir, let me look. I think I have a set of keys that will work." She jerked open a side drawer and scrambled through its contents. After a few moments she pulled out a ring with several small keys on it. She handed them to me.

"Thank you," I said. "I take full responsibility for this. If Ms. Brownley is unhappy, she needs to talk to me. You are not responsible in any way. Are we clear on that?"

Ms. Hall nodded, and looked relieved. "Yes, thank you, sir."

I smiled before I turned away. Clearly the woman was terrified of Cassandra. I would have to make sure Cassandra didn't make Terrie Hall the scapegoat for this. It would be entirely like her to try, I knew.

The keys unlocked the filing cabinets. I wouldn't go into the desk unless I couldn't find what I needed in the cabinets. I checked the labels on the drawers and found one labeled POS/INVOICES. I pulled it open and scanned the folders.

I pulled out four thick files that covered the past couple of years and set them on the desk. What I didn't see, however, was a file for the current fiscal year, which ran from July through June.

I glanced around the office, and my eyes lighted on the credenza behind Cassandra's desk. I had overlooked them earlier, but now I saw a number of folders in a standing wire organizer. I went over to look through them and found the folder I needed. I added it to the stack on the desk. They were bulky, and I knew if I tried to carry them back to my office like that, I would undoubtedly trip, and papers would go flying in all directions.

Ms. Hall supplied a large canvas bag emblazoned with the logo of a library vendor, and I stuffed the files into that. I returned the keys, thanked her, and waved good-bye to Delbert, who had been standing nearby the whole time, I realized. He was mighty curious. Good.

On my way out I encountered Lisa Krause near the reference desk. I paused to chat for a moment. I patted the strap of the bag over my shoulder when I noticed her curious glance.

"Homework," I said. "Purchase orders and invoices. I've got to get a handle on the budget, and I want to be ready for my meetings with you all on Wednesday."

Lisa grimaced. "Have fun. I hate dealing with budget stuff, especially spreadsheets."

"I'm not fond of them myself, but I have no choice. Have a good afternoon."

By the time I reached my office, it was nearly three. Diesel and Melba greeted me, and Melba asked about the bag. I explained, and she nodded. "Better you than me," she said.

Diesel came with me into my office and proceeded to give me an extensive summary of his activities since I had so callously abandoned him again. Melba brought me a fresh cup of coffee during the feline version of a tirade and grinned broadly. Finally Diesel settled down—after a considerable amount of attention on my part—and I was able to focus on work.

E-mail first, then the files, I decided. I couldn't let the e-mail get too out of hand. I had to respond to several inquiries about access to archival materials and had to explain there was no access at present. I jotted a reminder to myself to see about getting one of the reference librarians to oversee the archives a few hours a week, and then went back to e-mail.

I pulled out my notes from this morning's meeting with Forrest and the deans and looked through them. The major concern for the deans was that the resources for their divisions not be sacrificed to make up for the overspent budget. I had assured them I would do my best to ensure that all departments retained access to their most important electronic resources.

That was easier said than done. Cuts would have to come from somewhere. I looked at the staffing budget and made note of the savings from open positions. Those were frozen until further notice. The number I came up with covered almost a third of the overage. Where to find the remaining two-thirds?

I started going through the spreadsheet of library resource expenditures and compared it with the lists available on the library website. I was vaguely familiar with most of them, but since I hadn't been actively involved in any kind of management for nearly five years now, I felt I didn't know enough.

I leaned back in my chair and closed my eyes. My head ached again.

Cassandra, blast her, was the person I needed to talk to, in the absence of a serials librarian. As long as Cassandra remained uncooperative, I would have to take on the role myself to an extent. I decided that one position had to be filled, and soon. I made a note to discuss it with Forrest.

Back to the spreadsheet. I opened my eyes and leaned forward. I went through one resource after another on the ten-year spreadsheet. I paid particular attention to the increases from year to year, listed in a column for each year. The increases for most items were fairly standard, though there was an occasional higher percentage than in previous years.

One resource, Global Electronic Resources, increased at a steady 12 percent per year. Ten years ago, the amount allocated to it had been a hundred thousand dollars. The amount for the current fiscal year was a bit over two hundred and seventy thousand. That was a significant chunk of the budget.

I had never heard of Global Electronic Resources. The spreadsheet didn't indicate which resources they provided. I searched for the company website on the Internet, but what I found didn't help much. The website offered glowing recommendations from a number of colleges, most of which I didn't recognize, and stated that GER provided access to large collections of electronic books in all academic subject areas.

E-books. Well, that made sense. Over the past decade the Athena Library had beefed up its offerings of e-books, largely in the sciences but in the social sciences and humanities as well. I didn't know how large the e-book collection was, but I vaguely remembered hearing that it was around fifty thousand.

The problem with electronic resources and their prices that folk outside the library didn't understand was that, unlike the print edition, the money paid was basically a license. The library didn't actually *own* the electronic stuff. We simply had access to it, in varying degrees. Some access was theoretically perpetual; that is, once we licensed it, we retained access for the years paid. In other cases, if we stopped subscribing, we no longer had access.

Still, over a quarter of a million dollars to license e-books seemed exorbitant to me. I wondered how much new content the library had access to each year. Surely the collection grew over time. It would have to, in order to justify that kind of pricing.

Again, having Cassandra on hand to answer questions would be enormously helpful. She ought to be able to tell me how many e-books were in this collection.

The library cataloged all the e-books, I suddenly remembered. I ought to be able to search the online catalog and get at least a rough count of them. But would I be able to winnow out the e-books from other collections and databases?

One way to find out. I navigated on the Web to the library website and entered *Global Electronic Resources* enclosed in quotation marks in the search box for the online catalog. I knew it was the practice for many catalogers to include the e-book provider's name as part of the bibliographic record, so I should get some kind of number. I hit Enter and waited.

The results consisted of one hundred and sixty-three titles. I scanned through several screens of them. All appeared to be math, computer science, and engineering books. Those tended to be expensive, I knew, but for the amount of money there ought to be a lot more. I did a quick calculation, and we were spending over sixteen hundred dollars per book, if those were all the titles. There *had* to be more.

Since Cassandra was unavailable, I decided to ask Delbert if he had a list of titles from this company. There had to be one somewhere, and since his department had to catalog them, surely he had a list.

I looked up his number and called him. He answered right away. I explained what I wanted, although not why. "If you could scan it and e-mail it to me, I'd appreciate it."

He didn't answer right away, and I was beginning to get irritated. Then, all in a rush, he said, "Sorry, but I don't have one, you'll have to get it from Cassandra."

"That is a problem," I said, my tone barely polite. "Because Cassandra is out, I can't get hold of her. I need that list ASAP."

"Um, well, I'll see what I can do. Maybe she has a list somewhere in her files."

"Please look. You have my authorization to look in her office. Ms. Hall will give you the keys to her files."

"I don't know how long it might take," he said.

"I hope it won't take too long," I replied. "If necessary, I will contact the company and get it from them."

"Okay," he said. "I'll do my best." He hung up.

What was that all about? The man sounded worried.

After a moment's reflection, I decided I had better try to contact the company. I suspected it might be faster and easier to get the list from them.

Except that no one answered their phone.

THIRTY-TWO

||||||||||||||||||||||||||||||||||||||||||||||||||||||||||||||||||||||||||||

I double-checked the number on GER's website and dialed again. Still no answer. *Definitely odd.* I looked up the area code and discovered it was a New Jersey number.

I went back on the library's online catalog to have a more thorough look at those expensive e-books. Our default sort in the catalog was by descending publishing date, so the most recent books were listed first.

I blinked and peered at the screen. The first title in the result list had a publication date of twenty-three years ago. Surely that couldn't be right. I checked the sort, but they had been sorted properly.

After going through every screen of the list, I reached the end. The last title was a math book published in 1899. I clicked on the link for the book and was taken, after nearly thirty seconds, to a screen that informed me,

"Resource locked by user." Then the helpful words "Please try again later."

These e-books must be on a single-user license, and that meant only one person could use them at a time. I was curious why someone would be interested in a nineteenth-century math book, but research interests varied greatly.

I clicked at random on the link for another e-book and, after a similar wait, ended up at the same screen. My curiosity thoroughly piqued, I started at the end of the list and worked backward, checking access to every fourth title in the list.

Twenty minutes—and an even achier head, with sore neck and shoulders—later I had worked my way to the beginning of the list. Every single e-book I had tried to access was "locked by user."

I recalled that the ten-year-history spreadsheet included columns for cost-per-use for resources each fiscal year. I went back to it, found the line for GER, and scanned across from present to earlier fiscal years.

After I'd finished, I rubbed my eyes. Usage for these e-books started high ten years ago and increased every year, even as their cost increased. The cost-per-use varied from a high of two dollars and eighty-six cents to a low of twenty-seven cents per use.

That was phenomenal usage, I realized after I did some quick calculations. That would account for the resources being constantly locked.

But it was also suspicious, at least to me. I looked through the spreadsheet and examined the cost-per-use of other resources. None seemed to be as good or as consistent, except for the major journal collections.

A tap on my door pulled me out of my ruminations. I blinked and turned to see Melba standing a few feet away.

"You were so deep into whatever you were looking at I thought you were in a trance," she said. "What is so fascinating?"

"Budget figures," I said in a light tone. I wasn't ready to share my suspicions with anyone else. I wanted to make sure I had evidence of some kind before I said anything.

Melba grimaced. "They'd put me to sleep. Anyhow, that's not why I knocked. I wanted to let you know it's five o'clock, and I'm getting ready to leave. Will you be staying much longer? If you are, you may want to shut Diesel in here with you." She glanced down at the feline rubbing against her legs. "He's been with me most of the afternoon, but he's also been out to visit the cop on duty by the front door. They're buddies now."

"I've lost track of the time completely." I yawned suddenly. "Excuse me. No, I'm not going to stay. I need to clear my head for a while. Come on, Diesel, come to me and let Melba get going."

The cat meowed and rubbed against her legs again, but then he ambled around the desk to my side. I scratched his head, and he warbled. "Thanks again for everything, Melba. I'd never get through this without you."

She merely smiled and said *good night* before she turned and left the room.

"Okay, boy, give me a moment, and we'll be on the way home soon." I gave Diesel's head one more scratch before I turned back to the computer. I shut down everything except e-mail. I checked to see whether Delbert Winston had sent me anything.

He hadn't. Perhaps he was having trouble finding what I wanted.

Perhaps he doesn't want to find it.

"Maybe he doesn't," I said. "But until I have a better picture of what's really going on here, I don't know."

Diesel meowed, and I realized he thought I was talking to him. I laughed and logged off the network. It took me a moment to gather my things, and I made sure I had the canvas bag of files with me when we left the office and locked the door.

I closed and locked Melba's door in turn, and while I did so, Diesel went to bid his new buddy good night. I chatted with the young man for a moment, and then I headed for the car with Diesel.

Azalea had gone by the time we reached home, but she left dinner for Stewart, Haskell, and me. Stewart had the table set, and we ate about thirty minutes later.

I was poor company during the meal because my thoughts kept straying to the issue of Global Electronic Resources. I foresaw a long evening ahead, because I knew I would not be able to go to bed until I had some kind of answer, or at least a glimmer of one.

I surfaced from my reverie to hear Stewart say to Haskell, "Then the Queen of Sheba turned to me and said I had to stay for dinner and she hoped that I liked stewed goats' eyes and pickled cow tongue."

"What are you talking about?" I demanded.

Stewart chuckled at my expression of confusion. "I wondered whether you were really listening."

"Sorry," I said. "I'm preoccupied with work. Not something that has occurred often in recent years."

"Must be a real mess," Haskell said.

"I'm beginning to think it's worse than anyone realized," I said. "I can't go into details, but I suspect there's an embezzler on the staff." I shouldn't have said that, I realized a little too late. "You can't repeat that anywhere."

"Of course not," Stewart said. "I would think it was Peter Vanderwhatsit, if it was anybody. Otherwise, why did he just up and disappear like that?"

"Vanderkeller," I said absently, struck by Stewart's question. Why *had* Peter disappeared so abruptly? Because he knew his fraud was about to be uncovered, and he decided to skip the country before he could be caught? That was possible, I supposed, but from what I had learned from the vice president of finance, there wasn't any money actually missing. Not that they could find evidence of, at any rate.

I had thought he had resigned because he was simply too embarrassed to face the music. Peter had never liked owning up to mistakes. He had that much in common with Oscar Reilly. He had already suffered great embarrassment several years ago when his wife left him. Being blamed for fiscal ineptitude might have been more than he could handle.

"Earth to Charlie," Stewart said laughingly.

"Sorry," I said again. "Look, guys, I hate to do this, but would you excuse me? There's something I really have go to dig into, and until I do and find some kind of answer, I'm going to be distracted."

"Of course," Haskell said. "Do you think it's connected to the murders?"

"Almost certainly," I said, "if what I suspect is true. But I've got to keep digging."

"Dig away," Stewart said. "And if there's anything we can do to help, just name it."

"If you could keep Diesel entertained for the next three hours, that would help," I said, eyeing the feline by my feet. Inevitably, when I tried my hardest to focus on something, he decided that was when he needed immediate attention. As much as I loved him, I could do without that kind of distraction for a while.

"No problem," Stewart said. "Dante will be ecstatic. We'll take them both upstairs and let them play."

"Thanks." I rose. "I'll make it up to you later and clear the table before I go to bed, if you'll leave it all for me."

"Don't even think about it," Haskell said. "I'm taking care of it tonight."

I didn't protest any further, simply thanked them again, and hurried to the den. I got the laptop set up, pulled out the files and put them on the desk, and got to work.

I went through the folders and pulled out the purchase orders and invoices for GER. I discovered that the original licensing of their products occurred thirteen years ago, under the tenure of the director before Peter. She had been the library director when I was in college, and by the time she retired, she had to be around eighty, I guessed. She was an institution in herself, but I had heard that the last few years she had only a slender grasp on things, and the associate director, long since departed for a job elsewhere, had actually run the library.

There was no list of titles with the invoices, only a single line-item consisting of the name of the collection. *The GER Science and Math Collection.* The renewal date each year fell on December fifteenth. I paid particular attention to the most recent renewal and noted that the purchase order wasn't actually submitted until the second week of January. It bore Peter's signature, or to be more accurate, what looked like his signature, and a date of January thirteenth.

It must have been one of the last items he approved before he left, I supposed.

I went back through the folders and pulled out the purchase orders he had approved for the items that had put the library so overbudget.

There were five in all, various collections of journal back files and one new e-book collection. The total was just over half a million dollars.

Peter had scrawled his name on each one, and they all bore the same date, January thirteenth. I checked the calendar on my computer. January thirteenth was a Monday.

Was that the last day Peter was in the office? I couldn't remember.

I knew who would, however. I picked up my cell phone and speed-dialed Melba.

"Sorry to bother you at home," I said. "I've got a question for you. Do you remember the last day you saw Peter in the office?"

"I sure do," she said. "It was a Friday, January tenth. I remember telling him to have a great weekend. He actually smiled at me and said he planned to. He said he'd tell me all about it on Monday, but then he never showed up again." She paused. "Why did you need to know?"

"Just curious," I replied nonchalantly. "I was thinking about him, and I couldn't remember exactly when it was he left. I took the first half of January off, as you recall."

"Yes, you missed all the excitement of those first few days," she said. "I was never so surprised in all my life. Peter never seemed the kind to just up and vamoose like that."

"No, he didn't," I said. "I can't remember, did he leave a note? Or an e-mail?"

"E-mail," she said. "To the president, and he copied me on it, too."

"Do you recall exactly what it said?"

"Let me think." Melba was quiet for a good twenty seconds. "Yes, he said, 'Sorry I screwed things up, consider this my resignation.'"

"That was it?" I asked.

"Yes," Melba said. "I was surprised there wasn't more detail. He didn't even leave me a forwarding address for his personal mail. I've actually got a handful of letters from friends of his, and I don't know what to do with them. I keep thinking he might get in touch with me to ask me to send them on to him, but so far he hasn't. I tried calling his cell phone, too, but he never answered. The most recent time, I got a message that it wasn't a working number. Strange."

Definitely strange. I looked at the purchase orders Peter had supposedly signed three days after he left the library.

I suddenly had a feeling that Peter might not have gone voluntarily.

THIRTY-THREE

|||||||||||||||||||||||||||||||||||||||||||||||||||||||||||||||||||||||||||

"And you know another strange thing?" Melba said. "Well, not exactly strange, I guess, but a little unusual."

I wasn't really paying attention. My mind was racing over the possibilities. Could Peter be *dead*?

". . . Margie at the grocery store on the way home, and you should have seen the ring she was wearing. I've never been so envious in my life. Gorgeous blue stone."

I knew if I didn't get out of this conversation now, I'd be on the phone for a good twenty minutes.

"Sorry, Melba, I heard a beep. Somebody's trying to call me. I'd better take it."

"Okay, I'll tell you the rest in the morning."

"Sure thing." I ended the call and set the phone down.

I heard Melba's voice repeating Peter's message: *Sorry I screwed things up, consider this my resignation.*

Had it been Peter who caused the problems?

I wondered.

I looked through a year's worth of purchase orders. Odd how Peter's signature got so bad only within the last month or so before he left.

What about the date under the signature?

January thirteenth. Anybody could get confused and write the wrong date. I had done it often enough myself.

But just as often I wrote the day's date without even thinking about it. Especially if I were writing a number of checks, for example, or holiday cards. I didn't think twice about it, simply wrote the date and went on.

Perhaps the person who signed those purchase orders on Monday the thirteenth of January had done the same thing without realizing it.

I had no real proof, but I was convinced that Peter had not signed those documents, not when he didn't show up to work that day.

What about the date the purchase orders were created?

I picked up the documents in question and examined them.

They all bore the same date, January twelfth. The day before Peter supposedly signed them. A Sunday.

Peter didn't create purchase orders that I was aware of. I would have to check that with Melba, but I was pretty sure I was correct in this. I found a notepad and jotted that down. I would probably have a number of questions for Melba before I was done thinking this through.

Peter left in the middle of a pay period, I realized. What had happened to his final paycheck? He rarely took vacation time, so his final check would have included his regular salary along with payment for unused vacation. That would have been a pretty hefty check.

Where was it sent? And was it ever cashed or deposited?

More questions for my list, but how could I get answers? I couldn't simply call the payroll office and ask.

Perhaps Penny Sisson could find out the answers for me. *Good idea, Charlie.* I dashed off a quick e-mail to her, saying I was trying to tie up loose ends with the budget. Since Peter's salary was part of the library budget, I thought it was a pretty legitimate request if I went through Penny. I also asked whether she had any kind of forwarding address for him, or the address of a next of kin. I mentioned personal mail that needed to be sent to him.

What about Peter's house? His car? Surely he wouldn't have abandoned his house? He would want to sell it or at least rent it if he was leaving town for good.

I found a popular real estate website and searched for houses for sale or rent in Athena. I remembered Peter's address because I had been there several times for holiday parties.

No listing for it on the real estate site. That didn't mean it wasn't for sale or rent, though. Peter could have handled it privately, or it could already have sold or been rented.

One way to find out, but I felt slightly foolish. Should I jump in the car and drive to Peter's house? What might I find? No, I shouldn't do that. It was crazy. Exactly the kind of thing Helen Louise, Sean, and Laura would tell me not to do.

You don't have to go alone. There's a sheriff's deputy upstairs.

Would Haskell and Stewart think I had lost my mind if I asked them to go with me?

One way to find out.

All the way up to the third floor I debated with myself. Had my imagination run completely away with me? Was I seeing murder where there was none?

Peter was probably enjoying the sun in California right now. He had lived there for many years, and that would be where he'd want to go, I felt sure.

If he isn't dead.

I couldn't shake the feeling that something was terribly wrong.

Could I convince Haskell and Stewart to go along with this?

I paused on the third floor to catch my breath after my hurried climb. I almost turned back, feeling foolish again, but then I took a deep breath and approached Stewart's door.

I had to knock a couple of times, because it sounded like they were watching a movie with car crashes. Finally one of them heard, and Haskell came to open the door. He stood aside and motioned for me to enter the dim sitting room.

Stewart turned down the volume on the television set and froze the movie mid-scene. He then rose from the sofa and turned on more lights.

"Where are Diesel and Dante?" I asked when I realized I couldn't see them.

"They're snuggled up on the bed," Stewart said. "Neither one of them cares for action movies, and they wore themselves out playing earlier."

"I'll get Diesel for you," Haskell said.

"No, not yet," I said. "Actually, I need to talk to you both about something. Would you mind?"

"Of course not," Stewart said, and Haskell nodded. He pulled up a chair for me and then joined Stewart on the sofa. Stewart leaned against him.

"I don't want you to think I'm nuts," I said, "but I think there might have been another murder, a couple of months ago."

"What? Who? Who was murdered?" Stewart jerked upright.

"I think maybe Peter Vanderkeller," I said.

"Wasn't he the head of the library?" Haskell said. "The one who just up and quit one day?"

I nodded. "Yes. Except that I'm not so sure he left voluntarily. I'm afraid someone else arranged his departure."

"Why do you think so?" Haskell asked.

After a moment to marshal my thoughts, I gave them a summary of what little *evidence* I had. It didn't amount to a lot, except speculation, a series of *if*s, but I couldn't get over my uneasy feeling.

"What are you going to do about it?" Stewart asked when I'd finished.

"Go to Kanesha at some point," I said. "I don't want to talk to her about it yet, though, because it's all rather tenuous."

"You have some plan in mind, though, don't you?" Haskell asked.

I nodded. "I thought about going to Peter's house to see if it's inhabited. If someone is living there, I can ask them if they bought it or are renting and see if they have any information on where Peter is now. If it's empty, well, that could be evidence of a sort that I'm right."

"Or that he simply walked away from his life here and didn't look back," Stewart said.

"No, I don't think so," I said. "Peter had a thing about money. He was frugal, and I can't imagine him abandoning his house without trying to get at least some of his money back out of it."

"Good point. Since neither of us knew him, we'll have to take your word for that." Stewart rose from the sofa and tugged at Haskell's arm.

"Why are you doing that?" Haskell frowned.

"Because you don't think we're going to let Charlie go by himself, do you? Come on, Mr. Deputy, and bring your gun." Stewart grinned and batted his eyelashes at his partner.

Haskell stared at him for a moment, and I thought he was going to refuse. Then he, too, rose. "What are we going to do with the kids?"

"They can come with us," I said. "Diesel is used to riding in the car."

"I'll go get them." Stewart left the room and came back moments later with Dante in his arms. Diesel yawned as he padded behind Stewart.

Five minutes later we were all in my car. Stewart sat in the back with the animals, and Haskell was in the front passenger seat. He had strapped on his holster and gun, and I was glad he was with us.

Peter's house was in a neighborhood about a ten-minute drive away on the other side of town. A newer development, it had been built in the 1980s. The houses were large and on good-sized lots, though some had since been torn down and larger houses built in their place.

Daylight saving time wasn't for another week yet, and it was getting pretty dark by the time we reached Peter's house. I parked on the street in front. I cracked the windows for Diesel and Dante, and we locked them in. Dante barked until Stewart shushed him. Diesel meowed along with the dog, but he quieted when Dante did.

The house was set back from the street and obscured mostly from view by a high hedge and several trees. We walked up the driveway until we were even with the hedge, and I saw there were a couple of lights on inside. We paused but saw no signs of activity in the house.

"Good evening," a voice called from behind us. "If you're looking for Mr. Vanderkeller, I haven't seen him around lately."

We turned to see an older man, probably in his seventies, walking a large German shepherd on a leash.

"Good evening," I said, and introduced myself. "I used to work with Peter, and I hadn't heard from him in a while. My friends and I thought we'd drop by and see how he's doing."

The elderly man didn't introduce himself. "He's always kept to himself. Never has been much for talking to his neighbors." The dog whined, no doubt having scented, or heard, Diesel and Dante in the car not far away. "Quiet, Schnitzel," he said.

"So you haven't seen him lately?" Stewart asked.

I looked around for Haskell and didn't see him. Where had he got to? Then I spotted him lurking behind the hedge. I figured he didn't want to risk the neighbor seeing his gun. Good idea. The old gentleman might go home and call the police if he saw a man with a gun.

"No, sure haven't." The man scratched the side of his nose. "Reckon the last time wasn't long after New Year's Day. Saw him putting his garbage out one morning when Schnitzel and I were walking past." He paused. "Come to think of it, haven't even seen his car going in or out, either."

"Thank you, sir," I said. "I guess we'll go knock on the door and see if he's home."

"I hope he's all right," the man said, suddenly sounding worried. "I guess I ought to've checked on him, but he's always been so darn funny about that kind of thing."

"Don't worry about it," Stewart said. "We'll check on him. You and Schnitzel have a good evening."

We waited until he was about fifty feet down the walk before we joined Haskell on the other side of the hedge.

"Were you checking out the house?" Stewart asked in a low tone.

"Yes," Haskell said, "and I've already called 911."

"Why?" Stewart and I asked in startled unison.

"There's a body hanging in the kitchen, and it's been there for quite a while."

THIRTY-FOUR

Had I been a drinking man, I would have gone home that night and probably drunk an entire bottle of, well, something. As it was, I had to make do with a mug of warm milk and three aspirin.

As I was the only person present who was acquainted well enough with Peter Vanderkeller, I was asked to provide a tentative identification.

I say *tentative* because, well, Peter wasn't in the best condition after hanging in the kitchen for two months. I was pretty sure it was him, but to be absolutely positive they would have to use his dental records, or something. There was a note with the words *I'm sorry* scrawled on them. Not much of a suicide note, and I didn't believe it for a minute.

For one thing, Peter wasn't a tall man, and there was no chair or ladder anywhere close enough for him to stand on, in order to hang himself from the exposed beam like that. The killer hadn't thought that one through.

It would be a long time before I would be able to remember poor Peter without wanting to be ill in the bushes, the way I was that night.

Last night, really, though mercifully it somehow seemed more distant this morning. I'd had only about five hours' sleep, and I was up by five thirty trying to put the purchase orders and invoices back into their folders. I was going to hand them over to Kanesha later, along with a summary of my thoughts that led me to wonder about Peter and his whereabouts.

The news of Peter's death would not be released for several hours yet. Kanesha wanted time to investigate my suggested leads further before the announcement was made.

I still wasn't sure who had murdered Peter, or exactly why. Had he stumbled on the embezzlement and made the mistake of confronting the embezzler, who then decided the only way to avoid exposure was to kill Peter and make it look like he had committed suicide?

I had another sip of coffee. One sticking point was the overspending. Those invoices, all from legitimate companies for legitimate resources—unlike those from Global Electronic Resources—were authentic, I felt sure. Checking with the companies concerned would show that, but the question was, who okayed the purchases and when had they asked for the invoices?

The process would have taken a few days, if not a week or two, I thought. That argued premeditation on the killer's part, because it took time to set up the apparent motive for Peter's suicide.

The whole thing was cockeyed, a bizarre smokescreen created by the embezzler in order to hide his—or her—theft. I had yet to prove there had been theft, but investigation by the proper authorities into the Global Electronic Resources company would prove it was a fake. I was sure of that.

It was set up cleverly, though, and it had to involve more than one person. Whichever librarian was responsible—Cassandra, Lisa, or Delbert—had to have an accomplice in accounts payable. The vice president of finance had given me a quick lesson on how the college paid for such things as library resources. The vendor had to be set up in the accounting system. Otherwise there would be no payment issued. To be an approved vendor required certain paperwork, and someone had to have filled it out. The likeliest accomplice was therefore a person in accounts payable.

The only person I knew there was Melba's friend, Margie Flaxdale, and I had met her only the once. I didn't know how many other people worked in accounts payable, but the embezzler had to be working with one of them.

Peter Vanderkeller was the first murder victim. Oscar Reilly was the second. Why was Reilly murdered?

Because of his background in finance, I had to assume. He was made interim director because of the budget problems, and he presumably had the smarts to figure out something was fishy about the purchase orders and invoices. Had he then figured out who was responsible?

He must have. Being the man he was, perhaps he'd tried to blackmail the embezzler, and extort the ill-gotten gains from that person. The embezzler decided to kill again, to avoid exposure and to keep what he or she had stolen. Reilly was lured to the basement, probably knocked over the head, and then pressed to death between the shelves.

Okay, that made sense, even though my argument was still built on a series of *if*s. I tried not to think too much about the method of Reilly's murder.

The third murder victim—Porter Stanley. How did he fit into the picture?

The best I could come up with was that he either witnessed the murder, or Reilly had told him about the embezzlement scheme and had named the perpetrator. Stanley had then contacted the killer, no doubt expecting that with his size and intimidating personality, he could easily take over with Reilly out of the way.

Except that Stanley was shot to death, and there was no sign of his sister's jewelry anywhere. Had he recovered it from Reilly? If Reilly actually had it. I figured he must have. I wouldn't put anything past him, least of all stealing from his ex-wife and her wealthy family. I was sure he felt they owed him that much.

I spent nearly two hours getting all my thoughts organized in an e-mail to Kanesha, and when I finally clicked Send, I was ready to take a long, hot shower. Maybe the tension in my neck and shoulders would ease without my having to take more aspirin.

Dressed and ready for work, having breakfasted, I made the decision to leave Diesel home today. Haskell was still on guard duty, and Azalea was there, too. Between them, they would give him attention, and maybe he wouldn't be too upset with me. I was worried about what could happen on campus today, and I felt better knowing he was safe at home.

He meowed reproachfully—that's how it sounded to me—when I told him he couldn't come with me. I almost changed my mind because of the sad look in his eyes, but then I steeled myself. "No, sweet boy, you need to stay here today. Tomorrow, you can come with me." *Surely this will all be over by then.*

Melba was at her desk when I arrived. "Coffee's made. I'll get you a cup."

I thanked her and went into my office. She had unlocked the door for me. Always thoughtful. I had to guard my tongue around her today, because I couldn't tell her about Peter, not until the news was made public. She would be annoyed with me, but I had my orders. I set my briefcase down and logged in to the college network. On the way to work I had thought about the files Reilly had on that thumb drive. I hadn't double-checked those yet, and I needed to see if there was something I missed.

Melba came in with my coffee while I was scanning the list of folders and files. She set the coffee down on the desk.

"Where's Diesel? Surely you didn't forget him?"

"No, I knew I was going to be really busy today, and I thought it was better for him to stay home with Azalea."

"Well, I'll miss him, but you're probably right. I kept worrying yesterday he was going to slip out of the office, and I wouldn't be able to find him."

I looked up and nodded, smiling, then went back to staring at the screen.

"I never did finish telling you about me seeing Margie at the grocery store last night," she said.

"No, you didn't," I replied. I knew I'd have to let her tell me the story or she'd be annoyed with me the rest of the day, if not the whole week. I kept my eyes on the computer screen, though.

"Margie's always had a thing for jewelry. That's one thing we have in common. Like me, though, she hasn't had a lot of money to spend on it, although she has had a boyfriend for a long time. Never does talk about him, though. I don't even know who he is." She laughed. "Whoever he is, he must have a few bucks, because you should see the ring he gave her. She wasn't going to let me look at it, but I made such a fuss when I saw it, she had to. It looks like it belongs in a museum, old-fashioned really, but gorgeous. This huge sapphire, surrounded by diamonds. Whoever the boyfriend is, it must be serious, let me tell you. Wish I had a man that would give me presents like that."

I hadn't really been paying close attention, trying instead to find out whether Reilly had had copies of the GER invoices on his thumb drive. Finally, however, a few words got through. *Huge sapphire, surrounded by diamonds.*

Surely not, I thought, as a memory surfaced.

I looked up at Melba. "I want to show you something. Come around here so you can see my computer screen." I located the files of the jewelry pictures, and I clicked on the first one. I thought it was the sapphire ring, and it was.

"Did the ring Margie has look like this?"

"Exactly like it," Melba said. "Where did you get a picture of it? I don't understand."

"All I can tell you at the moment is that I think the ring belonged to Reilly's ex-wife. I don't know how your friend got it, but I have to let Kanesha know about this."

"Oh my Lord," Melba said. She stumbled around the desk to a chair and sank into it. "Oh my Lord."

"You can't breathe a word of this. Don't go near your friend today." I speed-dialed Kanesha on my cell phone.

She picked up right away, and I related Melba's story to her. "She works in the finance department. Accounts payable." I paused for her reply. "Yes, it fits perfectly. The boyfriend is the obvious culprit, I think."

I listened for a few moments longer, as Kanesha adjured me to stay in my office and out of the way. Things were going to start moving quickly, and she wanted me out of harm's way.

"Don't worry," I said. "I'm staying right here. You're welcome to take the ball and run, run, run." I ended the call.

"Charlie Harris, what in thunderation is going on?" Melba looked frightened.

"I'll explain everything later, I promise. You'll simply have to trust me for now." I paused for a deep, steadying breath. I could feel my heart rate pick up. "Also, we both need to stay here in our offices until I hear back from Kanesha, okay?"

Melba now looked even more frightened. "Dang, I wish I'd brought my gun with me."

"I don't think you'll need it," I told her. "The campus police officer is still on duty."

Melba expelled a pent-up breath. "Yes, thank the Lord, he is." She rose on slightly shaky legs. "I reckon I ought to try to get a few things done. Holler if you need me."

"You do the same. I won't be going anywhere, except to the men's room." I smiled in an effort to lighten the tension.

She nodded and walked out of the office on legs that were no longer shaking.

I turned back to the computer screen and continued my search through Reilly's files. It took me a few minutes, but I found the folder in which he had scanned copies of the GER purchase orders and invoices. I also found a brief document in the folder with several bullet points, the import of which was that this company needed to be vetted to make sure it was legitimate.

There was the proof that Reilly had at least been suspicious of these expenses.

I kept going through the folders and files, looking for any other indications that Reilly had found expenses he considered suspicious but came up with nothing. If there were other bogus items, he obviously hadn't found them yet.

Over the next few hours, until I heard from Kanesha again, I thought off and on about Delbert Winston. I had a hard time seeing him as a cold-blooded killer. An embezzler, perhaps, but not a killer. He had to be the one, though. How else would Margie Flaxdale have ended up with the ex–Mrs. Reilly's family heirloom? She had told Melba her boyfriend gave it to her, and Delbert was the only male among the three chief suspects.

When I finally did talk to Kanesha, I learned that Margie had lied to Melba about the boyfriend. There was no boyfriend.

There was, however, a girlfriend—Cassandra Brownley.

THIRTY-FIVE

On the Sunday after the arrests of Cassandra Brownley and Margie Flaxdale for the murders of Peter Vanderkeller, Oscar Reilly, and Porter Stanley, my family gathered at my house for our weekly meal. I had also invited Melba and Haskell Bates to dine with us. I knew everyone was curious about many of the details of the murder investigation, and I was prepared for a barrage of questions. I insisted, however, that the questions waited until we had finished our meal.

We adjourned to the living room, and everyone found a comfortable spot. Helen Louise sat beside me on the sofa, and Diesel stretched out over both our laps, his head resting against Helen Louise's stomach. Dante, now full of turkey, zonked out in Stewart's lap. I think we all felt a bit sleepy after a full and lively meal, but I had to concentrate to get my thoughts organized when I would rather be taking a nap.

"Did you suspect Cassandra Brownley all along, Dad?" Laura asked. "She sounds like a truly awful person, and a bully."

"I did, though I tried not to let my dislike of her color my judgment," I said. "She's a bright woman, but she let her evaluation of her own intelligence unbalance her. She thought she could bulldoze her way over anyone who stood in her path."

"She did do that for a long time," Melba said. "Until Charlie got in her way. She finally met her match." She chuckled.

"When Cassandra was first hired at Athena," I said, "the director was elderly and, frankly, no longer really up to the job. The salaries for librarians were low, and Cassandra wasn't happy. It wasn't long before she came up with the scheme to embezzle from the library budget."

"She had to have help, though," Helen Louise said. "And that's where Margie came in, right?"

"Yes, her plan wouldn't work unless she had an accomplice in accounts payable to make the fake company look real. I don't think she even thought of the scheme until after she and Margie met and became close."

"How did they get around the IRS? Even a fake company has to report earnings," Sean said.

"Margie did do tax returns, but she underreported the income, of course. They paid enough tax to look reasonably legitimate, but only just."

"How do you know all this?" Stewart asked. "I presume one of them must have talked."

I nodded. "Yes, Margie. Otherwise it would take Kanesha a lot longer to get at the truth. Kanesha is working with the IRS fraud investigators to uncover the full extent of their embezzlement."

"You mean it wasn't just the one thing?" Laura asked. "How much did they get?"

"That's the only one we know about," I replied. "There could be more, however. From the one fake line item, though, they managed to steal over one point seven million dollars over the course of a decade."

Frank whistled. "What I don't understand is why it took so long to figure out something hinky was going on."

"I know how you feel," I said. "But there are a couple of things to keep in mind. One is that Cassandra went to great pains to make this so-called resource look legitimate. She created fake usage reports to make it seem like the e-books in this phantom collection were used enough to make them worthwhile."

"That's pretty slick," Sean said.

"It is," I replied, "because nobody thought to question her on the statistics. Peter probably never did. He basically went with whatever his department heads advised him to do. With his own money he was parsimonious, but that frugality didn't extend to the college's funds."

"What was the other thing we should keep in mind?" Helen Louise asked.

"The fact that librarians, by and large, are not trained to be businesspeople, even though, in a sense, we do run a business. Most library schools, at least back when I went through one, taught a management course, and a course in statistics, but we didn't have courses in budgeting or finance of any kind."

"Opening the way for a smart woman like Cassandra

Brownley to take advantage of the general cluelessness of her coworkers," Alex said.

"Exactly," I said. "The problem for her little scheme was that, unbeknownst to her, Peter had been given instructions to trim the library budget for the next fiscal year by about fifteen percent. He apparently was reviewing resources and somehow stumbled on the fact that maybe these e-books weren't worth what they cost."

"Since Cassandra was the one responsible for the biggest chunk of the library's budget, he must have said something to her," Melba said.

"I have access to his e-mail," I said, "and I found a message from the first of December when he sent her a list of resources he thought should be canceled. Guess what was number one on the list?"

"Global Electronic Resources. Poor Peter." Melba shook her head.

"Yes, because that was probably when Cassandra started planning his murder. She wasn't about to let her cash cow be canceled." I sighed. "She came up with the scheme to get rid of Peter and then make it look like he resigned in embarrassment because he had overcommitted the budget by nearly half a million dollars."

"Didn't anyone think it strange that he would suddenly do such a thing?" Helen Louise asked.

"Yes, but no one dug any deeper because he simply walked off the job, or so they thought. Peter hated ever cutting resources because he truly believed in providing access to all the resources that our students and faculty need for their work. That was certainly one thing I admired in him.

"Cassandra arranged to be invoiced for several journal back-file collections and an e-book collection, knowing they would put the library way over budget. She apparently told the sales reps that Peter had authorized the purchases. The invoices were sent to her, and she created the purchase orders and signed them with Peter's name. Then she sent them to Margie in accounts payable."

I paused for a breath. "Cassandra couldn't risk the purchase orders getting to Peter, or the red flags would really have gone up. So she waited until the weekend that she and Margie killed Peter to do it, and then signed them the following day, the Monday when Peter didn't show up for work. They sent his e-mail resignation from his computer at home, because he was actually logged in to the campus network when they went to his house to fake his suicide."

"Stupid of her to have written the wrong date," Laura said.

"It was certainly careless," I said, "but it's the kind of thing one does automatically most of the time. She slipped up there, and analysis of the signatures on those purchase orders will probably prove that Peter didn't sign them."

"With Peter out of the way, they must have thought they were in tall cotton then," Melba said. "But along came Reilly."

"Right," I said. "Reilly, who was a finance person. He evidently caught on to the fact that something was hinky, to use Frank's term." I smiled at my son-in-law. "Instead of going to the president or to the VP for finance, he decided to try a little blackmail." I recalled the incident I had witnessed, when Cassandra came storming out of his office. I figured that was when he tried to put the pinch on her.

"In the middle of it all, the ex-brother-in-law shows up," Sean said. "Looking for the family heirloom jewelry that Reilly stole."

"That man really was a piece of work," Alex said, her nose wrinkled in disgust.

"Amen to that," Melba said in a decided tone. "Honey, you just don't know how nasty he could be."

"He paid for it," I reminded her. "Porter Stanley forced him to turn over the jewelry, of course. He had been shadowing Reilly for several days. Melba noticed him sitting in a parked car on the street in front of our building. Reilly never saw him, until I brought them face-to-face."

"Why did they kill Stanley?" Helen Louise asked.

"Because he knew they'd killed Reilly," I said. "He followed Reilly into the library that night and saw the murder. I don't imagine Stanley shed any tears over the dead brother-in-law, but Reilly had evidently boasted to him about his blackmail scheme. With Reilly out of the way, he attempted to carry on with the blackmail for himself.

"Cassandra went to meet him at his hotel and shot him. She found the jewels and took them, but she made the mistake of giving Margie one of the rings."

"And Margie let me see it," Melba said. "Really silly of her."

"They didn't know anyone else knew about the jewels, you see," I said, "but it was still a dumb thing to do."

"I can't imagine working with Cassandra and not wanting to bash her over the head with something," Laura said. "How could she get away with being nasty to people for so long?"

"Because they were terrified of her." I shared the

incidents Melba had told me about, when Cassandra sought revenge on coworkers. "They were afraid, even as a group, if they complained about her, she would do something terrible to them. Poor Delbert Winston hemmed and hawed when I asked him to look for some files, and he told me later he was too scared of Cassandra to do as I asked."

"Nasty," Helen Louise said. "So she was the one behind the pranks against Reilly? And the threats to you?"

"Yes," I said. "The woman couldn't stand to be thwarted. She wanted to keep Reilly riled up, and then they decided he had to die." I shivered suddenly. "I'm not sure whether they would have really come after me again, after that failed attempt with the gunshot, but I don't want to think about it."

Haskell finally spoke. "You were the only one who figured out the truth about Peter Vanderkeller, though."

"The more I thought about it, once I started digging into the budget and all those invoices and so on, I just had this feeling that Peter didn't go away voluntarily. I can't explain it," I said with a shrug.

"We're all thankful, Dad, that you did figure it out before those terrible women could harm you." Laura blew me a kiss. If she didn't have trouble getting up and out of chairs, due to her advanced stage of pregnancy, I knew she would have come to hug me.

"I'm thankful, too," I said. "Because I want to be around a long time. I've got grandchildren to spoil, after all." I looked at Helen Louise. "And a beautiful woman at my side."

Diesel sat up and meowed enthusiastically. We all laughed. Dante woke up in Stewart's lap and barked.

Sean stood. "I don't know about the rest of you, but I'm ready for another round of dessert. Dibs on the cheesecake."

"Not if I get there first." Frank jumped up and headed for the kitchen. Sean took off after him. Their wives exchanged amused glances.

"I'll go make the coffee." Stewart handed Dante to Haskell. He turned to me. "By the way, Charlie, Haskell is moving in." He winked at me, and Haskell's face reddened slightly.

"Welcome to the family," I said with a big smile.